THREE SWEDISH MOUNTAIN MEN

LILY GOLD

For everyone who's ever needed to run away

Three Swedish Mountain Men by Lily Gold
All rights reserved.

First digital edition published March 11, 2021
Copyright © 2021 by LILY GOLD

Ebook ASIN: B08YRTBHR9
Paperback ISBN: 978-1-7395867-8-2

5.2.23

AUTHOR'S NOTE

This reverse harem romance features graphic steamy scenes between multiple partners (don't be fooled by the cute cartoon cover — it's very spicy!)

While this is overall a sweet, steam-filled romance, it does touch on several sensitive topics. You can find a full list on my website at: www.lilygoldauthor.com. Happy reading!

CHAPTER 1
DAISY

I swear to God, the moose appears out of thin air.

One second, I'm minding my own business, driving up a winding road through a frosty, glittery pine forest. It's my first day in Lapland, and I arrived at my Airbnb a few hours before my check-in time, so I decided to explore the area. It's a beautiful afternoon; the roads are clear and empty, the mountains are towering around me, and the snow is falling in big flakes, fluttering peacefully down from the sky.

And then I turn a corner, and come face to face with a fucking enormous moose.

It's huge, twice as tall as my car, with long, branching antlers that look sharp enough to spear me. Its body is blocking the whole road. There's no way around it, so I smack my horn to scare it out of the way.

Which is a bad move.

As the noise of my horn blares out into the forest, the moose jumps, spins almost a full circle, and charges right at my car.

Swearing, I yank the steering wheel to the side and slam into reverse, sending the car spinning off the road and into the copse of trees. For a second, everything feels out of control as my tyres skid across the snow. I squeeze my eyes shut, bracing for impact—

And then a shockwave rocks through me. I hear the sound of breaking glass, and feel freezing air against my skin as my back windows shatter inwards. My seatbelt locks and cuts into me as I'm slammed forward. Before I can go flying through the windshield, the airbag explodes in my face, shoving my head back. My skull cracks against my seat. Pain rips up the back of my neck, and I scream as the car spins to a stop, creaking and groaning.

For a few seconds, I sit there, panting. Adrenaline is rushing through me in waves. My hands are still clenched on the steering wheel, my knuckles bleached white. Everything is eerily quiet. I can hear trees rustling outside, and the tiny pittering of thick snowflakes falling and melting against my windshield.

I try to move, but I'm pinned in place by the airbag. It hisses, deflating slowly in front of my face.

Closing my eyes, I take stock. I don't feel wet anywhere, so I don't think I'm bleeding, and nothing hurts enough to be broken. My neck burns as I try to turn my head, but hopefully, that's just muscle strain. I exhale slowly, feeling tears prick at the back of my eyes.

Not to be dramatic, but this has definitely been the worst week of my life.

Just seven days ago, I was in a high school art classroom, happily teaching seventeen-year-olds about charcoal smudging techniques. I went to the pub after work, and by the time I got home, there were news trucks outside of my house, and none of my friends would answer my calls. The school's head teacher had fired me via email, and my answering machine was full of messages from journalists. Someone had spray-painted *WHORE* onto my front door.

One email. That's all it took, for my scammy, slimy little ex-boyfriend to tear my life apart.

I expected the drama to blow over quickly, but it didn't. Over the next few days, the harassment got worse and worse, with more reporters banging on my door and angry neighbours shoving nasty letters through my letterbox. Last night, I finally broke. I had to get away. Sweden seemed like a good place to lie low for a bit. I've wanted to see the Northern Lights for years. I figured if I went far, far north, all the way up to Lapland, there'd be no chance that anyone would find me. And I'd be safe.

Obviously, I forgot to include wild moose in my calculations.

Dimly, I register the sound of tyres on gravel, and my heart jumps as I realise a car has pulled up in the road behind me. Thank God. There's the slam of car doors, and then footsteps run towards me. Two male voices are shouting, but I don't understand what they're saying. I see a dark shape outside my window, and then the driver's seat door yanks open. A man leans inside my car, scanning the mess. He says something in urgent-sounding Swedish, but I'm still so dazed by the crash, I just blink at him.

This guy looks like some kind of Nordic God. A gruff, grizzled face, a blonde beard, and ice-blue eyes. He might actually be Thor. When I just keep staring, he reaches into the car, cupping my cheek with a gloved hand, and repeats his question slower. His thumb brushes lightly over my cheekbone.

I finally get my mouth to work. "I—I'm sorry, do you speak English?" He raises a blonde eyebrow. There's a little *pfft* sound as the airbag deflates completely, hanging from the steering wheel like an empty plastic bag. I let go of the wheel, dropping my hands to my sides. My head is swimming. I try to remember the handful of phrases I memorised from my guidebook this morning. "Uh. *P-pratar du engelska?* Sorry, I—I don't understand what you're saying."

Thor turns to someone behind him. "She's a *tourist*," he says in English, his words dripping with utter disgust.

"Oh, in that case, we may as well just leave her to die then," a low voice drawls back. I fumble at the seat belt buckle, but my hands are too numb to click it open, slipping over the plastic. Thor reaches down and presses the button with one thumb. I shudder as the seatbelt slithers up my body, snapping back into its socket.

That was all that kept me alive. A strip of polyester. Without it, I'd probably be dead right now.

Shit.

Thor narrows his eyes at me. "You drive like an idiot," he growls out. "And your Swedish accent is the worst I've heard in my Goddamn life."

I sputter.

"Oh, move out of the way," the second guy mutters, and Thor gets shoved aside. "If she's dying, she may as well look at something pretty before she goes, instead of your ugly face." My eyes widen as a new head pops through the car door. He's just as hot as the first guy—all sharply-cut cheekbones and full, pouty lips. His eyes are a very light green, and his hair is a bright coppery-brown colour, falling in tousled curls over his forehead. He gives me a crooked grin, and a dimple peeps out from one cheek. My face heats.

I'm not sure what's wrong with me. I don't normally just blatantly check out dudes. Perhaps I'm actually dying in the snow, and my brain is just providing me a soothing hallucination of beautiful men as I slowly bleed out. That would be nice.

"I—I'm sorry," I say stupidly, because it's the only thing I can think to say.

"Aw, don't be sorry, honey," he says cheerfully, running his eyes over me. He has the tiniest trace of an accent, a gentle lilt that gives his words a pretty, sing-songy sound. "Are you injured? Does your back hurt?"

"I—" I roll my shoulders, and pain shoots up my neck again. "Not my back."

"Good." He reaches in and offers me a gloved hand. I take it, letting him gently tug me out of my wrecked car. "I don't like your chances of getting an ambulance up here right now." He pulls me out onto the road. Cold air stings my face as snowflakes flutter down, landing on my coat. I stumble as my feet hit thick snow, and he slides his other arm around my waist, keeping me upright. "You're okay," he says softly. "You're okay. Unlike the poor tree you just mowed down."

Bracing myself, I look around at the devastation I've caused. I'm half-expecting to see a giant carcass bleeding out into the snow, but judging by the line of hoof prints leading into the forest, I *just* missed the moose. Good for him.

Instead, I rear-ended into a pine tree.

"Holy shit," I breathe, taking in my car. It's not much—a second-hand, orange hunk of metal with a chipped paint job—but I've had it since I was a teenager. I saved up waitressing paychecks for years to buy this car. I took the ferry instead of a plane this morning, just so I could bring it with me to Sweden. And now it's so crumpled and cracked, it barely looks like a car at all. "Oh God. There was a moose—"

"I saw it," Thor grunts. "Eli saw it. The people back in the village bloody saw it. Apparently, the only person who didn't see it was you." I look up at him. He's got his arms crossed and his jaw clenched as he looks flatly back at me. "How exactly did you miss an animal that was two metres tall? You drive like an idiot. You could've killed it."

My mouth falls open. "*I* could've killed it? It could've killed me!"

He shrugs, like my death wouldn't be such a bad thing.

The redhead shoots him a look, then turns back to me. "Don't mind him, he gets all grumbly when his animals get hurt. What's your name, honey?"

I hesitate as my mind races. "Um. Uh. It's… Daisy," I settle on. I'm a terrible liar, and judging by Thor's quirked eyebrow, he thinks so, too, but the other man just smiles, offering me his hand.

"Daisy. That's pretty. I'm Elias Sandahl. Well, I prefer Eli," he says, giving my hand a firm shake. "And the big bear currently glaring at you over my shoulder is Cole. Sorry about him, he has severe behavioural issues."

Thor—Cole—grumbles something under his breath, patting the crumpled-in trunk. "Hope you didn't have anything important back here."

My eyes widen. I brought canvasses and all my paints with me, figuring that if I kept on painting commissions, I could hide up here for months. If anybody ever wants to hire me again.

Crap, crap, *crap.*

I run over and yank the lid of the boot up, staring in horror at all my broken equipment. All of my canvases are completely ruined, the frames splintered and the fabric ripped. Most of the paint looks fine, although one tube of cadmium red has exploded, spattering all of my stuff with dripping, vibrant crimson. It looks like a crime scene.

Eli comes to stand behind me, taking in the carnage. "Shit," he says.

I reach out to touch my suitcase, and my fingers come back red. The reality of my situation dawns on me. I'm stranded in a foreign country, with no car, no way of making money, and no clue where I am. I glance up at the sky. In the last couple of minutes, the snow has gotten even heavier, and the clouds are darkening ominously.

"*Shit,*" I echo.

CHAPTER 2
COLE

O f course she's a tourist. Of *course*.

I hate tourists. None of them can drive up here. They just roll in with their summer tyres and expect to be able to navigate ice and snow. I peer inside the broken window and fight the urge to swear. She's driving a foreign car, for God's sake. The steering wheel's on the wrong side. You'd have to be an excellent driver to drive the wrong kind of car on dark winter roads.

Which this girl clearly isn't. She probably barely passed her test. How hard is it to swerve without knocking down a tree?

I *hate* tourists.

I vaguely hear Eli flirting with her behind me as I examine the car. Her voice is soft and shaky as she answers. She sounds nervous.

She should be. She's lucky to be alive. I walk around the car, taking in the damage. The back window is cracked, and the trunk has been crumpled in like a tin can. She's left the key in the ignition, so I lean in and turn it. Nothing happens. Sighing, I pull it out, slamming the car door shut.

"Hey!" I look up. The girl is frowning at me. "What are you doing? Give me back my keys."

I run my eyes over her. She's tiny. If it weren't for the soft curves pressing against her pale pink ski jacket, I wouldn't even think she's old enough to drive. Even though she's about the size of a troll doll, she's got her arms crossed, glaring up at me like she's about to fight me.

I don't have time for this. "Why did you honk your horn?" I demand.

She blinks. "Because there was a giant moose in the road. I was trying to get it to move."

"You never honk at an elk. You'll just end up scaring it."

"Well, yeah," she mutters, "that was kind of the point."

I scowl. "Which do you prefer—a six-hundred-kilogram animal standing still in the road, or running around unpredictably?"

"Cole—" Eli starts.

I ignore him. "*And* you were driving too fast."

"I was below the speed limit!" She protests.

"When there's moose on the roads, you drive even slower."

"Well, sorry I don't know the *moose protocol*," she hisses. "This is my first time in the country." She starts stamping towards me, but just before she reaches me, she loses her footing, swaying precariously on her feet. My hands shoot out and grab her before she smacks into the ground. Jesus. She can't even stand up straight, for God's sake.

"How are you this clumsy?" I bark, setting her upright. "Are you driving drunk?"

"Can you please stop shouting? My head is killing me." She snatches back her keys and leans heavily against the hood of her car, rubbing her eyes. All the colour is drained out of her face.

Shit. She's not just clumsy. She's dizzy. "You hit your head, didn't you?" I say flatly.

Great. Now, even if I can get her car to start, she wouldn't be able to drive it.

"Sorry to inconvenience you," she mutters.

I sigh, reaching for her face. She jerks away from my hands. "What are you doing?"

"Seeing if you're bleeding." I tug her fluffy hood down, freezing when I get a good look at her face.

Oh.

She's beautiful. Really, really beautiful. Soft cheeks, massive brown eyes, and a little pink-valentine mouth. She shakes her head, and long, thick, chocolate-brown curls unravel from under her hood, falling all the way to her waist. Next to me, I see Eli twitch with interest.

"She's not bleeding," I tell him, my voice gruffer than usual. "But she's dizzy, and her car won't start."

He glances warily up at the sky. "We should head back to the town before the storm hits, then. Get her put up in a hotel and call her a doctor. She says she's staying in Kiruna."

I snort. "Of course, she is."

We've spent all day in Kiruna, stocking up on supplies. I hate it down there. It's swarming with tourists at this time of year, who all want to dog-sled and pet reindeer and put the Northern Lights on their Instagram stories. They look at the locals like we're a bloody museum exhibit.

Eli sighs. "Dude. Come on. The drive to the cabin could take almost an hour if the snow starts coming down hard. We might not make it."

"We'll make it," I say, with complete certainty.

"You don't know that for sure."

"Yes. I do." I open the boot of our truck, pulling out a tow strap. "If we go back to town, we'll get snowed in. I'm not spending *weeks* in that tourist trap." I strap up the girl's car, giving the cord a tug to make sure it's solid, then turn to her. "Keys."

"What?"

"Give me back your keys."

She looks startled. "What? No! Wait, what's happening?"

For a second, I wonder if she actually is stupid. Then I realise she didn't understand that whole conversation.

Tourists.

"You can't drive," I recap. "Your car is totalled and you have a head injury. Which means you have to come with us. There's a storm coming. We need to move now."

She takes a step back, crossing her arms over her chest. She's already shivering in her flimsy pink coat. "But where are you taking me?"

"Home."

Her eyes widen. "I don't know you. I'm not letting you drive me to your home!"

"Fine. Die here, then." I slam the truck boot closed.

Eli wraps his coat over her shoulders. "You don't really have a choice, babe," he says apologetically. "You're freezing already. When the wind picks up, you'll get hypothermia pretty fast. Promise we don't bite."

"I can just call someone to tow the car." She eyes me. "Someone professional. Not just some stranger on the street."

"Good luck with that."

"No one will be coming out in this weather," Eli explains. "Right now, everyone's headed home to wait out the storm. I doubt you can even get signal."

I hold out my hand again. "I'll ask one last time. Give. Me. Your. Keys."

She stares up at me, jaw working, anger burning in her pretty brown eyes. Snowflakes fall down between us, the flurry already getting faster. Without thinking, I reach down and tug up the hood of her coat again, covering her head.

She presses her lips together. Slowly, she opens her gloved hand and offers me the key. I take it and stick it back in the ignition of her car to unlock the steering, then head back to the truck, tugging the handle on the back passenger door. "In."

She gives me one last hard look, then climbs in wordlessly. I slam the door shut and head to the driver's side.

"Would it kill you to be nice?" Eli mutters, buckling in next to me. "She was just in a car crash."

"I'm saving her life. I think that's pretty nice of me."

"She's scared," he insists.

"You can cuddle her when we get there." I turn on the engine. "Do up your seatbelt," I order over my shoulder, then start the car.

CHAPTER 3
DAISY

I probably should have argued harder, I reflect, as I watch the snow-covered forest roll by outside the window. I think I read somewhere that your chances of escaping a kidnapping drop by ninety-five percent once they get you in the car. I don't know these men. They could be anyone.

Honestly, though, I'm really starting to not feel well. Now that all of the adrenaline has flooded out of me, I can't stop shaking. My brain is all slow and foggy, and my neck is killing me. I guess it's an after-effect of being slammed back against my seat.

"You're sure you can't take me back to the town?" I ask Cole, peering through the windshield. The terrain is getting steeper as we climb through the mountains. Fear clutches me. How high up do these guys live? I was told Kiruna, where I'm meant to be staying, is the northernmost town in all of Sweden, but we've been driving for a while now without any signs of stopping.

His hands clench on the steering wheel. "No."

"How do I know you're not kidnapping me?"

"You don't."

"Great," I mutter. "Fantastic."

Whatever. I figure I don't really have a choice. If he's right, and a storm is coming, I would've died anyway. At least getting axed into little pieces will be quicker than suffocating under several feet of snow.

I glance around the car. It's a worn, sturdy-looking truck with dark leather seats. There are winter coats stacked on the backseat next to me, and the trunk is full of cardboard boxes and tools.

I eye them suspiciously. "There's a gun back here."

"Yes," Cole answers.

"And an axe."

"Well spotted."

"Care to explain why?"

He turns a corner, and we enter an even thicker patch of forest. The trees are so close together they absorb the car's headlights, darkening the road.

"No."

Excellent.

Eli turns and tosses me a grin. "Don't worry, babe. We're taking you someplace safe. I promise."

Cole mutters something under his breath, and Eli rolls his eyes. The men start arguing in rapid Swedish, and I sink down in my seat, closing my eyes against my pounding headache.

I wake up with a jolt as the car cranks to a stop. I must have dozed off. The guys are both unbuckling and slipping into snowshoes.

We've pulled up in front of a decent-sized cabin, surrounded by sparse, frozen trees. The walls are made of red-painted wooden planks, and there are gold lights shining in the windows. It's like something out of a Christmas card.

I sit up in my seat to get a better view, and almost cry out as pain sears down my neck. It's even stiffer than it was before, and I grit my teeth against the tears that pop up in my eyes.

A blast of freezing air hits me as Eli opens my door. "Need a hand?" He asks cheerfully.

"I got it," I mutter, sliding out of the car and into the snow. I immediately sink almost to my knees. Freezing water soaks through the fabric of my jeans. Grimacing, I look around, taking in my surroundings.

Snow is falling from the sky, thicker than before. It's hard to see through the flurry of fat flakes. Apart from a big wooden storage shed, there aren't any other buildings nearby. I guess these guys must live completely isolated. Alone in the woods. No nosy neighbours hanging around to hear the screams of their victims.

Great.

Eli and Cole both lug crates from the boot of the truck and head for the front door. I try to follow, but when I step forward, my foot just sinks. I yank my back leg out of the snow and push forward again. It's like wading through quicksand. I only make

THREE SWEDISH MOUNTAIN MEN   **17**

it about three metres before my foot catches on something hidden under the snow. I lose my balance, tottering, then trip forward. I throw my arms out, bracing myself for a faceful of snow—

And a pair of strong arms wrap around my body. I'm lifted up and pressed against someone's chest.

I look up to see Cole carrying me, as if I'm as light as a kid. From this close, I can make out the soft blonde bristles shading his jaw. I watch a snowflake melt against his skin. "We don't have all day," he mutters, stalking ahead. He crosses the distance from the car to the cabin in just a few long steps, then very, very gently sets me down in the doorway next to Eli.

"Get her inside. I'm going to put her car in the barn," he says gruffly, then disappears.

Eli pulls open the front door and holds it for me. "After you," he says brightly.

Swallowing down nerves, I step inside the cabin.

I'm not sure what I was expecting. A blood-spattered abattoir? The bodies of all their former victims hanging from the ceiling on meat hooks?

It's actually a really lovely little home. The front door leads right into the living room. On the wall to my right is a set of closets and hooks, I guess for shoes and coats. To my left, there's a squashy-looking sofa and a couple of armchairs clustered around a coffee table. A cheerful fire crackles in a fireplace, and the wooden walls are hung with electric lights that emit a soft gold glow.

I take another cautious step inside, looking around. There are bookshelves lining the walls. A big dining table, surrounded by mismatched chairs. The living room is open plan, and I can see through to a small, brightly lit kitchen.

"Riv!" Eli calls behind me, pulling off his coat. "Look what we found!"

A man appears in the kitchen doorway, holding a steaming mug. I blink a bit as he steps into the light. Holy crap.

He's stunning. Deep brown skin, high cheekbones, full lips. He's wearing a white pressed shirt, open at the collar. The sleeves are rolled up, showing off impressively thick forearms dusted with dark hair. His eyes are sharp and cool behind a pair of thick-rimmed glasses. As he runs his gaze down me, I almost feel like I'm getting examined.

"Hi," I say, embarrassed. "Um. Sorry to barge in."

He ignores me and glances over my shoulder. "Eli. What is this?" His voice is calm and deep, without a trace of an accent.

"It's a girl." Eli helps me out of my coat. "I know you've been up here a while, but surely you must have seen one before."

A muscle tics in the man's jaw. "Why is she *here*?" He emphasises.

"Her car broke down. We couldn't just leave her in the storm, so we brought her back here."

"And now, what? She's just going to stay here?"

"What was I meant to do?" Eli gently pushes me into an armchair and bends to take off my boots. I try to push him off—I'm not a *baby*—but when I lean forward, pain sears through my neck, and I have to straighten, wincing. He gives me a sympathetic look, kneeling at my feet and tugging at the laces of my snow-covered shoes. "Should we have left her to die?"

"We don't have a guest room," the man says icily.

"Oh, she's only little," Eli says cheerfully. "I'm sure we can squeeze her in somewhere."

"*She* has a name," I cut in, getting fed up with them talking over my head. "I'm Daisy. It's nice to meet you."

The man's eyes flick over me again. "Riven."

The door behind me opens, and snow breezes into the hallway as Cole comes inside, stamping snow off his boots.

"Cole," Riven snaps. "What is happening."

Cole jerks his chin at me. "Check her out," he orders gruffly.

"What? Why?" Riven demands. "Who is this girl?"

I shake my head. I've had enough of this. Clearly, Eli is the only person who wants me here. "You know what, maybe I should just go. I'm sure there's a hotel or something nearby I can stay at."

I try to slide off the chair, but apparently, after everything that's happened today, my body has finally given up. My knees wobble and bend underneath me.

"Woah." Three pairs of hands grab at me; Cole's at my shoulders, Eli's at my hips, and Riven's at my waist. I don't know how he crossed the room so fast. I have to fight the urge to gasp as the three men push me back into the chair. It's overwhelming to be touched in so many places, with so many big, warm hands.

Eli squeezes my calf. "We think she hit her head in the crash. She's not feeling too good."

Riven's attention snaps back to me. "You're hurt?" He demands.

"My neck hurts a bit," I admit.

"You should've said." He turns and heads to the kitchen. "Put her on the table. I need her under the light."

I yelp as Cole's arms slide around me again and I'm lifted right off the ground. He carries me over to the dark wood dining table. "I can walk myself," I mutter.

"Did you learn recently? You're not good at it."

Riven washes and dries his hands, then comes to stand in front of me. I can't believe how big he is. Even though I'm sitting on the table, he still towers over me. All of the men seem unnaturally large; Eli is the shortest, and he's still definitely over six feet.

Riven's dark eyes are intent as he studies my face. "Are you nauseous? Confused?"

"A bit." Who wouldn't be confused right now?

"Head hurt?"

I wince. "It's killing me."

His lips turn down. "Hm." He takes my head in his hands. I jump a bit at his cold palms. "Alright. I'm just going to check your head and neck for injury. Please stay still. This might hurt."

CHAPTER 4
RIVEN

I am going to kill Eli.

It's his fault. It has to be. I don't know exactly how he planned to find a stranded girl on the road, but I'm sure he did it on purpose. It's just the sort of thing he'd do. He couldn't keep himself away from a beautiful woman if his life depended on it.

And of course, she has to be beautiful. It was hard not to watch as she and Eli peeled off all her winter clothes. Her thick coat and fluffy hood fell away, revealing smooth curves, long chestnut hair, and a sweet, heart-shaped face. She's wearing blue jeans that cling to her hips, and a tight thermal top that shows off her full breasts. I can see the pale line of her bra through the fabric.

And now she's sitting in front of me, and I have to touch her, feeling the creamy texture of her soft skin. She looks up at me, her doe-brown eyes unblinking as I manipulate her neck, turning it gently from side to side. My hand looks giant under her delicate jaw. She's tiny, probably barely five feet. I reach the back of her neck, and she winces a bit.

"Does this hurt?" I touch the tender muscle, pressing lightly. She nods, then lets out a little moan as I massage my thumb into the spot, feeling. I grit my teeth.

Yes. I'm going to kill Eli. Slowly.

Daisy must pick up on my bad mood, because she clears her throat awkwardly. "I'm sorry to bother you like this. This probably isn't how you wanted to spend your evening."

"It's my job," I say simply.

"You're a doctor?"

I nod, finishing up with her neck and turning my attention to her head. My fingers smooth through her hair as I feel across her scalp for a wound. It's like running my hands through silk. Her hair is ridiculously soft, falling all the way to her waist. As I carefully part it, looking for blood or swelling, the sweet scent of peaches fills my nose. My mouth literally waters.

She quivers suddenly, a shiver shaking down her spine.

I pause. "Are you cold? Would you like a blanket?"

"I'm fine."

"We can turn up the heat, it's not a problem."

"I'm not cold. Sorry. It just... it feels nice."

I stare at her.

She squirms, clearly uncomfortable. "So. Um. You're a doctor all the way up here? Is there even anyone for you to treat?"

"There are villages nearby. Some Sami settlements. I pay house calls, mostly, to people who can't reach the town hospitals." I finish checking her head. "Look up, please." She does, wincing a bit. Something twists in my stomach.

I put her through every test I can reasonably do at home, checking her balance, her reflexes, her pupil dilation. She passes every one with flying colours. Finally, I pull my pen out of my pocket to see how well she can track movement. I lift it in front of her face.

"Okay. I'm going to move my pen left and right. I want you to follow it with your eyes."

She nods, turning her head as I move my pen.

I catch her chin in my hand. "Hold your head still," I order quietly. She just looks at me, a little dazed. I keep my hand cupped under her jaw as we finish off the test, feeling her pulse batter against my fingers.

She can follow movement without any problem, so I step back, satisfied. "Very good." I clip the pen back to my pocket. "You don't have a concussion, although your neck seems a little sprained. You still have full range of motion, though. I wouldn't worry too much." Dusting off my hands, I head towards the kitchen cupboard we use as a med cabinet, rooting inside. "I'm going to give you some muscle relaxants for the pain. They'll make you drowsy, but it's best you sleep, anyway. Your other symptoms are probably just psychological shock. Near-death experiences tend to make you feel ill." I find the purple pill packet I was looking for, checking the expiration date. "You should feel more normal after food and sleep. Can you make her some food, Eli? Something hot?"

"Sure." He bounces off the counter. "You want some, too?"

"I already ate. I want to check out her car before the snow gets too bad." I hand her the pills. "Take two when you eat. Where are you staying? Kiruna?"

She nods.

"It will take a while for the roads down to the town to be cleared, but there's a settlement between here and there. A village. They have a mechanic. Do you have your wallet on you?"

She nods, obediently pulling it out of her jeans pocket and handing it over.

"Seriously?" Eli pipes up. "You made all that fuss about Cole towing your car, but you just give him your wallet?"

She shrugs. "I'm already here, now. If you guys *are* murderers, I won't need the money when you've hacked me to pieces."

My lips twitch in spite of myself. "I'm not robbing you. I'm going to call the mechanic. He won't be able to help until the storm is over, but it'll be quicker if we book an appointment now." I flip the wallet open, sorting through her cards. "I'll need your license and ID." I spot the edge of her license and go to slide it out.

She suddenly lunges at me, snatching the wallet right out of my hand. "Sorry, sorry, um, no can do," she babbles, wide-eyed. "I, um. Don't have one."

I feel an eyebrow raise. "You don't have a license?"

"Well, obviously I do." She swallows. "I just... don't want to give it to you right now."

"Why?"

"Because I don't know you, yet. You might be trying to steal my identity, or something!"

"O-kay," I say slowly. She twists to slide the wallet back into her pocket—then suddenly freezes, gripping her ribs. I frown. "Did that hurt you?" I reach for the hem of her t-shirt. "Let me see."

She bats my hand away. "What the Hell do you think you're doing?"

I blink. "Take your shirt off. I need to see your torso."

"What? No!" She skids back on the table. She looks legitimately alarmed, as if I'm about to rip all her clothes off her body. "It's fine. I just pulled a muscle lifting my suitcase earlier."

"Take it off," Cole growls from the doorway. "Don't be an idiot."

"Stop calling me an idiot," she snaps. "It's not *idiotic* to not want to take my shirt off, arsehole."

Eli snorts.

"I'm not trying to check you out," I say calmly. "I just want to see if you've hurt your ribs." She hesitates, and I reach for her again.

She slaps my hands away. "No! Stop!"

I try to push back my frustration. "Why not?"

She crosses her arms over her chest. "Because I said so! Isn't that enough? I told you, I'm *fine*."

I study her for a few seconds. She's breathing hard, her jaw set fiercely. She looks like she's about to fight me.

"Alright." I turn to Eli. "Cook her some food," I tell him, switching to Swedish. "I'm going to go check on her car. Ask her some questions. Find out who she is, what she's doing here. Get as much information as you can."

He gives me a lazy salute. "Right, boss."

Daisy slips off the table, wincing as pain jolts through her again. I pause in the doorway. I'm so used to Cole hiding bullet wounds and animal bites that I can't stop my mind going to the worse-case scenario. Internal bleeding. Shattered bone. Infection.

I feel like a prick for pushing her, but she was in a car crash. If it's serious, she could end up dying without immediate care. It's not like she can get whisked off to the ER in the middle of a storm. She needs to get looked at. "Try to convince her to take her shirt off," I add. "See if there's any bruising or cuts."

"You perv."

I roll my eyes and grab my coat, stepping into my snowshoes. "Just do it." I slip on my gloves and head out into the snow.

Thank God we have Eli. If anyone will make that girl comfortable enough to let me examine her, it will be him. It's usually a struggle to convince women to keep their clothes *on* when they're around him.

He'll get her talking, too. Eli can charm information out of just about anyone. I bet, before the hour's up, she will have spilled her whole life story.

Then we'll find out who this strange girl really is.

CHAPTER 5
DAISY

I watch as Riven disappears, then slowly uncross my arms from over my chest. Maybe Cole's right. Maybe I am acting like an idiot. But I don't trust these guys yet. None of them seem to recognise me, but they might just be pretending. If they know who I am, I'm sure as Hell not letting them see my boobs.

No matter how hot they are.

Eli starts clattering around in the kitchen, and I relax slightly. At least one of them likes me. "I don't think your friends want me here," I say drily.

He shakes his head. "Don't worry about them. Cole's been in a bad mood. For like, the last thirty years. And Riv has trust issues. But they'll both come around." He grins at me, sparking up the stove. "You're not a vegetarian or anything, are you, babe?"

"No. I can eat everything."

"Great." He nods at the big sofa. "Go make yourself comfortable. This won't take long."

I obediently drop onto the coach. The fire crackles at my side, warming my skin as I glance around me. It looks like all of the furniture is handmade. The cushions strewn across the sofa are embroidered with brightly coloured thread. The coffee table is made of a thick, textured oak, and even the coasters spread across its surface look like carved leather. With nothing else to do, I pull my phone out of my pocket, turning it on with a wince. I've had it switched off for the last couple of days. I'm too scared of the texts and emails everybody will have sent me. God knows what awful things they're saying. My screen lights up, and I wait for the slew of notifications—but there's nothing. I glance up at the corner of the screen. No bars. "You don't have any signal?"

"We do usually," Eli says, pulling a packet out of the fridge. "It'll be the storm."

That news settles heavily in my stomach. Well, I guess this is what I wanted, when I came up here.

A few days ago, after I got fired, I tried to hide from the reporters by going to my parents' house. They tossed me back out onto the pavement. As did every friend I tried to visit. Even worse, every single person I passed on the street recognised me. Brighton is a small city, and apparently, everybody had already read about me in the local news. As I trailed, crying, back to my flat, people started shouting at me across the road. Catcalling. Some even took photos. A gaggle of mums from the school I used to work at spotted me and practically chased me back to my flat, screaming about how they were going to sue me.

People even stared at me this morning on the ferry. My story had hit some major UK news stations by then. I was wandering through the food hall, trying to find a place to sit, when a teenage boy I passed moaned like he was having an orgasm. I almost threw up on the spot.

That's why I decided to travel up to Kiruna. It's literally in the Arctic Circle. I wanted to be as off-the-grid as possible. I didn't want anybody to be able to recognise me.

Well, now no one will be able to find my body, either.

Eli starts humming under his breath, a low, bass rumble. I watch him as he cooks. He's taken off his jumper, and he's wearing a tight grey t-shirt that clings to his broad shoulders. I watch his muscles roll under the thin fabric. I wonder if he's an athlete. He's very light on his feet, moving around the kitchen gracefully.

"What do you do up here?" I ask, picking up a pillow and squishing it to my chest.

"I'm a skiing instructor," he says over his shoulder. "In skiing season, I work down in the resort a few miles from here."

That explains that.

"I'm going to bend over now," he adds. "Make sure you pay *very* close attention to my ass."

I sputter. "I—what?"

He tosses me a dazzlingly white grin. "I can see you watching me in the window reflection. You gotta get better at perving, babe."

Heat floods my cheeks. "Um. I'm sorry."

He waves me off. "Hey, don't be embarrassed. Of course you want to look. You're only human. I'm sure it's not everyday you see a body so perfectly formed. So, please," he grins again. "Enjoy."

My face gets even hotter. "I thought you were bending over," I mutter. "Get on with it, then."

He laughs, bending to pull some plates out of the cupboard. I figure, since he's given me permission, I may as well enjoy the view. And it really is spectacular. His asscheeks are toned and sculpted, and his thighs—Holy shit. I don't think I've ever seen a guy with such thick, hard thighs before.

I swallow as he straightens. "Alright. Show's over, I'm afraid." He comes and sits next to me, setting my plate on the coffee table. Sausages and mashed potato doused in gravy, with a big spoonful of what looks like jam on the side.

I point at it with my fork. "What is this?"

"Lingon. It's a staple." He slings his arm over the back of the sofa. Even though he's sitting close enough for me to feel the heat coming off his skin, it's not creepy. Just warm and comforting.

For the first few minutes, I'm completely focussed on wolfing down my food. I haven't eaten anything since the roll and apple I nabbed on the ferry this morning. Riven's right; as I eat, the dizziness and fogginess in my brain start to dissipate.

Eli reaches over and rolls one of his sausages onto my plate. I look up at him, my mouth stuffed full. "Looks like you need it more than me," he says, eyes twinkling.

I blush, forcing myself to slow down. "So," I swallow my mouthful. "You're a skiing instructor. Riven is a doctor. What about Cole? Is he a gym teacher? Drill sergeant? Fascist dictator?"

He huffs a laugh. "Not quite. He works in wildlife control."

I frown. "Is he… like… a hunter?"

"Kind of the opposite. I guess you'd call him a ranger? He tries his best to keep the animals alive." He stretches out his shoulders, making a soft noise that sends heat panging through my stomach. "People call him if a moose is standing in their driveway and won't leave, or a mama bear gets too close to their house, or whatever."

My eyes widen. "A bear?"

"Yeah, you get all sorts up here. Bears. Wolves. Lynxes. Mooses. It's mostly mooses, though. They're ballsy."

I can't help smiling at *mooses*. Both Eli and Riven speak such good English, it's easy to forget that it's not their first language. It's kind of sweet.

"He has a lot of problems with tourists," he continues. "A lot of them end up hitting animals with their cars. Or they try to go hunting and don't kill the animals properly. Just leave them injured, running around the woods."

"Which is why he was so pissed off at me," I realise. "I could've killed the moose."

He shrugs. "Ah, he's just being a moody prick. Mooses walk on the road all the time. At least you didn't hit it." He whistles. "That's a goddamn nightmare. You'll be eating moose pie for weeks." He turns to me. "So, what about you? What do you do?"

"I'm a teacher," I say, then mentally slap myself. I shouldn't have told him that. If he figures out where I used to work, he'll be able to look me up. And then he'll find the news articles about me, and I'll be in a shitload of trouble. My heart starts to pound faster. I force myself to stay calm.

"Oh?" He says casually. "What do you teach?"

"You know. School."

He smiles. "I meant, what class do you teach?"

"Oh, is that what you meant?"

He looks at me narrowly. I take a huge bite of mash to occupy my mouth.

"So you work in a high school?" He asks after a moment. "Or elementary?"

I shrug. "I move around some."

"How old are the kids?"

I chase a lingonberry around my plate. "All different ages," I say breezily.

"I'm not getting anything else out of you, am I?"

"Well spotted."

He sighs. "Fair enough. How's your neck feeling? Are the painkillers working?"

I nod, rolling it around. "It's not as sore. It's still really tight, though."

"You know," he sets his cutlery down. "I am a trained masseur."

I raise an eyebrow. "Seriously?"

"Yep. Got my license as an anniversary present for one of our exes."

"Wow." That's one hell of an anniversary present. "Okay then. I guess." I lay down my empty plate. "Have at it."

He grins and settles himself behind me, pulling my hair gently over one shoulder. "You've got so much hair, Jesus."

"Yeah, I.... wait." I frown, replaying what he just said in my mind. "Did you say *our?*"

"What was that?" He rubs his hands together, warming them up.

"You said one of *our* exes. What does that mean?"

He hums. "I didn't say that. It's just my accent."

"You don't really have much of an accent."

"Thanks!" Before I can ask any more questions, he starts kneading my shoulders, and all the words die in my mouth. I gape like a fish as he rubs my sore muscles, loosening the day's tension. It feels *amazing.*

He chuckles. "What? Did you think I was lying about the training?"

I can't even speak. He keeps working on my shoulders for a bit, squeezing the tight muscles, then digs his thumbs into a harsh knot at the back of my neck. I gasp.

He stops immediately. "Too much?"

"Oh, no. No. No, no, it's great," I babble.

He hums and pushes into the muscle again, rubbing out the tension. I shudder all over. "There," I mutter. "Harder, please."

He frowns. "Babe, you're so tight. This must be really hurting you." He keeps working on the knot until the muscle finally relaxes, and I'm a half-melted lump under his hands.

I sigh. "You're a wizard."

"It's been said. Okay. Let me get the other side."

I shuffle up, and he slides his hands across the other shoulder. "You know," he says casually, kneading the muscle. "This would work a lot better if you took your shirt off."

My mouth falls open. I jump up from the sofa, staggering back. "Oh my God! You're just trying to get me topless!"

He has the grace to look sheepish. "Riven asked me to. He's worried that you're hiding an injury."

Fury boils in my blood. "Don't do that! Find something else to jack off to!"

He looks taken aback. "That wasn't what I was planning on—"

I cut him off. "Listen to me. I *don't want to*. What is wrong with you? Don't try to trick me into taking off my clothes! If I say no, I mean it!"

He puts his hands up. "Hey, I'm sorry. Sorry. We just want to know if you're hurt. Honestly."

"Do I really look that fragile? Would you be hovering over Cole like this?"

He shrugs. "We know what we can handle. But you're not from around here. And you're so small. We don't know what you can take."

"Well, it's shitty behaviour," I snap. "Don't do it."

He bites his lip. A reddish curl falls into his face. "I'm sorry," he says again. "Really."

I take a deep breath, trying to calm down. It suddenly sinks in just how vulnerable I am. I'm stuck here, with no one to call for help. The surge of panic that rises up in me overwhelms me. "I— do you have a bathroom?"

"Nope. We usually just piss in the snow." He gives me a tentative smile. I stare at him flatly, and he sighs, standing up. "I'll show you."

I shuffle back. "No. Stay there. Don't come with me."

He swears under his breath and sits back down. "That corridor." He points. "Second door on the left."

I follow his directions, stumbling through the dark corridor and practically falling into the bathroom. I lock the door behind me, put down the toilet seat, and slump onto it, trying to reason with myself.

There's no reason to be panicking. So far, the guys have saved me from a snowstorm, carried in my luggage, given me a check-up, and fed me. They even towed my car. If they wanted to hurt me, they would've done it by now. They're more than big enough to force me to do anything they want, and they've had plenty of opportunities.

I need to calm down.

There's a light tap on the door. "Are you okay in there?" Eli calls. "Are you trying to escape out of the window? The latch is a bit fiddly, you have to jiggle it."

I stand shakily and open the door. I'm immediately hit with the mouthwatering scent of warm sugar and cinnamon. Eli takes a step back, giving me space, and offers me a plate. "I made you a cinnamon bun to say sorry?" He tries.

I look down at the pastry. It looks delicious. "You made it?"

"Well. I put it in the microwave. But I did it very apologetically." He gives me a hopeful smile. "Look, I'm really sorry. I didn't mean to scare you. I promise mine and Riv's intentions were honourable, but you're right, it was shitty." He ruffles a hand through his hair. "If you want to be alone, you can spend the night in my room, and I'll take the couch, or—" He frowns. "Maybe... is that creepy, too? Um. We have a spare room I can drag a guest bed into, if you want to wait in the lounge? We don't get a whole lot of guests, we're kinda unprepared."

He looks so earnest, and so genuinely upset that he's scared me, that embarrassment blooms through me.

I hate that I've become this sensitive. A few months ago, if a man this hot had demanded I take my shirt off to *check me for injuries,* I would have whipped it off in seconds, and probably purred while he did it. I hate that I've gotten so scared of people. I *hate* it. It's not *me.* I feel like a little rabbit, jumping at every sudden noise, looking at everybody like they're a potential predator.

"No. No. It's okay. Thanks. I... don't want to be alone." I take the plate, heading back to the lounge. "Sorry for snapping. It's kind of a touchy subject for me, I guess." I curl back into my spot on the sofa, nestling into the cushions.

He plops down next to me, concern crossing his face. "What? Why?" When I don't say anything, his jaw goes tight. "*Why*?" He says again, his voice sharpening. "Did someone hurt you?"

I open my mouth, but no words come out.

He straightens. All of the lazy charm falls off him, and suddenly, he doesn't look quite so harmless. I don't doubt that this man could mess someone up in a fight.

"No," I say hurriedly. "No. Nothing like—whatever you're thinking. I shouldn't have said that." I rub my eyes. "I'm just tired. I'm talking too much."

He studies me for a few seconds, his face serious. I force myself to smile at him. For a second, I think he's going to push it, but instead, his expression softens. He opens his arms. "Want a hug?"

I blink, surprised. I don't know what I was expecting, but this wasn't it. I feel an odd tugging in my chest. I *do* want a hug, I realise. I kind of need one very, very badly. I've just had the most Hellish week of my life. I put down my plate. "I—um. Yeah. Okay."

He shuffles forward and wraps his strong arms around me. I don't even think before I bury my face in his shoulder, breathing in the scent of cinnamon sugar and pine trees. His t-shirt is soft and warm, and I can feel his heart beating steadily against my cheek. I melt into him.

I don't remember the last time I had a hug. Everyone who used to care about me hates me, now. Even my own parents wouldn't touch me with a bargepole.

Tears suddenly spring to my eyes. I try to swallow them down, but I can't. One tear drips down my nose, and then another. Soon I'm crying softly into his shirt. I can't stop.

Eli makes a sad noise. "Oh, sweetheart." He pulls me closer. "Shh. It's okay. It's okay." He starts rubbing my back soothingly. "You're okay."

I don't know how long I cry for. It feels like forever. He holds me the whole time, murmuring softly into my hair. Eventually, I run out of tears and pull away, hiccuping. "G-god." I wipe my face, embarrassed. "Sorry. I don't know where that came from."

He actually *laughs,* brushing a strand of hair away from my wet cheek. "Christ, what would it normally take you? A death in the family?"

"What?"

"You're lost in a foreign country, you were just in a car crash, you're injured, you barely missed freezing to death in a storm, and now you're trapped in an unfamiliar place with no way to contact the outside world. Trust me. Most people would cry at any one of those things." He squeezes me. "You're just exhausted, babe. Don't sweat it."

"Thanks." I snuffle. "It's BS, but I appreciate it."

"It's not BS." He wipes a tear off my cheek with his thumb. "I know you have no reason to trust me," he says sincerely. "But you *are* safe here. I promise."

I meet his gaze. The firelight flickers in his green eyes. His face is completely open and earnest. I can't help but believe him. Slowly, I nod.

He strokes another tear-track away, and I realise he hasn't let go of my face. I don't actually mind. It's nice to have his warm hands on me. His thumbs move up to my temples, and he starts rubbing circles, easing my headache.

"This okay?" He asks, his low voice rasping.

I nod, tipping into the touch. The fire crackles in the hearth. Outside, I can hear the muffled sounds of the storm. My breath gives a little hitch, still shaky from the crying, and he cups my cheek.

"You're okay," he says again, his voice low. I lean into his palm. I'm so tired. I let my eyes flutter shut, exhaustion slowly weighing down my body. I just want to curl up against him and disappear. Just for a bit.

Then, suddenly, he's ripped away from me. I open my eyes, looking down in horror at him sprawled on the rug. Cole is standing over him, his snow-wet boot planted in the middle of his chest. His face is murderous.

CHAPTER 6
ELI

Poor Daisy looks like she's going to have a heart attack. She shoots up, her eyes widening. "What are you doing?" She demands. "Get the Hell off him!"

"No."

She launches herself at Cole, trying to pull him off me. I've got to hand it to her—she's a fighter. She comes at him like a wildcat. Unfortunately, he's used to dealing with moose about fourteen times her weight, so he probably barely notices as she grabs his arm and tries to drag him away.

"What is *wrong with you?*" She hisses. "Have you lived in the woods so long you've turned into a bear? Get off him!"

"What the Hell do you think you're doing?" He growls at me. "We left you alone for half an hour! You can't keep your hands off her for that long?"

I put my hands up. "I didn't do anything!"

"He wasn't groping me," Daisy pipes up. "He was comforting me!"

"He hit on you while you have a *head injury*," Cole snarls.

"I don't! Riven said I was fine. And *I* was the one snuggling up to him, not the other way around." She tries again to shove Cole off me. "Get off him, you brute."

"It's alright, babe," I say. "We do this all the time. He's pretty easy to take down, look." I grab him by the ankle and yank, hard. Cole swears as he topples down on top of me. I grunt as all the air gets knocked out my lungs. "Jesus. You need to go on a diet, man. No more moose pie for you."

He shoves himself upright, eyes burning. "Come to the barn," he mutters. "Riven wants to talk to you."

Daisy offers me her hand. I don't need it, but I'm certainly not going to say no to any opportunity to touch her. I wrap my fingers around her tiny wrist, letting her help me to my feet, then brush myself off.

"See? No harm done. Cole wouldn't hurt a fly, really."

"Sure." She sounds sceptical. "Where are we going?"

"Not you," Cole orders. "Stay." He pushes her back onto the sofa cushions.

She sputters. "I'm not a dog!"

"We're going to talk about you. You can't come."

"We're going to look at your car," I explain, glaring at him. "You may as well stay here in the warm. Here." I pull a blanket out of the basket next to the sofa and wrap it around her. "Eat your cinnamon bun. We'll be back soon."

Her eyes narrow. This is not a girl who likes being told what to do. Noted. I smile at her as angelically as I can, until she sits back down, her eyes still suspicious.

Bored of this interaction, Cole turns on his heel and leaves, heading for the door.

I catch up with him halfway to the barn, stumbling through the snow. It's coming down thick, now. We don't have a lot of time. "Can you tone it down a bit?" I ask, as he storms ahead. "I was just telling her she was safe here. I don't think your random act of violence is really going to convince her."

"You shouldn't have tried to kiss her when she was drugged up and crying," he mutters.

"I wasn't going to kiss her."

"You were."

"I wasn't! I was drying off her face! She was upset!"

He cuts me a cold look. "You've never seen a pretty girl you didn't try to kiss."

"It's actually the other way around. A pretty girl never saw *me* and decided not to kiss me. That's hardly my fault, I'm just immensely kissable."

"Really?" He looks unimpressed. "You didn't even think about it?"

I scoff. "Well, I didn't say that."

Of course I thought about it. I've been thinking about it ever since I first saw Daisy. She looked adorable with her huge brown eyes, her cheeks pink from the cold. And then we got her inside, and I could see the rest of her. She's stunning. All curves and flowing hair. When she snuggled up with me on the couch, I got a close-up view of her soft pink mouth. So yes, I *thought* about kissing her. But I think about a lot of things. I wasn't actually going to do it. I'm not enough of a prick to kiss a scared, crying girl.

Cole's reaction is pretty interesting, though. Considering how much he seems to dislike Daisy, he certainly is protective over her.

I grin up at him. "That's sweet, you know. You swooped in like her knight in shining armour. It kinda seems like you *like* her—"

I grunt as he shoves me sideways into a pile of snow.

Cole towed Daisy's car into our storage barn. It's a big wooden building that we keep all of our vehicles and supplies in. One corner is full with chopped firewood covered with a tarp. In the other, we've got food; tinned and dried goods, and a ton of frozen meat. Daisy's car is parked up next to Cole's truck. Riven's got his head stuck in the bonnet.

"Well?" I pull the barn door shut.

"It's dead." He kicks the tyre. "It needs a heavy-duty mechanic. There's no way she can get it looked at until after the storm ends." He frowns. "Even then, she won't get far without giving up her license."

I remember the panic in her eyes as she lunged for her wallet. "Maybe it's out of date? And she thought we'd get her in trouble?"

"We're not traffic wardens," he mutters. "She didn't have any Swedish cash, either. Just English." I can see his mind ticking over as he tries to put the puzzle together.

Riven's always like this. He loves problem-solving. I guess that's what makes him such a good doctor. I'm personally of the opinion that when a gorgeous girl ends up in your house, you shouldn't question it.

"She doesn't know the language," he says slowly. "She doesn't have the right clothes, she didn't get her tyres changed. It's like she wasn't planning this." He glances at me. "Did she tell you what she does?"

"Says she's a teacher."

"What sort of teacher?"

"Dunno. When I pushed her, she just froze up. She clearly didn't want to talk about it."

"Isn't it the middle of the school year? She just abandoned her students to come drive out, completely unprepared, into the wilderness? It's like she suddenly had to drop everything and run."

"Sounds like she's in trouble with the law," Cole grits out. "We need to get her the Hell out of here."

"This isn't just your house," I point out.

When we first came across the cabin, it was more of a dilapidated shed. Between the three of us, we fixed it up into a real home; we installed plumbing and a generator, rebuilt all the walls and windows, added in the solar panels and under-floor heating. Riven covered the costs, and we split the labour between us. It's not like Cole can make any decisions about house guests all by himself.

"We should vote," I decide. "I vote that the sexy British chick stays as long as possible. Riven?"

We both turn to look at him. He presses his lips together. "I think, if she wants to stay, she should answer some of our questions. Or at least let us see some form of identification."

I throw my hands up. "Well, I think you're both being pricks. If she were a guy, would you be acting so bloody suspicious?"

Neither of them respond. They know the answer. If Daisy were a guy, she would probably already be asleep in a guest bed.

"Well, then," I say. "Maybe stop being so sexist."

Cole snorts. "Right. Because that's why you want her to stay. You're championing women's rights."

"I think women have the right not to freeze to death, yes," I bite back. "For God's sake, pull yourself together. She needs help. It's not *her* fault she's pretty."

Riven rubs his eyes. "She can stay until the storm passes," he decides. "Then Cole can tow her car into the town to get fixed, and she can book into a hotel."

"That could be days," Cole growls.

I toss him a grin. "I'm sure we'll find a few ways to pass the time."

We have an old collapsible guest bed tucked away in the back of the barn, so we take it with us back to the cabin. When we get inside, though, it turns out it's not necessary; Daisy's fallen asleep on the sofa, curled in a tiny ball under the blanket. Riv heads back to his office to do some work. Cole goes to clear stuff out of the junk room. I just stay in the lounge for a while, warming up by the fire, and watching the light flicker over her face.

CHAPTER 7
DAISY

I don't know if it's the exhaustion, or the drugs, or the wild Arctic air I've been breathing, but I have the oddest dream.

At first, I don't even know I'm dreaming. I'm still lying on the boys' couch, curled up in their blanket. I'm dozing, halfway between asleep and awake, when Eli steps into the room. His green eyes are shining. He smirks at me, then grabs the bottom of his shirt and pulls it up over his head in one smooth motion, letting it crumple to the floor. I feel my mouth drop open. He's covered in hard, cut muscle. My eyes trail across the strong pecs, the tight abs, and down to the tapered V of muscle leading below the waistband of his pants.

"Like what you see?" He smirks, coming to kneel between my legs. Heat slams through me as he tips up his mouth and starts pressing kisses up my thighs. "I want to taste you, sweetheart," he murmurs against my skin. "Want to fucking bury myself in you. Suck you and kiss you until you fucking burst all over my face."

My mouth falls open. "Oh," I whisper.

His mouth trails up, and up, sending tingles shooting through me, until his lips come to rest a few millimetres over my wet sex. Heat pools in me, and I give the tiniest tremble. He smiles against me, and leans in, licking a hot, firm stripe between my folds. My breath hitches gently, a soft sound of pleasure, and I wrap my fingers in his curls. He licks me again and again, pushing his face in deep. Warmth sinks into my skin, like I'm being dipped into a hot bath. All of my muscles weaken, and I slump back against the couch, feeling my cheeks start to flush as my breathing gets heavier.

The door opens again. Riven steps inside and comes to sit by me. For some reason, even though Eli's mouth is currently between my legs, it doesn't feel weird to have him so close.

"Daisy. You look flushed," he says with a frown, and starts running his hands across me with his gentle doctor's touch. Eli's tongue traces through my folds. An ache starts up, deep inside me, and I twitch involuntarily, shifting my weight to get the pressure right. Riv's frown gets deeper. "Let me just check that you're okay," he says quietly, bending to lift up my shirt. I try to protest, but before I can, my shirt and bra have disappeared. He stares at my naked tits, his dark eyes hungry. Slowly, he lifts a finger and traces it around my nipple, lifting goosebumps on my skin. I cry out as he gently pinches the hardening nub, tugging it away from my body.

Between my legs, Eli slips his hot tongue inside me. All of a sudden, the dull heat inside me bursts into flame. My eyes widen, and my hips start to move helplessly as I try to rub out the building ache. Eli's tongue slides in deep, and feels good, so good I'm struggling to get air in, but I need more. I need so much more. I'm throbbing and hurting, my breasts aching, my core clenching. I claw at the sofa cushions, a whine building in the back of my throat. Riv seems to understand, and starts kissing my neck as he alternates between squeezing and kissing my breasts, teasing me until it feels like my nerves are on fire. My body writhes, rubbing against itself as it tries to relieve the tingling pricks of arousal. I feel myself building towards a shivery, full-body climax. Oh, God. God. I can't take it anymore. My hips jolt once, twice—

"I'm going to—" I whisper breathily.

"No." A heavy hand lands on my shoulder. "Open your eyes, girl."

I do, and see Cole standing over me in just his underwear. "Oh, God," I breathe, still rocking my hips desperately over Eli's face. Him, too?

My eyes widen as he pushes down his boxers. His cock is huge and hard, stiffening slowly as he runs a hand across it. My mouth waters when I see the smooth, delicate skin. I want him in my mouth. I want to taste. "Please," I choke out.

He reaches down and touches my bottom lip gently. "I want you to take it all."

I stare. "I don't think—"

"You can take it," he says roughly. My head tips back on a gasp, my mouth going slack as Cole pushes gently inside. I wrap my lips around the head of his dick, feeling him shudder deliciously as I start to lick up his warm, salty taste, groaning in pleasure.

Eli suddenly flutters his tongue against me. I cry out, spasming. Shivers hurtle down my spine, wracking through me. I can't handle it anymore. I twist my hands in Eli's hair, closing my eyes as I start to come, every muscle in my body shaking helplessly with release as wave after wave of pleasure shudders through me—

"Daisy?"

I jolt awake, sweating, with my hand between my legs. Tingles are rushing over my skin. I'm hot and trembling, and there's an ache low in my belly. For a few seconds, I don't know where I am. I look around me, wide-eyed, taking in the wooden walls, the beams on the ceiling, the big oak dining table. Eventually, my eyes land on Eli, and my stomach flips. He looks just as hot as he did in my dream, in a white t-shirt that clings to his biceps, and a loose pair of sweatpants. His curls are ruffled like he just got out of bed. I glance at the window. Morning sunlight filters through the curtains. I slept the whole night through.

Eli smiles at me. "You okay, sweetheart? You were squirming around a bit. Thought you might be having a nightmare."

I look down. I'm covered in a blanket, thank God. I pull my hand away from my crotch. Christ, I'm actually wet. I can feel the cold stickiness clinging to my thighs.

I don't even remember the last time I had a sex dream. Let alone one I woke up wet from. I swallow, wiping my hand slyly off on my thigh. "No. No, I'm fine."

He frowns. "Hey. You're all pink, babe. Did you catch a cold out in the snow?" He reaches over, and his fingertips brush my fore-head. I jerk back, heart racing. I don't think I can handle his hands on me right now. The image of his head between my thighs slaps over my vision, so vivid I have to blink it away.

He puts his hands up. "Sorry, sorry. Didn't mean to spook you." He points a thumb back to the kitchen. "I'm making pancakes. You want one?"

I clear my throat. "Yeah. Yeah, a pancake would be great."

"Great. They'll be about ten minutes, so you've got just enough time for a shower. I left a towel out for you."

"Thank you," I squeak, sliding off the sofa and hobbling towards the bathroom. My little pink suitcase is in the hallway, so I stop to grab some clean clothes before shutting the bathroom door behind me.

I look around. I was in here just last night, but I was so freaked out, I didn't even notice the shower. It's built to look like the inside of a sauna; the walls are made with light-coloured wooden planks, and there's a little bench built into one side. I find the water knob and turn it, gasping under the burning hot spray. Powerful jets of water pummel me, beating away the tension in my body. I close my eyes and just stand there for a moment, basking in it, then look around for something to wash with. There's a little shampoo rack fixed to the wall, lined up with three bottles. One black, one white, one green. I'm sure Eli wouldn't mind me using his; I just have to work out which one it is. I pick up the black one and pop the cap, smelling it. The scent is hot and musky, like whiskey and spice. I close my eyes, inhaling. It's *delicious,* but it doesn't seem like Eli's thing.

I try the white bottle. It smells fresh and clean, like sheets and soap. This one's a possibility. So is the green one, which is scented like fresh-cut pine. I stand there for almost a minute, holding the bottles and deliberating under the hot flow of water, before I manage to shake myself out of it.

Jesus Christ. What the Hell is wrong with me? Is it something in the air? Is there less oxygen at this altitude, or something? Why on Earth am I standing in a strange man's shower, huffing his shower gel?

I squeeze a bit out from the black bottle, wash myself down, then get out and dress quickly. When I step back into the kitchen, braiding my hair, Eli's standing at the stove holding a sizzling frying pan. The sweet, buttery smell of pancakes hits my nose, and my mouth immediately starts to water.

I finish tying off the end of my plait. "Can I help? Do you want me to set the table, or something?"

"Don't worry about it, babe. Just sit down." He tosses me a sideways look. "How are you feeling?"

I rub the back of my stiff neck. "Okay."

"Still hurting, huh?" He flashes me a grin. "If you're gonna lie, you should get better at it. We have plenty of experience dealing with Cole. The guy once got bitten by a moose and didn't tell us until two days later, when he *literally started dying* from blood poisoning."

I roll my shoulders. "Kinda sore," I admit.

He licks some batter off his thumb. "You know, that massage is still on the table."

"Dream on."

He laughs easily. "Oh, trust me, I will. Hey, check it." He shuffles the pan a couple of times, then flips the pancake high in the air, catching it neatly. I watch his big bicep flex under the sleeve of his t-shirt.

"Very nice," I manage.

He tosses me a bright smile, then turns back to the food.

"Morning," a low voice rasps. I look up to see Riv standing in the doorway, his dark hair rumpled. He's wearing thick-framed glasses and a tight white t-shirt that practically glows against his black skin. I didn't realise just how built he was last night. He's even more ripped than Eli. The muscles in his arms are like ropes. He pours himself a mug of coffee, slaps Eli on the shoulder, then comes to stand by me. I jump when he stoops, taking my neck carefully between his hands.

"Wha—"

He slides his thumbs under my jaw and gently moves my neck to each side. I'm suddenly surrounded by the scent of him; clean and fresh, like crisp linen straight out of the drier. It makes me want to bury my face in his shirt.

"I thought you gave me the all-clear?" I say weakly, as he turns my face under the light.

"Double-checking never hurts," he murmurs. As he pulls back his hands, I could've sworn his thumb brushes my cheek. "Here." He presses two more pills into my hand.

"Um. Thanks." Eli slides a plate of pancakes in front of me, tugging at the end of my braid. "Thanks," I say again. "Really. You two are being so kind."

I say the *two* quite pointedly. Eli snorts, sitting down next to me. I start wolfing down my food.

Riv goes to the stove to make up his plate. "I radioed down to the nurses in town," he says over his shoulder. "Apparently, the snow is forecasted to stop by this afternoon."

I perk up. "That's great!"

Riv winces. "It's not as simple as that. Even though the storm might have passed, it doesn't mean that you'll be able to travel."

Eli nods out of the window. "We'll have to dig ourselves out, first. And then wait for the roads to be cleared."

"Down in the city, they have snowmobiles, but all the way up here, the government just pays farmers to use their tractors," Riven adds. "God knows when they'll get to it." He takes a deep sip of his coffee. "It does mean that cell phone reception should be back up, though. There must be so many people worried about you."

I poke at my pancakes. "I doubt it. No one even knows I'm here."

He raises an eyebrow. "Not even your family?"

"They stopped speaking to me."

"No friends?"

Not anymore. I smile grimly. "Nope."

"No boyfriend?" Eli asks lazily. We both look at him, and he shrugs. "Just wondering. It seems like important information."

"No. I don't have a boyfriend."

He sighs. "You poor thing. If you ever want to fix that—"

"Shut up," Riven says, closing his eyes.

Call me, Eli mouths, winking. I snort, using my last piece of pancake to sop up the leftover jam, then sit back in my seat, fully satisfied.

"So, what happens now? What do you guys do when you can't leave the house?"

Eli leans forward, meeting my eyes. "How do you feel about Uno?" He asks very seriously.

CHAPTER 8
DAISY

Riven's right; the storm does stop. By noon, the snowfall is just a gentle pitter, and by two, the skies are completely clear. The guys all convene in the lounge, getting ready to shovel snow before it freezes. I tag along and start getting dressed, too.

"We really can handle it ourselves," Riven says, frowning. "I don't want you to aggravate your neck."

"My neck is fine," I insist. "Really. The pills worked; it doesn't even hurt anymore."

He gives me a stern look. "Just because you're not experiencing pain, doesn't mean that you're not injured."

"I'll be careful," I promise. "Seriously. I'm not going to sit around like a princess while you do all the work."

He sighs, handing me a shovel. It's so big I struggle to lift it. Jesus. Being around the guys makes me feel like I've shrunk.

Everything about them is big; their bodies, their equipment, their furniture. And, unfortunately, their clothes.

"You can wear your little pink jacket as an undercoat," Eli says, sifting through the hall closet. "But you'll need something on top until you work up a sweat."

I peep under his arm and see that the closet is full of skiwear, tightly packed together. "Wow. You have so many jackets."

"Get one every tournament," he says distractedly, pulling out a red jacket, holding it up against me, then shoving it back in.

"You compete?"

"He's a national champion downhill skier," Riv cuts in, tying his bootlaces. I get a brief glimpse of tight, rounded glutes as he bends over, before forcing myself to look away, my face heating.

"Here you are." Eli pulls out a puffy white jacket with his name emblazoned across the back. "This one's a bit small for me, so it might not completely drown you." He helps me into it, and I try to fasten it up, but some of my hair gets tangled in the zip. I wince as my scalp burns, trying to tug myself free, but the strands are wedged tight in the little zipper.

Suddenly, I feel big hands on my shoulders. I go very still as the dark scent of spice and whiskey fills my nose. Cole carefully eases the zipper free, then twists my hair together in a ponytail, tucking it down the back of my coat. His fingers are unbelievably gentle, sending sparks rushing across my skin. I swallow through my dry mouth as he steps back.

"Thank you," I say.

"Why is she even coming?" He grumbles. "How is she going to shovel snow when she can't even dress herself?"

I scowl at him. "Oh, I'm sure *she* can learn. *She's* not totally stupid." I might be small, but I'm strong.

He raises an eyebrow, pulls a pair of gloves out of his pocket, and tosses them over his shoulder at me. "Just try not to freeze," he mutters.

Finally, we're all suited and booted, and we step out into the snow. It's the first time I've properly seen where the boys live, and the view takes my breath away. We're midway up the mountain, looking down over forests of pines. Everything has been blanketed in snow, and the whole landscape glimmers, flashing delicate blue and silver as it reflects the early spring sunlight. I look up. Peaks rise around us, looming over our heads. "Wow."

Eli grins. "Sweet, right?"

"More than sweet." I look around, taking everything in. My fingers itch for a paintbrush, and I wince as I remember my mangled canvases. I'll have to make sure to get some great reference photos before I leave. "What's that over there?" I point to a dilapidated stone hut on the edge of the drive. Eli follows my gaze.

"Oh. That's the shack. It's where the previous owner kept firewood and supplies and stuff. It was way too small for us, so we built the barn instead. We should really get around to knocking it down."

There's a clanging noise, and I turn to see Cole grab a ladder attached to the side of the cabin. Heaving his rake over one shoulder, he starts climbing up onto the roof one-handed.

I watch him go. "Is that safe?"

Riven shrugs. "He's not died yet." He turns to Eli. "I'll take the barn. You two do the drive?"

Eli nods. Riv disappears towards the huge shed while Eli and I tramp down to the road. A strong wind breezes past us and I shiver, even through both my coats. "Jesus. How cold is it?"

Eli stamps, tilting his head. "I'd say about minus twenty?" He hazards cheerfully.

"How do you know?"

He shrugs. "This is what the snow sounds like at minus twenty. Don't worry. You'll soon warm up." He passes me my shovel. "Now remember. Lift with your legs."

Half an hour later, I am a snow shovelling machine. *Heave. Lift. Drop. Heave. Lift. Drop.* I heave and lift and drop over and over again, clearing the snow as fast as I possibly can. It's tiring work, and all of my muscles are aching, but I don't care. I throw myself into it. I want to pull my weight. And I want to show Cole that I'm not completely useless.

A trickle of sweat drips down the back of my neck, and I stick my shovel in the growing pile of displaced snow, straightening to unzip Eli's jacket and tie it around my waist. I look around, panting. A little wave of triumph hits me when I see the section that I've cleared is almost as big as Eli's.

He's stopped shovelling too, and is leaning against a pine, looking at me. Not doing anything. Just looking.

"What?" I call.

He shakes his head. "Nothing. Just watching you."

I huff, turning back to the snow. "Creep." I dig my shovel back into the snow and heave to lift it up, all the muscles in my arm shaking.

Something hard thumps into my back, almost knocking me over. I whip around to see Eli patting together another snowball. "What was that for?!"

He shrugs. "You called me a creep. That's not nice. I'm very offended." He bends for more snow, and I take in the view. He's taken off his jacket, too, so I can see his sweater-covered muscles in all their glory. His high cheekbones are stained pink from the cold, and his coppery hair is ruffled. He looks *delicious.*

I wipe snow off my shoulder. "If you don't wanna be called a creep, maybe stop staring at me."

"But you're so nice to look at." He straightens. "Here. Catch."

"Catch wha—"

He pulls his arm back and lobs the snowball right at my face. I gasp as it hits my cheek, so cold it almost feels like a burn. Without thinking, I drop my shovel and jump, grabbing a branch of the pine tree spreading over us and shaking it hard. Eli yelps as a pile of snow slides down over him.

"Shit!" He bends and grabs at the snow, balling up another sloppy snowball, and I dash for cover. The snowball flies right by my face, clipping my ear, and I frantically grab my own lump of snow to chuck back at him.

Soon, we're in the middle of a full-blown snowball fight. We batter each other, not pulling any punches. He's not holding back because I'm smaller than him; he's using every ounce of strength in his giant athlete's body to beat me. And it's *fun*. So much fun. I feel like a kid. Eli is so playful, it's bringing out a light-heartedness in me that I haven't felt in months. I've been so worried about my scummy ex, it's like I've forgotten how to just enjoy myself. And now this man, with his lazy smile and constant teasing, has brought that part of me back out of hiding.

I love it.

I peek out from the tree I've been hiding behind, sending my own missile flying towards him and hooting in triumph when it hits him dead in the forehead. He scowls, shaking snow out of his hair like a wet dog, then bends and sweeps up armfuls of snow, packing it together. My eyes widen when I see how big the ball is getting. "Don't you dare!" I shout over the wind. He grins, scooping up more and more snow. I drop to the ground to make my own giant ball, but when I look up again, he's standing, hefting a lump of snow bigger than my head.

"Any last words?" He calls.

I back up slowly, holding my hands in the air. "Eli—"

He lifts his arms back to throw, and I turn on my heel and run. I barely get three steps away before the giant snowball hits me in the back. Knocked off balance, I trip on one of my snowshoes, skid, and slip over, landing on my ass. I groan and roll over, looking up at the pale blue sky. My blood pounds in my ears. Freezing snow falls down the back of my jacket.

I feel more alive than I have in a long time.

There's a crunching sound as Eli jogs up to me, panting. "Wipe-out," he crows. "You good?"

I can't resist messing with him. I wince, propping myself up on my elbows. "I'm not sure. Think I twisted my ankle."

The smile drops right off his face. "Shit. Really? RIV—" He steps closer, giving me the opening I need. I grab at his knee and yank, pulling him down just like I saw him do to Cole last night. He lands on top of me, our limbs all tangled together. "Mother*fucker*."

"Sorry," I giggle. "It was too tempting."

He tuts. "Babe, if you wanted to get under me, you could've just asked." He settles himself more comfortably on top of me. I push at him, but he just makes himself even heavier, pinning me to the ground. He bends so close his curls brush my face. Little forks of electricity flicker in my belly. My eyes trace over his twinkling green eyes, cataloguing the tiny starburst of freckles under his eyebrow, the faded scar on his cheekbone.

"Do you surrender?" He practically purrs.

"Never," I whisper.

"*Reaaally,*" he draws the word out.

I can't breathe right. His chest is pressing against mine; I can feel the solid muscle crushing my breasts. My stomach flips over and over as his eyes drop to my mouth.

I want to kiss him, I realise. I want to kiss him so badly my lips ache. I want a bit of his sunny happiness for myself. His lashes lower, and he dips his head until our lips are almost brushing. I let my eyes fall shut, tilting my mouth up to his, and a low, appreciative rumble rattles through him. He bends lower, his lips barely grazing mine—

I reach out, grab a handful of snow, and stuff it down the neck of his jumper.

He chokes and shudders as it slides down his chest. "Oh, *Jesus*—"

"Never!" I announce again, grinning.

He scowls at me and twists to scoop up his own handful. I cringe, expecting a faceful of snow. Instead, he just gets a tiny pinch between his fingers. My heart stutters as he leans forward, his eyes very intent on my face, and touches the freezing crystals to my lips. I whimper at the freezing sensation. A breath knocks through his body at the sound, all of his muscles tensing. His hand spreads over my neck, tilting my jaw up.

"Let me get that," he rasps.

I nod, letting my eyes flutter shut as he finally kisses me.

It's a tiny kiss, as if he's sipping the snow right back off my lips. The feeling of his hot mouth on my freezing skin is almost orgasmic. I sigh, gripping hard into his shoulders, and kiss him back, hard. He groans, wrapping his arms around me and pulling me into him.

Eli kisses exactly how I expected him to: playful and nipping and sweet. A thrill washes over me as he presses a tiny kiss to my bottom lip, then sucks it slowly into his mouth, his hands stroking me through all of my layers. He clearly knows what he's doing. My ex-boyfriend Sam always kissed me the exact same way, like he was following a routine; five seconds closed-mouthed, ten seconds frenching, rinse and repeat. Eli's much more natural, moving on top of me, responding to every little twitch of my body and sigh that leaves my lips.

The scent of pine fills my senses as he nudges my lips open with his and slips his tongue against mine. My head spins. I grab a fistful of his sweater, and he makes a deep purr in the back of his throat. The sound rumbles through me, making my stomach flutter and my breasts ache.

Without thinking, my hands drift to the hem of his sweater. I slip off my gloves and slide my fingers under the hem of his shirt, feeling his burning skin and hot, hard muscle. The snow at my back is freezing, seeping through my ski jacket; but the man on top of me is like a furnace, radiating heat, and I just want to cuddle up to him. I run my fingers across the ridges of his muscles as I kiss him, and he shudders over me, letting loose a low moan right by my ear. His lips leave mine, trailing down my cheek and across to my throat. His curls tickle my skin as he starts pressing hot, sucking kisses down the side of my neck. I can feel wetness starting to pool between my legs, and arch as he hits a particularly sensitive spot.

Suddenly, he stills, then pulls back, ignoring the little whine I make when his lips leave my skin. He pushes some hair behind my ear. "Hey. It's tingling."

I open my eyes, blinking through the lust hazing my brain. "Huh?"

"It's *definitely* tingling," he says, staring intently at my neck. "Shit. That's so cute."

"What's tingling? Your dick?" I buck my hips, feeling the hardening bulge between his legs.

He grunts, grinding down on me in return, and my mouth falls open on a pant. "Not *tingling*. *Tin-gel-ing*." He strokes a finger behind my ear, making me shiver, and I realise he's brushing his fingertip over my tattoo. It's a tiny fairy silhouette, about as long as my fingernail, tucked behind my ear.

"You mean Tinkerbell? I got her after I went to Disney a couple years back."

"*Tinkerbell*. She's called Tingeling in Swedish." He tips his head, taking me in. "Hm. It's fitting. You're both about the same size."

I narrow my eyes. "Not a massive fan of the height jokes," I warn.

He grins impishly. "Aww. What are you gonna do? Kick me in the ankles?"

"Probably someplace higher. I think if I stretch, I can *just* about reach your balls."

"Thank God. Imagine the tragedy, if you couldn't reach my balls!" He nuzzles into my neck. "Baby, you're shaking. You're getting too cold. C'mon." He kisses my tattoo. "Let's get you warmed up." He stands and takes my hand. The world tips in a blur of white as I'm pulled upright. He puts both of our shovels under his arm, and we trail back to the house. My whole body is humming. My lips are tingling. I can feel heat coursing through my veins, lighting me up inside.

What the Hell was that? I peep up at the side of Eli's handsome face as we stamp through the snow. What happens now? Do we just go inside and pretend it didn't happen? Do we kiss again? I don't think I've ever kissed a stranger outside of a nightclub before. I couldn't help myself. It seemed so natural.

Eli squeezes my hand. "Relax, Tink. You want some hot chocolate? I make it from scratch."

I shake my head, like I can toss out all of the loud, clamouring thoughts knocking around my brain. "*Please*."

We step back into the cabin. Riven's already there, sitting at the kitchen table in front of his laptop.

"Have fun?" He asks, not bothering to look up.

I blush, toeing off my boots. "Eli's a child. He started a snowball fight."

"I'm sure he's enjoying having someone to play with," he drawls, then nods at my phone. "I put your phone on charge. Someone called Sam keeps calling you."

My head jerks up. "*What*?"

He blinks, taken aback by my reaction. "I didn't mean to pry. His name popped up."

I shake off my coat and half-run across the room to swipe my phone. A text from Sam glares up at me, and my stomach drops. I quickly delete the message without looking at it. "He's my ex-boyfriend. We broke up a few months ago, but he still won't leave me alone."

Eli whistles, setting a pan on the stove. "That's shitty."

"Yeah. It really is."

Pretty much everything about Sam was shitty, to be honest. I met him about four years ago, at an art show. He swept me off my feet. The longer we were together, though, the more he changed. He was jealous. He kept trying to cut me off from my friends. He didn't let me speak to other men. I know a red flag when I see one. I gave him some time to clean up his act, and when he didn't, I left.

And then he showed me exactly how shitty of a person he was.

Sighing, I roll through the rest of my notifications. I have hundreds, mostly texts from old acquaintances who have seen me on the news. There are outraged emails from my students' parents. Multiple missed calls from the school. I delete them all, trying my best not to look at them, then open up the email box for my painting business. After my big scandal, I'm not expecting any clients; but I guess all publicity is good publicity, because I have a handful of portrait commission requests. Well, three, to be exact, and then a couple of emails from people calling me a slag. Because this is my life now.

Eli puts his chin on my shoulder and holds a square of chocolate against my lips. His curls brush my cheek. "What's that?"

I quickly delete an anonymous message with the subject line DIE YOU SLUT BITCH, clearing my throat. "Um… my commissions email. I have a couple people who want paintings done." I open my mouth, letting him pop the chocolate inside.

"Commissions?" Riven's fingers pause over his keyboard. "I thought you were a teacher?"

I lick my lips. "I'm… ah. Taking a break from teaching right now. I really only do it for the money. My degree is in Fine Arts. I always wanted to be a painter."

The stove crackles, and Eli goes to check on the hot chocolate. I can practically see the wheels turning in Riv's head as he pieces the jigsaw together. "Oh? And that's why you had all that painting equipment in your car?"

I nod. "I actually came up here to paint the Northern Lights. I always wanted to see them, and I needed a holiday, so I figured now was the right time."

"Hm." He purses his lips. "Is there a big market for oil paintings nowadays?"

"You'd be surprised. It's a pretty common wedding gift. People like to have portraits of their families, and stuff. I prefer land-scapes, but—" I shrug, uncomfortable with the line of question-ing. "Whatever gets the clients, I guess."

He taps his full bottom lip with the end of his pen. "Do you have a website? I'd love to see some of your work."

There's no way in Hell. "It's under construction," I say brightly. "Sorry."

He frowns slightly. "How are you able to get clients if your website is down?"

I open my mouth to try to answer, but luckily, Eli interrupts the interrogation, plonking four steaming mugs on the table. He strokes a hand lightly down my arm. "Wanna check out your bedroom?" He murmurs in my ear. "Cole set it up last night. Probably more comfortable than our sofa." He pauses. "Defi-nitely more private."

I think I see Riven roll his eyes. I jump at the chance to get away, picking up two hot chocolates. "Lead the way."

Eli shows me down the hallway to a door I haven't seen before, standing aside to let me inside. I get a brief glimpse of a little cot bed and a lamp, before Eli dumps the mugs on the floor, spins me around, and pins me up against the wall, his mouth slanting over mine in a deep, slow kiss. His lips are soft and taste like chocolate, and I sigh, melting under him.

CHAPTER 9
COLE

I love storms.

They make life so much simpler. You stay inside with the fire going. You read books, you watch the snow fall. You eat simple meals and go to bed early. No shopping. No strangers. No work. We always lose signal, so no phones or television. It's good for you. Cleans your brain out. Helps you reset.

Or it did.

The girl won't stop laughing.

I put down my book for the fifth time, trying to keep my annoyance in check.

I'm used to living with two other men. Riven's quiet enough, and even though Eli can be loud, at least his voice is low enough for the radio to drown out. I forgot how high-pitched girls' voices are. Daisy's laughing, and it sounds like a damn bell tinkling, easily cutting through the cabin's walls. It's setting me on edge.

I don't like her. She's far too evasive. Last night, when Eli asked her name, she clearly lied to him. She's refusing to tell us anything about her life. God knows what secrets she's hiding.

Eventually, the sound dies down. I turn back to my book, flipping a page. I only get a few lines in before Eli must say something *hilarious*, because she just collapses into giggles again.

Gritting my teeth, I stand up, scraping my wooden stool across the floor. I can't handle this anymore. It's too damn annoying.

I follow their voices to the guest room I set up for her in our old junk closet. It's pretty simple; just a bed, a chest of drawers, and a lamp. It's hardly luxurious, but I don't see how she could need much more than that. They've left the door open, and I stop outside to look in.

Daisy and Eli are sitting on the bed, poring over a card game. As I watch, Daisy plays a card that makes Eli let out a long string of swear words. She giggles, shoving at his shoulders.

Jealousy spikes into me. Which is odd. Eli is always surrounded by women. They stick to him like flies. In skiing season, he practically sleeps his way through the ski resort. It's been like this ever since we were kids—everyone has always been drawn to him. I've never cared before. In fact, growing up, we had kind of a pact: if we needed to meet a bunch of people, he would go ahead and charm them all, so I could slink back into the shadows and wait until we could leave. He knew talking to strangers wasn't my scene, just like I knew being alone wasn't his. We fit together well.

But now, watching him grin at Daisy, laughing with her as if they've been friends their whole lives—I'm jealous. And I have no bloody clue why.

As I watch, he wraps a hand around the end of her braid and tugs, dipping to kiss her exposed neck. She gasps, biting her lip. I feel my dick twitch as he runs his mouth over her soft skin.

Shit. Shit, shit, shit.

It's been so long since I've watched Eli with a woman. Apparently my body is still just as into it. Her breathing picks up as he kisses her, her creamy tits swelling against the low-cut neckline of her tank top. I can't ignore the ache in my balls as pink flushes up her cleavage. Eli murmurs something into her skin, rubbing his curls against her cheek, and she laughs again, the sound pretty and bright.

I can't handle it anymore.

I stomp into the room. "Can you *please shut up*," I grind out. They both jump, pulling apart. "Your voice is giving me a headache."

Eli rolls his eyes, looping an arm over her shoulder. "For God's sake, man—"

"No," Daisy cuts him off. "No, it's fine. It's a good thing you let me know, Cole. I'd hate to talk too loud and give you a migraine."

I run my eyes over her. She's practically naked in her summer pyjamas. She shifts under my gaze, tugging down the hem of her tiny shorts.

"What the Hell are you wearing?" I grunt.

She looks up, eyes flashing. "*Excuse* me?"

"You came on a trip to the Arctic Circle, and bought *that*?" I glance down at her suitcase, lying open on the floor. It's full of lacy, frilly things. It looks like she barely packed at all. Just grabbed handfuls of random stuff. I think back to her winter gear. It was brand new, and I could've sworn I saw it on an Inter- sport rack a few months ago. She bought it in Sweden.

"Stop looking at my underwear." She reaches over and knocks the lid to the case shut.

"Are all your clothes like this?" I demand. "Did you pack for a summer vacation?"

"You guys have heaters in every room," she points out tersely. "I might even last another hour without freezing to death."

"I mean it. You didn't plan to come here, did you? This wasn't a planned holiday."

Her cheeks get hotter. "What does it matter?"

"It matters, because it means you lied to us about why you're here."

"Knock it off," Eli says, frowning. "Leave her alone, man."

I ignore him. "Who are you?" I demand.

She blinks. "W-what do you mean? I'm Daisy."

"How old are you? Where do you live? What do you do?"

"I told Eli. I'm a teacher." She fiddles with the corner of the quilt. "I'm from London."

"Yeah? What do you teach?"

She opens her mouth, then closes it again.

Eli stands up with a sigh, squaring off against me. "I'm serious. Leave her."

I can't believe him. We've been burned before by a lying woman. And Eli got hurt more than any of us. I can't understand why he can't learn to protect himself. "You heard her, right? She practically admitted to hiding shit."

He shrugs. "She doesn't have to tell us anything."

"But—"

"*Stop*," he orders, staring me down.

I'm speechless. Eli doesn't pull shit like this. He's usually far too easygoing to fight with me or Riv. He raises an eyebrow, then jerks his head towards the door.

"Seriously?"

"Yes."

A few beats pass. He doesn't back up.

Jesus. "Just keep it down," I mutter, turning to go.

I stomp back into the kitchen. Riv's sitting at the kitchen table on his computer. I set the kettle to boil and clatter through the cupboards for some coffee. My mind is whirring. This isn't right. It can't end well. Daisy's clearly hiding things from us, and that makes her a threat. We should be treating her like a liar, not opening up to her. I pour two mugs of coffee and bring them to the table.

"Eli's made a move," I mutter, setting them down.

Riv doesn't look up from his screen.

"Riven."

"And this surprises you?" He holds out a hand for his drink, still tapping at his keyboard with one hand. "Was there any chance of them *not* hooking up?"

"He'll get attached."

"The last time I checked, Eli is more than capable of having casual sex."

I shake my head. "He's not having sex with her. They're like… kissing, and playing games, and shit. He looks really happy." Eli's had plenty of one-night-stands in the last five years. He doesn't usually act so cuddly with them. "He's too trusting. It's like he didn't learn anything from the last time this happened."

Riven hums.

I clench my fists. *"Riven."*

He finally meets my eyes. "What do you expect me to do about it? Shall I lock her up in her room? He's an adult. If he wants to mess around with her, let him."

I drop into an armchair, looking out of the window. "I don't trust her."

"Shocking."

"She's lying about who she is. She lied about her job." She's not a good liar. She gets all pink and shifty.

Riv sighs, closing his laptop. "I know. And you can stop worrying. I got a message half an hour ago that the roads to the village are cleared. We'll go tomorrow, get her car in the garage. She should only be with us a couple more days after that."

All of the muscles in my chest unclench. "Why the Hell didn't you open with that?" I growl.

The corner of his mouth ticks up. "It's sweet when you worry about him."

"Piss off."

He laughs, taking a sip of his coffee. I slump back in my chair. A few days. Just a few more days, and she'll be gone. I can stay out of her way for a few days.

Another peal of muffled giggles echoes through the walls. I rub my forehead, making a mental note to pick up earplugs tomorrow.

CHAPTER 10
DAISY

The next day, Cole pulls into a small parking lot behind a garage. The roads down to Kiruna, where my Airbnb is, still aren't clear yet, but he's driven us down to a local settlement, towing my poor beat-up car behind him.

I peer out of the window. "Are you sure I won't be able to find someplace to stay here?"

"We don't like tourists," Cole grunts. "Don't think anyone will have put their room to rent."

"You're stuck with us a bit longer, Tink," Eli says, patting my knee. "Don't worry. The roads to town should be cleared in a couple days." His hand lingers a moment, heavy on my thigh, and I feel my stomach squeeze. I study him out of the corner of my eye, tracing his square jaw and unruly hair. I'm a bit taken aback by the strength of my crush on him. I don't think I've ever connected with someone so quickly. We spent all of yesterday evening huddled together in my little bedroom, playing card games, drinking, and talking. And kissing. Just a bit. He only left after Cole barged in, with a wink and a slow, lingering brush of lips.

His green eyes catch mine, sparkling, and for a few seconds, I can't look away.

Riven twists around in the front seat. "Daisy?"

I lean forward. "Yep!"

He holds up a shopping list. "When we do a supplies run like this in storm season, we always stock up on enough supplies to last at least a month, just in case we get stuck."

My eyes widen.

"It's incredibly unlikely to happen," he assures me. "But better safe than sorry. Think forward. Is there anything you'll need in the next month or so?"

"No. I don't need anything special, I'll just eat whatever you guys have."

"Not just food. Toiletries, or anything from the pharmacy?"

"No. I'm good."

Riven's dark eyes don't leave mine. "Are you sure?" He presses. "You're good for over a month, if it comes to it?"

"Um. Yes?" I don't know why he's pushing this so hard.

"There's nothing that you might need in the next month, or so?"

"... No?"

"He's asking if you need tampons," Cole intones from the driver's seat.

A couple beats pass. Then I burst out laughing. "I have some in my suitcase. Thanks, though."

"Alright." Riven twists back to face forward. I try to smother my laughter. "You've got all of our numbers. It'll start getting dark around three, so we should try to leave before then. If you wander off alone and get lost, just ask someone where the main square is."

"Got it."

Everyone pops open their doors and gets out of the car. I look around. We're in a small car park full of worn-looking cars. Across the road, I can see lanes of houses. Frozen air fills my lungs, and I take a deep breath.

"Come on, Tink. Let's go inside." Eli takes my hand, tugging me across the car park to the little glass-walled office. A bell chimes as we step over the threshold. Inside, it's clean and cosy; there's a waiting area with plush leather seats, and a vending machine shoved in the corner. A man with silvery hair is sitting behind the counter, glaring at his computer like he wants to set it on fire. There's a bowl of toffees by his hand.

"*Hej, Ulf.*" Eli saunters up and nabs a couple before the man yanks the bowl away, grumbling something. "No, I didn't break another snowmobile," Eli answers in English. "In fact, it wasn't even me this time!" He unwraps a toffee and pops it in his mouth. "My friend Daisy wrecked her car. We had Cole drag it out back."

Ulf drags his eyes from Eli to me. "*Friend,*" he grunts.

"She's *very* friendly," Eli grins, slipping the other sweet into my pocket.

I elbow him in the side. Ulf sighs, forcing himself up from his chair. "ID?"

Shit. I turn to Eli. "Um. If you've got somewhere else to be, I can handle this by myself."

He shrugs. "I don't mind staying with you. I don't have anything to do."

I bite my lip, trying a different tack. "It's just… I could use some time alone? You know—after being trapped inside the past few days. I'd like a bit of breathing room."

I'm worried I'm being rude, but he just shrugs and wanders off, heading back out into the snow. I guess after living cooped up together for so long, the guys understand the need for space.

I hand Ulf my ID and license, my heart thudding. He scans them, and my throat tightens as his frown deepens. His eyes flick between my face and the license. A few long seconds tick by. I brace myself, expecting him to say something—but he just types something into his computer, and then hands them back without comment. I heave a sigh of relief. He doesn't recognise me.

God. I hate living like this.

"Right." He heaves himself out of his desk chair. "Let's see it." We head outside into the car park. He whistles when he sees the mess of my car. "The Hell did you do to it?"

"Moose."

"Ah." He tugs open the bonnet and examines the engine. I hang around awkwardly as he fiddles around inside, then moves to the boot. My phone buzzes in my pocket, and I pull it out, staring at the text flashing across my screen.

Sam: *Please, babe. Just give me another chance.*

I delete it, then shove the phone back as Ulf straightens, dusting off his hands. "It will be a lot of work. I need to order some new parts. It will take at least two and a half weeks if the weather is good. Longer if there are more storms."

I nod, my heart sinking. "How much do you think it'll cost?"

He says a number that makes my jaw drop. That amount would wipe out my savings completely. There'd be no chance of me renting a room in Kiruna while I wait. Crap. What the Hell am I going to do?

Eli flashes into my head. I'm sure that he wouldn't mind me staying with the boys, but there's no way the others will want me sticking around for a couple of weeks. I can't just live on the streets until the car's ready, but there's no way I'm going home without it, either.

I'm screwed.

Sighing, I take the quote Ulf prints off for me, pay the deposit, then head back outside. I need to think. I start walking through the cobbled streets, my mind whirring.

The village is beautifully picturesque; an odd mix of modern and traditional. A bank with an illuminated sign is squashed between old-fashioned looking bars with lanterns hanging in the doorway. There are kids playing in the snow on the streets, zooming past on little sleds.

"Hey!" Someone calls. I turn around automatically. I'm walking past a little pub. The doors are shut against the cold, but clusters of people are sitting outside at small metal tables, wrapped up in blankets. Orange heaters glow down over their heads as they sip their beers and chat. A man stands up from one of the tables, staring at me. His cheeks are red, and he's wheeling on his feet. He studies my face, then drops his eyes over my body, staring hard at my chest.

Shit.

I give him a weak smile and turn to walk away. He shouts something after me, and I increase my pace, my heart thudding in my throat. Footsteps ring behind me, getting faster, and I jump when a hand lands on my shoulder. Wincing inwardly, I turn to face him. He's middle-aged, probably in his fifties. Greasy blonde hair clumps over his head, and his eyes are watery and bloodshot from drink. He mumbles something garbled and mean-sounding. I might not understand what he's saying, but catcalling has a very specific tone to it.

"I'm sorry. I don't speak Swedish," I tell him. He shouts again. I see a few people around the square glancing over at us, wide-eyed, and cringe. Shit. This is the last thing I wanted when I came up here. Attention.

He paws at my coat. "I'm sorry," I say, stepping back again. "I—I don't know what you're saying."

My shoe catches on the icy cobbles, and I stagger backwards. He grabs my arm. His stubby fingers press painfully into my skin, even through my thick jacket.

Part of me is in shock. This can't be happening. We're in public. I'm not about to get assaulted in broad daylight in front of an entire square full of people. But no one seems to want to do anything. He tugs my arm, yanking me into him so I fall across his front. Hot, yeasty beer breath fans all over my face as he clasps me to him. I try to shove him off, but he's twice my size, and it does nothing as he reaches for the zip to my coat. He tugs at it, like he wants to rip it right off me. Anger flashes through me, and I lift my heel, stamping hard on his foot.

CHAPTER 11
RIVEN

I close my eyes and breathe through my nose, trying to keep my annoyance under control. "I told you," I say patiently, "you can't go walking in the snow. Your ankle is unstable, and your bones are too brittle."

Anna, the grey-haired elderly lady I'm currently treating, scoffs. "I've been walking around just fine for the last ninety-five years."

"That's kind of the problem," I mutter, prodding the swollen skin.

She gives my shoulder a light slap. "Don't be so rude," she scolds.

I sigh, stretching out my back. I'm kneeling on the floor of Anna's kitchen, prodding at her ankle as she lounges in her favourite chair. It's the fifth time this year that she's called me in for an injury. I don't even know why she bothers; she never actually does anything I recommend her to.

Her grandson is standing at the stove, making tea. "Grandma, please don't hit the doctor. What does she need, Riv?"

I sit back on my haunches. "An X-Ray. As soon as the snow to the city gets cleared. Until then, ice it for fifteen minutes every hour, and take the painkillers I left last time." I eye the sealed pill bottle on her counter.

"I don't need *painkillers*," Anna huffs. "I'm not a child."

"They're not just for pain," I explain as patiently as I can. "They also reduce swelling. If the swelling gets too bad, your whole ankle could dislocate. You want that?" She grumbles under her breath. I look back up at the grandson. "And for God's sake, keep her off it."

"Sure thing."

I straighten, shaking both of their hands, then head back out into the snow.

My mood is dark as I trudge through the streets. I love my job, but this is the worst part. Anna needs hospital treatment, and until the roads clear, I can't give it to her. It's so frustrating to not be able to treat patients properly.

I turn a corner into the main square, heading for the pharmacy. Out of nowhere, an arm slings around my shoulder, half-strangling me.

"Alright?" Eli asks.

I shove him off me. "Aren't you supposed to be with Daisy?"

"She told me to piss off," he says cheerfully, falling into step next to me. "Said she could sort out the car by herself."

"She's probably hiding her ID again," I mutter.

"Yup."

My eyes slide across to him. He looks like a self-satisfied cat, happy and lazy. There's a smudge of Daisy's shimmery pink lip salve streaked on his cheek. "So, what? Are you two together, now?"

"Of course not." He looks at me sideways. "Why? You like her? I saw you looking at her earlier."

"I look at a lot of things."

He sighs. "It's okay, man. You don't have to become a monk because of one bad relationship."

I scowl. "It wasn't just *a bad relationship.* It ruined all our lives, for years."

"Well, maybe this is exactly what you need." He steps out in front of me, blocking my path. "Clearly you're not ready for something serious."

"I won't ever be." I push forward, trying to get past him. He just starts walking backwards. "Eli—"

"*So,* why not just try her?" He insists. "Baby steps, right? No commitment, just a casual fling before she has to leave. And there'd be two of us. That would take some of the pressure off."

"Should we be having this conversation without her? You don't even know if she's interested in me, yet."

He snorts. "Trust me. If she's into me, she's sure as Hell going to be into you. Tall, dark, handsome doctor?"

"It's not going to happen."

He grabs my shoulder. "Don't you miss it?" He says, his green eyes suddenly serious. "I do. It feels like there's something missing. What if it's her?"

I try to shake him off. "Eli, I have a job to do."

"Just think about it," he says, letting me go. "I'm gonna go get some food."

He saunters off, disappearing around a corner. I watch him go, my head spinning. His words repeat over and over again in my mind. *It feels like there's something missing. What if it's her?*

He's right. I do feel something missing. I've felt it for the last five years, like a hole in my chest. We've built a little family up here, away from civilisation, but it's not complete yet.

The image of Daisy pops into my head. She's certainly beautiful. It's been Hell having her wandering around the house, to be honest. It's kind of difficult to focus on work when there's a woman walking through the hallways, all soft curves and creamy skin and long, thick hair. I'm not used to having that kind of distraction around.

But that's all she is. Beautiful. That doesn't mean she has any special connection with any of us.

My phone buzzes in my pocket. I pull it out, checking the screen. Unknown number. I slide it open to accept the call.

"Dr Nilsson."

"Riven, darling," my mother croons in her thick American accent. I stop in my tracks.

"Mom? Are you okay? Whose phone is this?"

"Oh, I'm fine, darling. It belongs to one of the maids. I knew you wouldn't answer if you knew it was me calling. You've been ignoring me the last few days."

"I haven't been ignoring you. Phone service is down again."

"God. I don't know why you keep living in that awful place. They're practically medieval."

Anger spikes through me. "You didn't seem to have an issue raising me here."

"Yes, but things are different, now. We can afford a better lifestyle."

I sigh. "What did you want? I'm busy right now."

"You're still coming over this June, aren't you? I want to organise a party."

"No. Sorry."

"But we had plans!" She whines. *"You can't just make plans and cancel them like that!"*

"We didn't have plans. You told me I was coming over. I said I wasn't. You ignored me."

She huffs. *"Would one little visit really hurt so much? We miss you, Riven."*

"Yes. I'm a doctor. If I just disappeared for three months, it would hurt quite a lot of people."

"Well, all those native people have their own herbal medicines and whatever, don't they?"

I grit my teeth. "Sorry, I'm not coming. Is there anything else, or can I go do my job?"

She sighs. *"Look, darling. I know you're still angry. And your father and I have apologised about the little issue we caused with Johanna. But it's been years. Isn't it time you finally forgave us?"*

My heart freezes in my chest. "It wasn't a *little issue*," I hiss, "she destroyed the lives of everybody I care about. And you both *helped* her do it."

"Well, the situation was difficult. It was your fault for involving her in that threesome thing you do. It was bound to end in tears, Riven, honestly. We were just doing what we thought was best for you."

I close my eyes. "No, I will not be coming home this summer. Mom, I'm sorry, I really have to work." I hang up.

My phone immediately buzzes again. I slide it back into my pocket, rubbing a hand over my face. I hate talking to my parents. Every time, I end up absolutely furious. I'd cut them off completely, if they didn't keep making donations to the local hospital. But—

"WHORE!"

A shout from across the square shakes me out of my thoughts. It takes me a couple seconds to pick out where the voice is coming from. A drunk old man is standing outside one of the local pubs, ranting at some poor girl. He steps back, unblocking her from my view, and I catch sight of a familiar pale pink coat.

Daisy.

I don't even think before I take off across the square, running full-pelt. As I get closer, I can hear the disgusting things he's saying to her. "I thought of you when I came last night," he slurs. "You're just a little slut, aren't you? Here." He paws at her pocket. "Gimme your phone. I'll give you my address. You can come over later, yeah? Don't worry, my wife won't mind."

Daisy pulls away, confusion all over her face. "I'm sorry," she says. "I… I don't know what you're saying."

"Don't be mean," the guy mumbles, pushing forward. "C'mon. Gimme your number. I'll pay you to come over." She tries to step back again, and he grabs her arm. "How much do you want, huh?" He yanks her into him, and she falls across his front.

Anger flashes across her face. "Don't touch me," she hisses, then stamps on his foot, hard.

The guy howls. "You little *bitch!*" He spits.

"Hey!" I bellow. "What the Hell are you doing?" They both look over. Relief floods Daisy's face. I pull her behind me and turn on the man. He's clearly pissed out of his head. His cheeks and nose are red, and his eyes are glazed. "You don't touch her, you don't talk to her, you don't fucking *look at her,*" I snap. "Do you understand me?"

The man looks between the two of us. "Doctor, your girl is a whore," he garbles. "She's made me come so many times."

Daisy shivers. I draw her closer to me. "Get the Hell out of here, you piece of shit."

"She likes it in the ass," he crows. "She likes to take it hard up the ass. You take her up the ass?"

I snap. I step forward and grab the guy by the collar, shoving him backwards. "You come near her again, and I will call the police. You're sexually harassing women in broad daylight. There are plenty of witnesses."

He stumbles back. "Police won't care," he mumbles, then belches. "I'm just tellin' the truth. She's a whore."

"Fuck. Off."

Grumbling under his breath, he turns and staggers away through the snow, heading back to the pub. I take a couple of breaths, trying to calm down. The protective instinct running through me is so strong that it surprises me. I haven't been this angry for as long as I can remember. I squeeze my eyes shut, taking a breath through my nose, then turn to Daisy. She's standing rooted to the spot, her arms crossed tightly over her chest like she's trying to hide herself from him. "Are you alright?" I rough out.

"What was he saying?"

My lip curls. "Unpleasant things."

"Oh." She wilts. "I thought so. But I didn't know for sure, so I didn't know what to do. I didn't want to kick him in the nuts if he was just a weird old man. But then he grabbed me." She bites her lip. "What was he saying, exactly?"

"You don't want to know."

Her face hardens. "Riven. I'm serious. What. Was. He. Saying."

I sigh. "Just a bunch of sexist bullshit. Ignore him."

"*Tell me*," she insists.

"You really want me to translate?" She nods, brown eyes wide. I rub my face. I don't even want to say it. "He called you a… prostitute. He said that you, ah…" I try to word it nicely, "enjoy anal sex." Her face whitens as all the blood drains out of her cheeks. "He's just drunk and talking crap," I assure her. "He probably says it to every pretty girl he sees." She looks down, swallowing hard. Her shoulders shake. For an awful second, I think she might be crying. I put my hand on her back. "Hey. You're okay."

When she meets my gaze, her eyes are dry. Her mouth is set in a firm line. "Of course, I'm okay," she says fiercely. "I've had much, much worse."

My stomach twists. "Believe it or not," I say slowly, "that doesn't make me feel much better."

"I wasn't trying to make you feel better." She crosses her arms over her chest and glares across the street, pursing her lips into a little pink heart shape.

I hesitate. All of my appointments are done for the day. I still have a few more errands that I need to cross off my list, but I can't leave Daisy alone like this. I'm not leaving a woman to wander through a foreign town by herself after she just got sexually harassed.

"Are you hungry?" I ask suddenly.

She blinks, then nods cautiously. "I guess?"

"Want to go get some lunch?"

"I… okay."

"Come on." Without waiting for her, I start striding across the road. I'm used to walking with Cole and Eli, but she struggles to keep up with her shorter legs. Her foot hits a patch of ice, and she skids. I grab her before she can hit the ground, wrapping an arm around her waist. Glancing around, I see us getting quite a few curious stares. Most people around the village know me. I'm sure the gossip mill is already churning. Great.

"Come on," I say again, a bit more gruffly, hurrying her across the square.

CHAPTER 12
DAISY

Riven takes me to a small, traditional-looking pub with a wooden sign swinging outside the door. Inside, it's warm and full of gold light. The walls are covered with reindeer antlers and flickering gas lamps. A red-hot fire crackles in a big stone fireplace.

A beaming middle-aged woman with pink cheeks scuttles up to us and leads us to a table near the back of the room. There are a few other groups scattered around; mostly men laughing too loudly over their beers, but a couple of families, too.

I jump when I feel hands on my shoulders. Riven gently slips my coat off for me, hanging it on a hook hammered into the wall.

"Thank you."

He inclines his head, pulling out my chair. "How do you feel about eating reindeer? As far as meat goes, it's about as ethical as you can get." He smiles up at the woman. "It's Charlotte's specialty."

I shrug. "I'll try anything once."

He says something to Charlotte, who grins and runs back off to the kitchen to start the order. Riven pours us both glasses of water from a tap on the bar, then settles back into his seat just as the food arrives. He's ordered two big bowls of steaming stew, full of potatoes and meat and carrots. I suddenly realise how hungry I am. I pick up my spoon and dig in. The stew is thick and rich and savoury.

"This is delicious!"

"I'm glad you like it." He puts a piece of bread on the edge of my plate. "Eat."

"Thank you."

I'm a bit nervous. I've not spent any one-on-one time with Riven. Ever since the first day, he's been polite; but he's made it clear that he doesn't actually want me here. He doesn't say much as we eat, mostly focussing on his phone. I take the opportunity to study him, watching the firelight play over his sharp cheekbones and dark brown skin. He really is unnaturally good-looking. Under his coat, he's wearing an expensive-looking black sweater that fits snugly to his body, straining a little on his broad shoulders and biceps. His thick-framed glasses reflect the light of his phone screen as he bows his head. The whole package is one-hundred-percent sexy doctor.

A few tables over, a group of drunk men suddenly erupt into song, their voices booming through the room. People from other tables join in, laughing and raising their cups. Riven smiles faintly, but doesn't look up from his phone.

"What are they singing?" I ask. Everybody seems to know it. Even the little girl the next table over is happily singing along.

"*Ja, må han lever.* It's like Happy Birthday."

"Oh!" I clap with everyone when they finish. "It sounds more like a drinking song."

"It was one, originally, I think." He frowns, scrolling through his screen. There's a line between his dark eyebrows. I have to fight the sudden urge to reach over and stroke it until it goes away.

"Riven, is something wrong?"

He glances up. "Hm? Ah. No." He puts his phone in his pocket. "Sorry, I'm being rude."

"Not at all! I can occupy myself. I just thought… you looked kind of upset." I tilt my head, studying his face. "Are you okay?"

His lips part. He pauses for a moment, like he's trying to work out whether or not to tell me. "My parents keep messaging me," he says eventually. "My mother is trying to get me to come home for the summer." His face twists. "She's now resorted to offering me money."

I cut a dumpling in half. "Wow. She must really want you back. Does she live near here?"

He shakes his head. "America. My mom's side of the family are from the US. Hence the name. She insisted if I was going to have a Swedish surname, she should get to pick my first name. I guess she wanted something more exotic than Anders or Mattias." His lip twists.

"Wait. So you're American?"

"My dad insisted on raising me here as a kid, but my parents emigrated back to LA when I was a teenager. Mom thinks that if she can just get me to visit, I'll be so amazed by the pool and her yacht and her mansion that I'll never want to leave. She's convinced that there must be something wrong with me, wanting to live up here in the cold, away from all the malls."

"You don't really seem like the mall type."

He smiles drily. "No."

"I was wondering why you didn't have a Swedish accent. Eli only has a tiny one, but it comes out sometimes."

He nods. "I was raised bilingual. Eli and Cole learned English in school."

I take another spoonful of stew. "Did you live in America at all?"

"Just for two or three years, while I was in high school. I came back here when I graduated to study medicine."

"It must be hard, being so far away from your family."

"Not at all. My dad is…." he smiles grimly. "Well. Maybe you know him. Hans Nilsson."

The name does sound familiar. I think about it. "Wasn't he in the news a few years ago? Something about a rapper?"

Riven nods stiffly. "He's a lawyer."

It all falls into place. "He's the lawyer who got that rapper off the murder charge!"

Riven looks down at his bowl.

I remember that case. It was an ugly story. A really famous rapper stabbed his girlfriend to death when she walked in on him with another woman. The crazy thing is, the guy literally confessed to the murder; but somehow, his lawyer still got him acquitted. It was in all the papers.

"How did he do it?"

Riven shrugs. "He has a reputation for winning impossible cases. Whenever a really, really rich person screws up, he's the first person they call."

"Even if they did it?"

He huffs a bitter laugh. "Especially if they did it. He specialises in getting innocent bystanders put in jail."

I lean back in my chair. "Shit."

"So you can imagine, I try to avoid family barbecues. Every so often, though—" he grimaces when his phone buzzes again. "Well. My parents have donated a fair amount of money to the local hospitals. I can't stop talking to them altogether."

I take a sip of my water, my head reeling. "Is that why you came up here?"

He shrugs. "When I was in America, I was surrounded by very rich people, and nothing felt real. Out here—" he jerks his head at the door. "People have less, and everything is a lot simpler. People take care of each other. They know human beings are more important than bank accounts."

"Wow." I look down at my bowl. I'd wondered why Riven decided to work so far up North. Now it all makes sense.

Charlotte bustles up, holding a candle in a carved candlestick. She plops it down between us and lights it, saying something in Swedish to Riv. He shakes his head, but she just chuckles, nudges him, and wanders off again.

"What did she say?"

He sighs. "That she's never seen me with a girl in here before. And if we're on a date, we should have romantic lighting."

I snort into my stew. "Well. I'm honoured to be the first girl you bring here."

We eat quietly for a bit. Now that I think about it, the situation is kind of date-like. Especially with the yellow candlelight flickering over our faces and hands. I don't remember the last time a man took me out to eat, one on one. Sam was never big on dates.

As if he can hear my thoughts, Riven suddenly reaches across and takes my hand. My breath dissolves in my lungs. I watch with wide eyes as he brings my fingers to his face, examining them with a frown.

"You should put your gloves back on. You're losing circulation." He touches the pad of his thumb to my little fingernail. "They're going blue."

I sigh, frustrated. "How come you can handle the cold so well, and I'm so bloody fragile?"

"You're not fragile. Just small. You need some more weight on you."

"I lost a lot of weight recently," I admit.

"By accident?"

I nod.

"Were you ill?" He brings my fingers to his mouth, blowing on them. The jolt of heat in my belly surprises me. I press my thighs together under the table.

"No. It's just been a rough few months. That's why I came up here. To get away."

"Bad breakup?" He cups his hands around mine, warming them up. I shift in my chair. It feels ridiculously intimate.

"You could say that."

"What happened?"

"Did you notice how I stopped asking you personal questions when you started looking uncomfortable?"

His eyes twinkle in the candlelight. "I think I deserve some information about the strange woman I've brought into my home."

"I'm a five foot girl who apparently can't eat a bowl of soup without my fingers dropping off. I think you three big strong mountain men have the advantage in this situation."

He smiles properly, then, and I sit back, a bit stunned. His smile is beautiful. Big and white and shining. My heart literally thumps in my chest. I can't help smiling back.

His phone rings again, the shrill beep ruining the moment. Riven sighs, sitting back and pulling it out of his pocket. He glares at the screen.

"Maybe you should answer it," I tell him. "If your parents are trying this hard to contact you, it might be important. Maybe something's happened."

He nods, standing slowly and heading outside. I finish off the rest of my bowl, sopping up the broth with the last slice of bread. I've only just licked the last bit of butter off my fingers when Charlotte reappears.

"How did you like the food?" She beams, stacking up our bowls.

"It was delicious, thank you!" I fumble for my wallet. "Um, do you take card? I don't have any Swedish cash on me."

She chuckles. "Yes, we take card. We are not in the dark ages. But you do not have to pay. Dr Nilsson always eats free." She tuts at Riven's empty chair. "Where did the man go?"

"He just went to take a phone call."

She sighs. "You must be patient with him. He does not have much practice with the women."

"I can tell."

She throws back her head and laughs heartily, then squeezes my cheek. "You are very pretty."

"Oh." I flush. "Thank you."

"It is good for him," she says. "To find a girl. He works so hard. He looks after so many of us in the village." She conjures a cloth out of nowhere and starts wiping down the table. "When my boy was sick last year, it was storming. We couldn't take him to the hospital. Dr Nilsson slept on our sofa to look after him all through the night. He is a very good man."

My heart warms. "I think so, too."

She reaches across and squeezes my hand. "Please tell him he must come back again soon. And I expect him to bring you with him."

When I step outside, I find Riven standing near the entrance to the restaurant, leaning against a streetlight. It's gotten so much darker since we were inside; the sky is now a deep blue, quickly heading for black. He's still on the phone, speaking harshly. I can tell by the set of his shoulders that he's not happy.

"There's no amount. I told you, no. It's not happening," he snaps, ending the call and dropping the phone into his pocket. I watch him take a deep breath, closing his eyes.

I come up behind him, crunching through the snow. "Riven?" His eyes flicker open again. "Hey. Are you okay?"

A muscle tics in his jaw. He nods, but I can tell he's lying. Behind his usual calm mask, he looks really, really upset.

My heart hurts. Without even thinking, I step forward and pull him into a hug. The top of my head only reaches the middle of his chest. He's still for a few seconds, frozen—then he wraps strong arms around me, pulling me even closer, locking his hands behind my back. For someone who seems so reserved, he's an excellent hugger.

We stay like that for a while. Snow flutters down over us, and I hear laughter and chatter as people pass; but we just stand in the middle of the pavement, holding each other. I rub his back slowly through his coat, feeling the tension trembling in his body. His clean, warm-linen smell washes over me again, and I bury my face into him.

Eventually he pulls away, his chest expanding with a big breath. His usually calm eyes look unnaturally dark in the dying daylight. He licks his lips.

"You look like you needed that," I smile. "I—"

I break off when he puts a gloved hand on my cheek. His thumb strokes over my cheekbone, wiping off snowflakes. He doesn't say anything. He's breathing harder than usual, every muscle in his body tense.

"Riven?" I whisper. "Are you o—"

He bends and presses his lips to mine.

The world goes mute. It sounds like an exaggeration, but I mean it; as soon as Riven kisses me, it's like someone has shoved a pair of sound-cancelling headphones over my ears. All I can hear is my own shaky breath, and the soft bristle of Riven's stubble stroking over my cheek. His kiss is soft at first, a warm, closed-mouth press that sends heat jolting through my veins. Without even thinking, I twist both hands in the lapels of his coat and surge up, kissing him back, hard. He groans, the sound rumbling through his chest, and tangles a hand in my hair to pull me even closer. His fingers massage the back of my neck as the kiss deepens, becoming long and sliding. It would be completely perfect, but soon my calves start to shake. At least when I kissed Eli for the first time, we were lying down. Riven is the tallest of all the men. Eventually, I can't take it anymore and start to pull away, but he just wraps his arms around my waist and picks me up, easily lifting me up onto a step without breaking contact with my mouth. We kiss harder, and harder, until I'm panting into his mouth, rubbing against his front, practically seeing stars. I've never had a kiss quite like this, before. It feels like the kind of kiss you see at the end of a movie, when the hero's chased the heroine down to the airport and arrived in the departures lounge just before she gets on her flight. I wrap my hands around his neck, sucking on his bottom lip.

"Daisy," he mutters, and I shudder, pushing up even closer. Closer. I want to be closer.

"There you two are!" A bright voice suddenly calls from across the square.

We pull apart, gasping for air. For a moment, I can't look away from Riven's dark eyes. He's looking at me with an expression I can't begin to understand on his face. A mixture of softness and confusion.

"Guys!" The voice comes again, and I snap out of it, my eyes flicking over his shoulder as Eli and Cole come crunching through the snow towards us.

Shit. Did they see us kissing? From the angle they're coming from, it's possible that all they saw was Riven's back. Eli doesn't look like he noticed anything, swaggering up with his usual dimpled smile. He's carrying a cardboard box, looking very pleased with himself.

Guilt blooms in my stomach. I'm not guilty that I kissed both of them; I'm not in a relationship. I can kiss who I want. But it feels a bit unfair, since they're so close. This could make living arrangements very awkward.

Especially since Riven doesn't seem to want to let me go. His grip on my waist just gets tighter, as if he wants to pull me away from the other two.

"Riv," I mutter. "Get off."

Slowly, he straightens, reluctantly dropping his hands. "Did you get everything?" He asks. Cole nods.

Eli lifts his box. "I got drinks!"

"He bought enough booze to last us until next year," Cole adds drily.

"Yep." Eli shakes the box gently, and I hear the glass clink of bottles. "We're partying tonight!"

Cole takes the box off him, presumably before he breaks something. "Let's get going. I'm not driving on half-cleared roads in the dark." Without waiting for us, he goes stamping off down the street.

Riven reaches over and adjusts my scarf, tucking it carefully back under my coat. I shiver as his leather gloves touch my throat. "Come on," he says quietly, putting a hand on the small of my back. Eli joins us, flanking me on the other side.

"Have fun without me?" He asks brightly.

"I… um…" I flounder. I'm packed between two hot, muscled men, both of whom I've kissed today, and that fact is kind of melting my brain. "Yeah. Riven and I ate stew."

"Saucy."

We make it to the car, and I help the boys pack up the boot. Just before I climb into the backseat, my neck prickles. I can feel someone watching me. I turn and see the old man from before, standing right in the middle of the road, just staring at me.

My heart freezes in my chest. Did he follow me?

It wouldn't surprise me. In the week before I left England, I had plenty of creepy men following me around Brighton. Shuddering, I climb inside and slam the car door shut, huddling in my coats. For a second there, I let myself forget what I was running from.

But I guess I can't ever run away from the truth.

CHAPTER 13
DAISY

Eli cooks spaghetti and meatballs for dinner, and I make a Cesar salad to go with it. After we eat, we all crack open the booze and migrate to the fire. The boys have a record player, and me and Eli sift through their piles of old rock records, picking out what to play.

To my surprise, Cole is out here too. He's not saying much; just sitting in the armchair by the window, drinking his whiskey and watching the snow fall outside. He has a book on his lap, but he's ignoring it.

As I flip through old record sleeves, I watch him out of the corner of my eye. There's something mysterious about him that I can't put my finger on. When we first met, I assumed he was just a prick—and he is that—but there's something deeper to him. Another layer. He looks almost sad as he stares out of the window, watching snowflakes flutter to the ground. Lonely.

Eli sets a record on the turntable, then pulls a plastic crate out of the fridge. It's full of tiny glass bottles, like the spirits you'd buy on an aeroplane. "Alright. Let's get you a drink."

I eye the little bottles dubiously. "*Snaps*?"

"You bet. It's kinda like vodka flavoured with herbs, I guess. Let's start you off easy." He checks a label on one of the bottles. "How does orange peel and cinnamon sound?"

"Delicious."

"Right." He twists off the cap and pours the bottle into a little glass. "Here you go, babe."

I sip it tentatively. It burns going down, but it leaves a pleasant, spicy aftertaste. I smack my lips. "Nice."

Eli pours his own drink, then slumps down on the sofa next to me. "So. How was everyone's day?"

Riven plucks a bottle from the box. "Well, my mother called, and offered me twenty thousand dollars to come home."

Eli whistles. "Shit."

"Yeah." Riven's mouth is grim. "It's the last thing I want to do, but the local hospital could really use that money. I don't know what to do."

"Hold out until she offers you more," Eli shrugs. "She can afford more than that." He points at me. "What about you, babe? How was the garage? Is your car gonna be okay?"

I pull a face. I was so worried about the creep outside the pub that I completely forgot about the mechanic. "Bad. It's *so* much more expensive than I thought it would be."

Eli nods. "Pretty much everything is expensive in Sweden. Taxes."

"If you don't have the money, we can cover it, it's fine," Riven adds.

"No. Absolutely not. No way in Hell." I'm already indebted to these guys, as is. The last thing I want to do is take money from them. "I can afford to get the car fixed myself; the only problem is, it'll use up all the money I had saved up for the trip. I wouldn't be able to rent a room anywhere. I'd just have to go straight home again."

I have to hide a shudder at that thought. I can't go home, back to all the awful, judgy neighbours, and the journalists banging down my front door. I can't.

"Didn't you say you had commissions?" Riven asks. "Will they be enough to pay for the rest of your trip?"

I nod. "I can't work in my car, though."

Eli slaps his thighs, standing. "Well, then. That's it. You'll just have to stay."

I blink. "Stay?"

"Yeah," he says simply. "Stay with us until you've finished your commissions, Tink. That way, there's no rent, and you can save up the money quicker."

"I don't want charity—" I start.

"It's not charity. We want you here, as a guest. We're inviting you to stay. Right, guys?"

He looks at the other two. Riven hesitates for a few seconds, then nods.

I turn to Cole. I'm not imposing on him anymore if he doesn't want me to. It isn't fair. This is his house, too.

He considers me over the rim of his whiskey glass, his smoky blue eyes considering. "Why did you really come here?" He says suddenly.

I squirm. "I told you. To paint the Northern Lights."

"Don't bullshit me."

I take a breath. "I… wanted a place to get away from everyone." I fiddle with the hem of my shirt. "A place without internet."

"We can get internet."

"You know what I mean. Someplace remote, where people would be less plugged-in. And no one could find me."

He narrows his eyes. "You ran away."

I nod. There's no use denying it.

"Why?"

"I can't tell you."

"Why not?"

"I don't want you to know."

His lips tighten. "Are you in danger?"

I consider. Honestly, I don't know. I *feel* like I am. The creep in the village today seemed to prove that theory. But maybe I'm just being paranoid.

Either way, my hesitation is apparently enough to convince him. "Until your car is fixed," he mutters, standing and picking up his bottle. Then he just leaves without another word.

"Bye, Nalle!" Eli calls. "We love you!"

There's a low grunt in response, then the door slams shut.

"So, I'm still not *super* convinced he likes me," I say.

Eli shrugs, leaning over to refill my little glass. "As we say, *smaken är som baken.* Taste is like a butt."

"What?"

"Divided."

"What?"

He shrugs and clinks his glass to mine. "*Skål.*"

"*Skål,*" I echo, then choke as the *snaps* burns down my throat. "*Jesus.* What was that?"

He checks the bottle. "Peppercorn and dill. No?"

"Absolutely not."

He tips his head back and laughs. In the corner of the room, the record player switches track. I don't recognise the tune, but it's a ballad, slow and crooning. I yawn, stretching, and let my hair fall in a curtain over my face as I curl up on the sofa.

"Aww," Eli says, his voice soft in my ear. "Our baby's getting tired." He tugs me into the crook of his neck, and I breathe in the scent of him.

Our baby. What a weird thing to call me. It makes my insides quiver.

Riven sits down on my other side with a sigh, setting his glass on the coffee table. Eli grumbles but moves up to give him space. I snuggle back into the sofa cushions. God, this is the life. Fire crackling in the fireplace. Snow falling outside the windows. And a hot man on either side of you, keeping you warm. I could fall asleep right here.

I've actually just started to drift off when Riven pulls my hair away from my neck and presses his lips to my throat.

I'm immediately wide awake. My heart pounds in my chest as heat burns through me. I don't move a muscle as he runs his hot mouth over my neck, pressing his lips over my fluttering pulse.

On my other side, Eli starts idly playing with my bra strap, running his thumb under the fabric. I swallow hard. Holy shit.

Riven leans a little closer, his stubbled cheek rubbing against the sensitive skin of my throat. Eli inches in, tracing his finger down my neck, sending tingles shooting through my skin. I open my mouth, but no sound comes out.

I cannot believe this is happening. I'm sitting between two men making a move on me, and neither of them knows the other one is doing it. This is simultaneously the hottest and most awkward experience of my life.

I squeeze my eyes shut and force myself to pull away. "Wait. Stop." I look between them, my cheeks flushing. "Guys. Um. I have to tell you something."

Both men look amused. "Yes?" Riven prompts.

"I, um…" God, why is this so hard to get out? I feel my cheeks heating.

Eli tilts his head. "What is it?"

I wince. "I kind of—kissed both of you?"

The two exchange a glance. I run a hand over my face. "I just got caught up in the moment. And you're both so hot. And I'm... well, I'm not *sorry* I did it, I can kiss who I want, and it's all just casual anyway so it's not like either of you has some kind of *claim* on me but I get that it's weird because you're both best friends and I didn't mean to make things awkward between the two of you so I just thought you should know—"

Eli puts a finger on my lips. "Oh, my God, stop before you explode. He already knows, Tink."

I blink. "What?" I turn to Riven. "What do you know?"

"I knew that you and Eli had been together when I kissed you in the square," he says calmly, taking a sip of *snaps*.

"*How?*"

His lip tips up. "You weren't exactly subtle," he points out. "Besides," he gives Eli a fondly irritated look. "He told me. Very excitedly."

I scramble to understand. "But... then... why did you kiss me?"

He sets his drink down again and takes my hand between his warm fingers. Slowly, he starts to massage my hand, relaxing all the tendons of muscle. It feels so good my eyes drop half-shut.

"It's been a while since we did this," Eli says by my ear.

"Did what?" I whisper. Eli's teeth graze my earlobe, and I shudder. "*Oh...*" I can't stop the moan falling out of my mouth.

Both men take identical deep breaths. Riven's fingers tighten on my hand. "You're right," he tells Eli. "I have bloody missed this."

The redhead grins.

"Missed wha'?" I practically slur, as Eli's warm breath ghosts over my ear. Riv brings my hand to his mouth and presses a hot kiss right in the centre of my palm. Desire spikes through me.

I push away from them both, shaking my head to clear it. "Okay, will you please just tell me what's going on?"

Riven sits back and picks up his drink again, like nothing just happened. "We always used to share women," he says casually, taking a sip.

I stare at him. "Share as in—you both had sex with her?" I look between the two men. "At the same time?"

"All three of us. Cole, too." Eli kisses my bare shoulder. "Not just sex."

Riven shoots him a look, but I barely notice. My head is spinning with all of this new information. "Why?"

"We've been best friends since we were kids. We've shared pretty much everything," Eli says flippantly. "It just sort of happened, the first time around. And it felt so good that we kept doing it."

"And… it gets you off?"

His green eyes darken. "God, yeah."

"But what are you guys getting out of it?" It kind of sounds like they're getting the raw end of the deal.

He shrugs. "There's nothing hotter than watching a girl getting more and more turned on. And when you're seeing her with someone else," he blows a hot breath over my ear, making me shiver, "You get to really enjoy the show."

"Only if you want to, though," Riven amends. "We don't want you to feel pressured because you're staying here." He picks up my hand and resumes his massage. When his thumb rolls against my palm, I arch, sighing.

It seems ridiculous that just a couple of days ago, I was slapping Riv's hands away from me. Now, I want them on me more than anything. After he defended me in the square, I feel more than safe with him. And I swear my lips are still tingling from his kiss. If he keeps up the hand massage, I'll probably crawl into his lap and purr like a cat.

"I've never really thought about threesomes," I admit. "They just never crossed my mind."

"Think about them now," Eli suggests. "We'll wait."

So, I do.

I wasn't always so nervous about sex. Before I met Sam, I used to love being sexually adventurous. I loved men. I loved my body. I loved trying new things. I lost that part of myself for a while, but now I've got a chance to get her back. No one here knows me. I can do anything I want.

So why not?

A little sparkle of anticipation shivers down my spine. I lick my lips. "I… okay then. I'll give it a try. Please."

Eli relaxes. "Thank God. I thought you were offended."

My eyes widen. "Why would I be offended?" Having two drop-dead gorgeous men trying to sleep with me is actually doing wonders for my ego.

"We don't want you to feel used, is all," Riven says.

I scoff. "I've been used. Trust me. Choosing to have sex with two sweet, sexy men is not being used."

Concern floats across Riv's face. "What do you mean?"

Jesus. I couldn't keep my mouth shut if my life depended on it. "Nothing. Forget I said anything."

His frown deepens. "Daisy…"

I take the plunge and just grab the hem of my shirt, yanking it up to reveal my bra.

That shuts him up.

"Holy shit," Eli rasps, his already deep voice lowering. I slide back against the sofa cushions, letting them both get a good look. "You are…"

"Incredible," Riv says quietly. His intense gaze trails all over my bra.

Eli traces his thumb over the lace fringing the cups. "Riv. Look at the little flowers," he whispers. "God. You are cute as Hell."

I squirm. My breasts suddenly feel uncomfortably full and heavy. I want them in his hands. I clear my throat. It's a very odd feeling, to be half-naked in front of two fully dressed men while they chat about your body. "How do we do this, then? Do you just—spit roast me like a pig on a stick?"

The men exchange a glance, then both burst out laughing.

I scowl. "What?"

Riven lifts a hand and strokes gently down my arm, feeling my skin. "We can do that, if you like. But maybe we could start off a little slower."

My heart is thudding in my throat. "Like what?"

Riven nods at Eli. "Kiss him," he orders.

I don't even have time to turn around before strong arms wrap around my shoulders, and I'm pulled into a warm chest. I close my eyes, breathing in the scent of pine. Eli's lips meet mine in a hot crush, and I sigh as his tongue curls over mine, plundering deep in my mouth. Red firelight flickers over us as we kiss slowly, languorously, taking slow open-mouthed sips from each other's mouths. His fingertips skim over my naked back, drawing tickly patterns over my skin, making me shiver.

My head is floaty and my skin is heated when I finally pull away from him, heart pounding. I turn to look at Riven. He's watching with dark eyes, slowly palming himself through his jeans. I don't even think before I lean forward and press my lips to his as well. He cups my jaw and kisses me back hungrily, his tongue sliding hot and possessive against mine. Behind me, I hear Eli make a little punched-out sound. There's a rustle of fabric. I hope to Hell he's getting naked.

Riven's hands smooth down over my back to the curve of my waist, sending waves of goosebumps rolling over my skin. When he reaches my hips, he grips them, yanking me onto his lap. I straddle him, kissing him harder, and harder, until tension starts building in my belly and I'm trying not to rub into his lap. I'm so hot, all over. Behind me, I feel warm fingers on my back. My bra strap is unlooped, and the cups fall away. Eli's big hands wrap around me, cupping my breasts. I bite my lip, arching into him, then moan as Riv sucks on my tongue.

"Christ," he breathes against me, watching as Eli starts slowly squeezing my tits. "I think we should relocate."

"Let's stay here," I whisper, my eyes falling dreamily shut. "I always wanted to shag in front of a fireplace." Eli suddenly tugs one of my nipples, sending a bright spark flying between my legs.

"*Ah!*" I gasp, my body jerking between the two men.

Riv closes his eyes. Eli presses his forehead to my back. "I'm going to die tonight," he announces. "Tink, pick me out a pretty headstone, won't you? Don't let Cole do it, he'll just dump me in an unmarked grave."

A thought strikes me. I run my fingernails down the back of Riven's neck. "Should we ask Cole? If he wants to join?"

Yeah, I don't like the guy. But as long as he kept his mouth shut, I think I'd definitely like *screwing* him. It would be like getting nailed by Thor's hammer.

"I'm pretty sure he doesn't," Riven says gently. "He's, ah—still warming to you."

"Oh." I try not to let my disappointment show. It quickly melts away as he leans in, brushing his lips against the shell of my ear.

"You want me inside you?"

I nod, blood shooting to my cheeks at the thought.

Eli slides off the sofa. "Turn her around," he says, and Riv grabs my hips. They seem to know what they're doing, so I just let them gently manhandle me. I end up sitting in Riv's lap, his naked chest against my back, facing the fire. As he pulls back my hair and starts sucking on my neck, Eli drops to his knees in front of me, kissing up the inside of my leg. I close my eyes, loving the feel of his hot lips on my skin. "You might want me to loosen you up a bit first," he says. "Before, you know, the spit-roasting. Riv's pretty big."

"Eli…" Riv sounds exasperated.

"What? Am I supposed to pretend not to notice? I don't go temporarily blind every time you take your clothes off."

I arch, grinding back into Riv. Holy shit. He's not kidding. Riv hisses in a breath through his teeth, cupping my jaw and pulling my mouth to his. The kiss starts off chaste, but soon devolves into something filthy and wet. Our tongues slide together, and his hands smooth over my tits and waist and hips, squeezing and feeling. Between my legs, Eli's mouth climbs higher. His thick curls brush up to my thighs, and I clench my muscles as he pauses, his open mouth millimetres over my quivering pussy. His hot breath ghosts over me, sending tingles rushing over the sensitive skin. My hands fly out. "*God.*"

Behind me, Riv wraps a thick forearm around my front, pinning my arms to my sides. "Is she wet?" He asks calmly.

Eli nuzzles between my legs. "Oh, yes." He presses a kiss to my entrance.

"Good."

"I bet we can get her wetter, though. I want to see her dripping."

"Hello?" I squeak. "I'm right here."

"Sorry, love," Eli blows another hot breath over my sex. It feels almost like feathers, brushing my sensitive nerves almost imperceptibly, and I squeeze my eyes shut, feeling more wetness pool between my folds. Eli laps it up slowly, then smiles, licking his lips. "Jesus, woman. You taste like heaven." He leans in again, and his tongue finally roughs over my clit.

"Oh, *God*." My whole body jerks. He pulls back a little, running the very tip of his tongue around my hood, brushing it with *almost* enough pressure. "Please, please."

He hums, giving me another teasing lick. It's not enough, so I start slowly rubbing myself against his mouth. He groans deeply. "Yeah, babe," he mumbles, pressing a sweet kiss between my legs. "God. That's right. Take what you need." I do, drawing little circles over his face with my hips. Apparently, that drives him absolutely crazy. He starts groaning and shifting around, panting hard into me, as if he's too turned on to even stay still. I peep down and see that he's stroking himself slowly through his tight black boxers. Even covered by fabric, it's obvious that he's seriously packing. "God," he mumbles, nibbling lightly on my sensitive nub. I flinch against him, and his hand grasps at my thigh. "Oh my God, babe. You're perfect, perfect." He licks a stripe between my labia. "Bloody perfect."

"T-take them off," I rasp.

Without lifting his mouth from me, Eli hooks a finger in the waistband of his underwear and shucks it off. I watch as his erection bounces free. He's thick and swollen. The smooth head shines in the gold firelight, a drop of pre-come glistening on the tip. My mouth aches at the thought of my lips around it. He drops a hand, palming himself roughly.

"Don't," I whisper. "Wait for me."

His hand spasms, but he lets it fall by his side. "It *aches*," he moans, kissing between my legs again.

I sigh, letting my head fall back on Riv's shoulder—then whimper as he wraps his hand around my jaw and turns my neck to the side, pressing his mouth to my throat and sucking at my beating skin. At the same time, Eli slips two fingers inside me. I squirm as he works them in and out, curling them to stretch me open as he licks my sensitive nub harder and faster, lapping at me with his rough tongue. The tension building inside me breaks, and I can feel myself rushing towards release faster than I ever have before. I bend and twist, but I have barely any range of movement.

"I'm gonna—Riv, Eli—I can't—"

Riv holds me even tighter to his chest, his muscled arms like iron around me as he rolls my breasts in his hands. I buck against him. I want to grab Eli's head and shove him into me. I want to curl my fingers in his hair. But I can't. All I can do is give myself up to the feeling of two mouths on my body. Four hands squeezing me. Skin sliding over mine. It's too much. I can't stop shaking. My hips are jerking and twitching under Eli's mouth. I start rocking over him, riding his face, helplessly rubbing my wet pussy against his mouth, and he lets out an agonized sound.

"Oh my *God*," he groans, desperately burrowing his face in closer, getting his cheeks and mouth and chin wet as he kisses and licks and nibbles at me. My eyes fly open. It's too much. Too much sensation. I dig my nails into Riven's forearms, panting for breath— then Eli locks his lips around my clit and sucks, *hard*. My back arches, and I half-scream as I fall apart.

CHAPTER 14
RIVEN

Feeling Daisy shake with pleasure against me is so goddamn hot, I almost lose it right there, with her ass jerkily rubbing my growing hard-on through my jeans. I tighten my grip on her wrists. I can feel her pulse fluttering against my thumbs. She squirms on top of me, sweating and crying out as Eli keeps licking her, milking out the climax. Eventually, though, she starts to shudder with overstimulation. Her hands jerk in my grasp, so I let them go, and she grabs his head, pushing it away.

"Oh my *God.*" She breathes, sitting up on my lap. Her cheeks are flushed, and her hair falls loose around her shoulders. "What the—"

Eli stands, wiping off his wet mouth, and grins at me. "Think she's ready for you."

Daisy squeaks as I give her nip one last little twist, then stand, switching positions with Eli. He turns her in place, draping her legs over the arm of the settee, while I quickly lose my jeans.

Daisy's eyes widen as she notes my lack of underwear. I snap open the condom Eli hands me and roll it on, then come to stand between her knees, putting a hand on each thigh, gently parting her legs. She's pink and glistening in the firelight. I can feel my heartbeat in my throat.

"Yes?" I ask.

"Yes," she breathes. "Please."

I trail my fingers down her shining labia, carefully spreading them, drinking the sight of her in. This will be the first time I've had sex with a woman in over five years. I thought I might never again. I want to enjoy the moment.

She shifts, restless. Wetness drips and sticks to her legs. She wants to rub her thighs together, to get a bit of pressure to relieve the ache, but I brace her legs firmly, letting my cockhead nudge her clit very, very lightly. It twitches angrily, and she chokes, trying to buck against me. "Get in me. Now. God. *Now.* Please. Please, Riv—"

"Shh." I stroke her thigh, then reach down to trail my finger very delicately through her folds, tracing the contours of her soft skin. She moans, shivering, then reaches out and grabs my hand. "Please," she whispers, her brown eyes melting into mine. "It hurts."

Well, we can't have that. I finally line myself up, swallowing through my dry throat. Very slowly, I push into her.

She feels incredible. Soft and wet and burningly hot. And she's *tight*, too, so much so I have to slide into her in increments, giving her time to stretch and take me. She tosses her head back, a pink flush spreading down her neck and chest. When I'm fully sheathed inside her, she goes still.

I force myself to stop. "Am I hurting you?" I ask quietly.

"No. Feels good," she mumbles, shifting around. "Full." She twists to look at Eli. "You, too, please."

"So polite," he teases. "Where d'you want me, babe?"

"My mouth," she says hoarsely.

He doesn't need telling twice. I try to hold myself steady as he slowly slides into her mouth, but as I watch her full, pink lips curl around his length, my hips jump, and I can't help thrusting slightly into her. She whines.

"Shit," I hear Eli mutter under his breath. I grip onto the arm of the sofa, my knuckles turning white, trying to keep my body under control. "Ready, Riv?"

I give him a nod, then roll my hips back and slam into her, hard. She cries out in pleasure, her back arching. I grab her thighs, wrap them around my hips, and start up a heavy, pounding rhythm of thrusts. She moans and twists, pushing her pelvis up into mine as she sucks on Eli. I can see her head bobbing enthusiastically as he thrusts into her mouth. She's clearly loving this, throwing herself into it as she tastes him. Her cheeks are pink, and his face is screwed up in pleasure.

I'm amazed at how easily she falls into the swing of things. Finding someone to do this with is more complicated than just scouting out a girl who's willing; we need to all be on the same wavelength, or the rhythm will be off, and the sex will just be awkward and clunky. I swear to God, it's never been this easy. It's like she was made to match us.

I tighten my hands on her thighs and drive into her, feeling her walls clamp down hard on me, sucking me in. She feels like heaven, slippy and hot and greedy around my dick. Through it all, she keeps licking at Eli. Judging by the noises coming out of his mouth, she's good. Maybe too good.

"*God.*" I glance up to see him pulling gently out of her mouth. She whines, arching after him. Her lips are red and wet, and my balls ache at the sight of them. "Sorry, babe," he says. "I can't handle much more of that." He swallows. "Not ready for this to end." She presses a sucking kiss to his tip, and he groans, running a hand over his eyes.

"Daisy," I ask, fighting to keep my voice level. Like I'm talking to a patient. "Do you often have multiple orgasms?"

"Yeah," she gasps. "When I'm alone, anyway. But never when I'm with a g—"

I roll my hips, hitting the sensitive tissue deep inside her. She cries out, her head falling back, and I feel her clench down as she starts to come again, her thighs locking around me.

"Pretty," Eli mutters, watching with hungry eyes as she tosses her head back. "Pretty, pretty, pretty girl. Look how pretty she is."

I nod in agreement. Still coming, she grabs him by the neck and yanks him down to kiss her. The two of them kiss sloppily while I piston into her, screwing her right through the climax, slamming over and over again into her tightness.

Eventually, she pulls away from Eli. Her full tits shudder as she heaves for air. "Riven—" She tries to squirm away from me. "I can't—"

"Relax," I command. "You can."

"I can't do it again, I, I—" I drop a hand to tickle between her legs, and heat rises in her cheeks. "Holy shit." Her eyes widen. "Oh, oh, oh my God—p-please don't stop, Riven, please, please."

I don't stop. I keep going, pounding into her, gritting my teeth. She cries out with every thrust, arching like she's being electrocuted. Eli stands and presses the head of his dick back against her lips. She opens her mouth and swallows him down, sucking at him frantically, like she can't wait to taste him again. I can feel my balls tightening and set my jaw. I can't hold out much longer.

Apparently, neither can the other two.

"Shit, I'm gonna come," Eli says. "Baby, baby." He touches her shoulder. "You want me to pull out, honey?"

She can't talk, but she makes a disapproving sound around his dick.

"Yeah?" He pants, his hips stuttering. "You wanna take it, babe?"

She nods. He throws back his head and shouts as he comes. His hand fists in her hair, pulling, and I guess Daisy must like that, because the slow wave of a third release finally hits her, his come still filling her mouth. Her sex clenches around me like a vice, gripping me as her walls start to pulse, and it's suddenly all too much. I roar as I finally let go, my eyes slamming shut.

After over five years of rubbing myself off like a teenager, coming inside a woman—especially a woman this unbelievably sexy—is almost overwhelming. My hips batter into her as I explode, losing all control. My mind goes empty and gold and *sings* like a struck bell, and I keep pumping into her, holding her thighs tightly against me until my balls feel completely drained.

When I finally slump back into my body, I realise Daisy's still moaning and gasping. I open my eyes to see Eli on his knees, sucking at one of her tits. He looks up at me and grins. "One for the road."

"You never know when to quit, do you?" Still catching my breath, I carefully slide out of her. She wriggles and chokes, body jerking, as Eli keeps playing roughly with her breasts. I grind up against her, adding to the pressure.

"I can't," she whispers. "I can't, I can't, ooh—" Her hand flails out weakly, coming to tangle in Eli's curls. "Please. It feels so—"

"Sh. You're almost there, sweetheart." I stroke her thigh, rubbing harder against her. Her mouth falls open with a gasping frown. I hold her hips steady as she shudders, whimpers, then falls off the cliff one last time. This time, both me and Eli get a front-seat view as pleasure wracks her body, twisting and shaking through her. Her lashes flutter, and a mascara-stained tear track streaks down her cheek. Eli dips to lick it up, then nuzzles into her neck.

How did we get this lucky?

She's still moaning softly as I slide my hands under her and lay her on the floor. Eli flops down next to us. I dispose of the condom, and then we all end up in a tangle on the rug, panting. Eli's lying behind Daisy, his face buried in her hair. She's plastered against my front, her tits crushed against my chest. The fire crackles in the stone fireplace, heating our bodies. I close my eyes, stroking my hand slowly over her hip as she catches her breath. She's still flinching and twitching with little aftershocks. Her cheeks are flushed, and her brown eyes are all glassy and hazy. She looks wrecked.

"Our poor baby," Eli mumbles. "Did we break you, Tink?" He smooths some hair off her face.

"Holy crap," she whispers. "Um. Wow." She rolls over a bit, trembling. "I've never come that many times."

He presses a quick kiss to her lips. "That's what we like to hear."

"Are you alright?" I ask her.

She looks at me through her lashes. "What do *you* think?"

"We didn't overwhelm you?"

She shrugs. "Maybe. Maybe I like being overwhelmed." She tilts her head onto my shoulder. "How was it for you?"

Eli grins. "The best sex I've had in years. Hell, I think Riv saw God there, for a bit. Thought he was gonna pass out."

Daisy turns to me. "Do you, um, think Cole heard?"

"He might be in the barn. But probably. Does it bother you?"

She shivers. "No," she says, biting her lip. There's something she's not saying, but I don't think now is the time to press it.

I stand. "Put her in my bed," I tell Eli, switching to Swedish.

Eli frowns. "Why not mine?"

"Because I don't trust your laundry skills."

"Screw you, I did my sheets yesterday!"

"Do you even know how the machine works?"

"Yes!"

Daisy frowns. "Hey. Don't speak another language when you just screwed me. It's rude."

"We're talking about how hot you are," Eli assures her, swinging her up in his arms. "I'm only putting her in your bed if I can come too," he informs me.

I roll my eyes. "Fine." It's big enough for the three of us.

Daisy snuggles into his chest as he carries her through the hallway and into my bedroom. I flip on the light.

My room is a little messy. Everything is clean, but there are notes all over the desk, and a few piles of books stacked against the wall. Even though I keep buying more bookshelves, I can never keep up with my book-buying habit. It's probably a diagnosable addiction at this point.

Eli carries Daisy over to the king-size bed, plopping her right in the middle of the white quilt. She rubs her face into my pillows. "Are these silk?" She mumbles.

"They keep Riv's hair pretty." Eli tosses back his own curls. "Of course, mine don't need as much work. I'm a natural beauty."

I don't say anything, just enjoying the view of her curled up in my sheets. She's still completely naked, pink and sweaty. Soft brown waves of hair float over my pillows. She wriggles under my gaze, pressing her thighs together. "What?"

"You look great in my bed."

She blushes and stretches out her arms. "Come on, then. I want a double cuddle."

I lift the cover and slide in beside her. She lays her head on my chest, curling up into a little ball. On her other side, Eli presses up against her back, spooning her. She grabs his hand and tugs it to wind around her, so he's holding her tightly, then sighs happily.

"What do you think?" Eli mumbles. "Did you feel like a pig on a stick?"

I snort. She shakes her head, snuggling closer into me.

"I feel happier than I have in a long, long time."

CHAPTER 15
DAISY

I wake up in heaven. There's no other word for it. Everything around me is soft and warm. I'm lying on a ridiculously comfortable mattress, covered by a squishy quilt, and on either side of me is a hot, naked, muscled man. I have to fight the urge to pinch myself. There's no way this is my life. I don't get this lucky.

Eli is lying in front of me, his curls falling over his eyes, breathing steadily. He's pushed the quilt off in the night, and it's laying low around his hips. My eyes follow the trail of fine hair leading down to his half-hard dick.

Jesus. Talk about morning wood.

"Morning," a low voice grumbles behind me. I roll over. Riven's awake, propped up on his elbow, an open book on his lap. He hasn't put his contact lenses in yet, and he's wearing his thick-rimmed glasses. His hair is rumpled around his head. My mouth practically waters. He looks sinful. Like a sexy, off-limits professor, or something.

"How did you sleep?" He asks, smiling slightly. He looks so hot that I can't stop myself from tipping my lips up and kissing him. He tenses for a second, surprised; then cups my cheek, deepening the kiss. I sigh, melting into him. He drops his hand under the cover, sliding it down between my breasts and over my stomach.

"How are you feeling?" He murmurs, his fingertips running tickly little circles on the sensitive skin. I arch my back, pushing into him. "Sore?"

"If I say yes, will you give me a private examination?" I whisper.

He chuckles, tilting my head to trail his hot mouth down my throat. I close my eyes. I can feel myself getting wet again under the covers.

"I think I gave you hickeys last night." He touches his fingertips very lightly to my neck. "I might have gotten carried away," he admits. "I couldn't help myself. The noises that you were making…"

I shake my head. "I bruise like a peach. And we're in the middle of nowhere; it's not like anyone's going to see them, anyway." I actually kind of like the idea that he's marked me up. There's something so possessive and primal about it. He dips his head again, biting my throat softly, and I twist under the sheets as fire flickers through me. Reaching up, I grab him by the back of the head, tangling my fingers in his thick hair—

There's a sudden shrill beep from the corner of the room. Riven groans, pulling away reluctantly.

I reach for him. "No. Come back. What is it?"

"My radio. Someone's trying to get a hold of me." He looks over his shoulder at the radio, hesitating.

I sigh. "You should go, then. It might be an emergency."

He looks surprised. "Yes?"

"Of course. I'm not getting between you and your patients. Someone might need help."

He studies me, dark eyes hot and melted behind his glasses, then presses a kiss to my shoulder and slides out of bed. I watch, my mouth practically watering, as he pulls a pair of grey sweatpants over his muscled thighs. Before he leaves, he picks up his pillow and whacks it down onto Eli's face. Eli springs up, shouting a stream of swear words.

"Shut up," Riven orders. "I've got to take a call. Keep Daisy company."

Eli blinks his green eyes at me, his face relaxing into a lazy smile. "Hey, pretty girl." He rolls closer and drapes an arm around my hips, pulling me closer. "Did Riv kiss you?"

"Um. Yes?"

"You poor thing." He cups my cheek and kisses me gently. It's not like his usual, sensual, sliding kisses; this one feels softer, more intimate. It's a good-morning kiss between two lovers. The thought of that fills me with a soft, warm glow when he finally pulls back. "There. Hopefully that will cancel out his terrible technique."

I laugh, trailing a hand down his bronzed chest. "I'm not picking sides. You're both equally good kissers."

"Sure, sure." He tuts, stroking my throat. "Look what a mess he made of your neck. What is he, a vampire?"

"I'm sure my thighs are just as bad, thanks to you."

"Let me just check." He dives under the quilt before I can grab at him. I close my eyes as his curls tickle down my belly. My mouth falls open as he presses a tiny kiss between my legs, then pops his head back out again.

"You're right," he says sadly. "You look completely ravaged. Sorry about that."

I'm about to demand he finish what he started, when I notice a flurry of white outside the window. "Oh, *no*."

Eli trails his fingers over my thigh. "Not usually the response I get when I'm in bed with a girl, but okay."

I point at the window. "It's snowing again."

"Yep. It does that a lot, in the Arctic Circle."

I glare at him. He grins, hooking an arm around me and reaching for his phone. "Heavy snowfall tonight or tomorrow," he reads from the weather app. "Yep. Looks like another storm."

"God. How do you handle it? Being stuck here all winter must feel like you're in prison."

He shakes his head. "This isn't anything like a prison. I would know."

My lips twitch. "Why, you been?"

To my amazement, he nods. "Check my prison tat." He twists, showing me a tattoo on his bicep that I didn't notice last night. I lean in for a closer look. It's a bit faded, but still clear; an even, four-pointed star done in black ink.

I run my fingertips over the lines, watching his thick muscles tense. "Are you serious? You got this in jail?"

"There's not much else to do in there," he says. The bitterness in his voice surprises me. "And some of the guys are very artistic." He frowns, making a little move with his shoulders, like a duck flicking water off its back, then flops back down on the mattress. "You like tatted guys, honey?" He drawls, slipping back into his lazy, easygoing persona. "I can get more."

I refuse to be distracted. "What happened?"

He smiles wryly. "You're not meant to ask *what happened*. You're meant to ask *what did you do*."

I shrug. "Whatever it was, it can't have been that bad."

"Why do you say that?"

"Because you're not a bad person."

His eyes soften a bit. "God, you're sweet."

"Maybe I'm being too trusting. Is this the part where you tell me you're all murderers working together? You charm women up to the cabin, Cole takes them out with an axe, and then Riven dissects them for their organs?"

He nods, but his smile doesn't reach his eyes. "Don't look in the freezer. It's full of kidneys. No, it was, uh, possession. Coke. I was in for a year."

Holy *shit*. A whole *year*? "How old were you?"

"It was only a few years ago." He thinks. "Five, I think? I was twenty four."

My mouth drops open. That's so recent. "Oh my God, are you okay?"

"Yeah. Not a high point in my life. But what can you do?" He grins, cheek dimpling. "Missed the women the most."

I narrow my eyes. "You're full of shit."

"You're not the first to tell me," he admits, stretching out on top of the pillows. He looks at me from under his lashes, green eyes twinkling. "You're supposed to ask me if I did it, you know."

"I am?"

He nods. "You're terrible at this. I don't want to just monologue about my tragic past all by myself. I'll get shy."

"Sorry. I didn't know audience participation was required." I curl up next to him, putting my face on his pillow. "Did you do it?" I whisper.

He rolls closer. "Nope." He whispers back. "I was framed."

My eyebrows shoot up. "Seriously?"

He nods. "I was just in the wrong place at the wrong time. Some rich bitch with a great lawyer and a party drug habit blamed it on me."

"And you did a year with a bunch of drug criminals? Oh my God, Eli."

His jaw tightens. "You know the real kicker?" He reaches out to play with a strand of my hair.

"What?"

"It was Riven's dad who put me in jail."

We stay in bed for another hour or so, messing around, then I eventually force myself to get up and take a shower. I've literally just soaped myself up when there's a rough banging on the door. I sluice myself off quickly and wrap myself up in a towel to open the door.

Cole is standing on the other side, arms crossed over his chest. He scowls at me.

"Sorry, did you need the bathroom? Give me a sec, I'll just dry off—"

"How long does it take to have a bloody shower?" He barks.

I check the clock on the wall. "I've been in here two minutes."

"How the Hell am I meant to get to work if you're taking up all the hot water?"

When I first got here, I would be irritated at him for being such a prick. Now, though, I guess I'm getting more comfortable around him, because he just reminds me of a grumpy old man. I look at the coffee in his hand. "Look, maybe you should cut down," I recommend, lowering my voice. "I hear too much caffeine can make you irritable. That's clearly a major issue for you."

His scowl deepens. "It's my first cup."

"So… this is just your personality?" I suck in a breath between my teeth. "God. That's pretty unfortunate, isn't it?"

"Get out of the bathroom."

"Kay."

Cole leaves for work after his shower, and Riven holes himself up in his room, answering phonecalls, so Eli and I spend the day lazing around the cabin. We make brunch—eggs, bacon, and avocado toast—then settle on the rug in front of the fire to play some more card games.

After last night, I can barely keep my eyes off him. He looks incredible, his square jaw highlighted by the flames, his wild auburn hair all lit up gold. Every time he leans over to stoke the fire or add some more wood, I get an excellent view of his biceps.

I run my fingers over the soft, worn rug. Just a few hours ago, I was laying here naked and panting, while two men took turns licking and kissing and sucking all over me. A blush rises to my cheeks at the memory.

"What are you thinking about?" Eli murmurs, his eyes flicking up from his hand. "It looks dirty."

My blush deepens. The fire heats my skin almost uncomfortably. I squirm, fanning myself.

Eli's smile turns wicked. He drops his cards and leans forward to grab my chin, kissing me slowly. We end up sprawling on the pillows, leisurely making out, our game forgotten.

· · ·

As the day goes on, the snow starts to fall thicker and faster outside the windows. I guess Eli was right about the storm. "When's Cole getting back?" I ask, biting the inside of my lip. He just shrugs. I frown. "But… what about the storm? What if he gets caught in it?"

"He won't. The guy has crazy weather-prediction skills." He puts down another card. "Anyway, he's a ranger. He can handle the cold better than any of us. Your turn, babe."

I try to settle back into the game, but I can't concentrate. There's a bad feeling in my gut. I'm sure something is wrong, but I can't put my finger on it. After losing three more games in a row, I give up.

"Where *is* he? The snow's getting really bad, now." All I can see out of the window is a thick flurry of white.

"He's probably staying in the village overnight." He touches a knuckle under my chin. "Relax, Tink. He'd have called if he was in trouble."

I don't like the idea of that. What if he *can't* call, for some reason? What if he's hurt himself? What if he got attacked by an animal, or he slipped on ice and cracked open his head, or—

Suddenly, the lights sputter and turn off. The cabin turns dark and shadowy. The only light is the grey reflecting off the snow outside the window, and the flickering orange of the fire.

"Shit. That'll be the generator." Eli jumps to his feet. "Gimme a sec, I'll go refill it. I guess Riv forgot."

I sit back. "What's wrong with it?"

"Probably just ran out of fuel. Don't worry, we have a backup, and a ton of charged batteries. Even if it's broken, we're not gonna lose power." He heads out of the room.

I get up and drift over to the window. In the background I can hear Riv talking rapidly on the radio. Even though his voice is urgent, the sing-songy lilt of his Swedish soothes me. I lean against the windowsill and let my mind wander as I watch the storm. I've never seen so much snow in my life. It whirls and flurries so fast, all I can see is white, except for one little smudge of grey in the distance.

I frown, squinting through the falling flakes. There's definitely something there. A dark shape is moving slowly towards me. As I watch, it stumbles.

Holy shit. It's a person.

I lean even closer into the window, pressing my nose against the glass. I recognise the broad shoulders and giant, hulking silhouette.

It's Cole.

He's clearly struggling. He's got something big in both of his arms, and every few steps, he pauses, doubling over. Judging by how slow he's moving, it looks like he's hurt.

I don't even think. I head to the door and grab my boots and a pair of snowshoes, then bundle myself up in my winter gear. My hands fumble on the poppers of my coat. My heartbeat is rushing in my ears. I'm not moving fast enough. He's *hurt*.

Eventually, I'm fully dressed. I look around the porch for something I can use to help, and my eyes catch on a sled leaning by the door. I grab it, brace myself, and open the door, heading out into the snow.

Oh my God, it is so cold. I've never felt cold like it. Even through my coat, I feel like I've just had a bucket of ice water sloshed all over my body. Snowflakes swarm against my face, stinging my skin like a hive of angry wasps. I remember too late that I probably should have put on goggles, but I don't have time to go back and get them. I have to reach him. Mashing my eyes shut, I push forward towards his silhouette. As I get closer, I see that he's clutching his shoulder with one hand, carrying a bundle with the other.

His eyes are wide behind his goggles when I finally reach him. I trip over the edge of my snowshoe and almost fall. His free arm shoots out to grab me, and I see the pain cross his face.

"You idiot!" He roars over the wind. "What the Hell are you doing?"

"Shut up." I tug the sled to his feet. "Put it on."

He carefully lowers the bundle onto the sled with a grunt of pain. I grab the rope and start tugging it back towards the house. He grabs for the rope. I pull it away from him. "You're injured."

I guess his shoulder really must be hurting him, because he lets me drag the sled back to the house, heaving it through the thickening snow. The wind is at our backs, so it's much easier this way. We make it to the front door, and he tries to turn the handle, but his numb hands keep slipping. I open the door for him, and we fall back into the cabin.

He starts shouting before I've even shut the door behind us.

"What the Hell is wrong with you?" he bellows as I pull off my gloves. "You don't go out in a storm! Are you stupid? You could've died!"

"*I'm* not the one currently dripping blood all over the floor," I snap. "Jesus, are you okay? What happened?" I shove the sled in the corner and reach over to help unzip his coat. He's shivering convulsively, his hands shaking.

"Stop." He bats me off. "Don't touch me."

I peel off the coat and wince when I see his sweater. There's red staining his shoulder. "Let me see. You should probably put pressure on it, or something. What happened? Did you fall?" I reach for him, and he flinches away. "Stay still. We need to see how bad it is, Cole—"

"STOP!" He steps back, grabbing the door handle. "I have to get back out there."

My jaw drops. "*What?*"

His face is dark. "Visibility was too bad to drive the car to the barn. I need to cover it."

"Are you *insane?* You're injured!"

"I'm fine."

I push past him, standing in the way of the door. "Absolutely not. There's no way."

He shoves his goggles up onto my head. His blue eyes are burning with rage. "What the *Hell* makes you think you can tell me what I can't do?"

"You're weak, you won't make it!" I point at the red seeping through into his jumper. I swear the stain is already bigger. "Look how much blood you've lost! Cole, I'm serious, it might be really bad."

He tries to slide past me. I block his path again. "I have to get the car out of the snow," he repeats slowly, like I'm an idiot. "Get out of my way."

"No."

His eyebrows shoot up. "Are you going to dig it out of a snow-drift tomorrow? Are you going to pay for any damage? Will you defrost the engine?"

"Sure. I'd love to. Now go *sit down*." I try to push him into the living room, but he grabs me by the shoulders and shunts me to the side, hissing through his teeth as the movement jogs his arm. I watch in horror as droplets of blood spatter onto the cabin floor, but he just ignores them, pulling his goggles back down over his face.

I can't stop him. He's too big; I feel like a little chihuahua nipping around his ankles. His hand closes around the door handle, and I do the only thing I can think of. I run back into the lounge, raise my voice, and shout "Riven!" at the top of my lungs.

CHAPTER 16
COLE

"You're an idiot," Riven mutters between his teeth as he pulls down the neck of my shirt.

"I'm fine," I force out. My shoulder hurts like a bitch, but it's not like I've never gotten injured before. And I hate being fussed over.

My eyes flick to Daisy. She's hovering a few feet away, her face pale.

"You're not fine," Riv barks. "Take your shirt off."

Eli gasps and cover's Daisy's eyes. I take a deep breath through my nose. I'm not in the mood to deal with either of their shit right now. "No."

"You want to get blood poisoning again?"

"Come on, Nalle," Eli wheedles. "Do what the nice doctor says. If you're good, he might even give you a lollipop!"

I scowl. "Don't call me that."

Of course, Daisy's ears perk right up. "What does it mean?"

Eli grins. "Teddy. Everyone calls him Cole, but it's actually a nickname. His real first name means 'bear' in English. But he wouldn't hurt a fly, so when he gets all grumbly like this, I call him *teddy*."

She raises an eyebrow. "Your first name literally means Bear? Jesus, did you come out of the womb growling?"

"If you don't remove your shirt in the next ten seconds," Riven says crisply, snapping on a pair of gloves, "I will cut it off you."

Wincing, I pull off the fabric. Pain rips down my shoulder, and I feel warm blood gush across my skin. Daisy gasps softly.

"Go, if it bothers you that much," I growl.

She folds her arms. "No way. I'm not leaving."

Riven bends, washing blood off the area with warm water, and I feel his breath on my skin as he examines the bite. "This is nasty," he mutters, his fingers testing the edges of the wound. "What was it? Another moose?"

"Couple months ago, he found a moose that had eaten a shit ton of fermented berries off a bush, and gotten drunk," Eli mutters to Daisy. "It got into the car park of a local school and smashed through half the cars until Cole managed to tranquillise it. Took a nice bite out of his shoulder, too."

"It was a mother," I say gruffly. "We found her calf nearby. They're not usually so aggressive."

Riven stands upright, frowning. "This isn't a moose bite. Unless your elk somehow developed canines."

"Husky," I grit out through my clenched jaw.

Riven hisses in a breath. Husky bites are almost as powerful as wolf bites. He pulls a tube out of his kit. "I'm going to apply a localised anaesthetic so I can take a closer look. Check nothing has gotten into the wound. Did it look rabid?"

"Of course it didn't look *rabid,* we don't have *rabies* in this country."

"I had to ask."

"Yeah," Eli drawls. "We'd hate for you to turn irritable and aggressive."

"If you're not going to say anything useful, why don't *you* cover the car," I spit.

"Are you kidding? There's no way in Hell I'm going out in that." He turns to Daisy. "Hell, I can't believe you did. Will you save me if *I* have a near-death experience? Because that's pretty hot. I'm sure I could come up with something."

"No one is going anywhere," Riven snips. "The snow's coming down too badly now. Did you lift something? The edges of the wound look torn open."

"No."

"He was carrying all that equipment," Daisy says, nodding to the sled by the doorway. I glare at her. She glares right back.

Riven gives me a flat look. "Well, you're going to need stitches. Eli, can you take Daisy to your room?"

"Nope," Daisy announces. "I'm staying here." Her eyes narrow. "So he can't lie."

"It can be a bit gory," Riven warns, snapping on a fresh pair of gloves.

She snorts. "I'm a teacher. I'm not squeamish. We once had a pregnant teen give birth in one of our classes." She sits on the arm of the sofa, watching as Riv applies a stinging antibiotic cream.

"You need to stay in your lane," I mutter.

She rolls her eyes. "Oh, for God's sake. Stop acting like I snitched on you. You're the one being an idiot here, not me, *Teddy*."

Riven sews me back up, and I grit my teeth, trying to ignore the fact that I'm being watched like a bug under a microscope. "There." He ties off the bandage, giving my uninjured shoulder a squeeze. "Now, as your doctor, I would like to recommend you go to the hospital and get this seen as soon as the snow clears."

"I'm not doing that."

"I figured." He sighs, peeling off his gloves and dropping them in a yellow disposal bag. "Well, I'm done here. I have patients waiting who actually want my advice. Call me if he starts frothing at the mouth."

Eli gets up, stretching. "I'm gonna go work on the generator some more."

"It's not working?" I look around. The lights are still all on.

"We're using the backup right now. It's not a big issue; I think the filters just need to be cleaned."

I nod, and he leaves, his footsteps echoing down the hallway. I lean back against the sofa cushions, finally letting my eyes fall shut. My shoulder burns under the numbing cream. I know I should go clean myself up, but I'm too tired to move.

A hand touches my arm. I open my eyes. Daisy's standing over me, her long hair falling around her face.

"Come by the fire," she says quietly, tugging me up and leading me closer. "You're still shivering."

"I'm fine."

"You look like an extra from *Saw*. You've got blood all over you. At least let me clean you up." She points to a roll of paper towels and a bowl of water she's laid on the rug.

"I can just take a shower."

"Didn't you listen to anything Riven said? You can't get your stitches wet." She glances at my shirt and sweater, crumpled on the floor. "When I'm done with this, if you give me your clothes, I'll get the stains out."

"How do you know how to get blood out of clothes?"

"I do this really odd thing, where I bleed out of my vagina for a week every month? I don't know why, it's weird. Now *sit*."

I don't even have the energy to argue with her. I feel heavy, like all my bones are made of lead. She perches on the sofa arm next to me, dipping a paper towel in the water. She's so close I can smell her—the sweet scent of peaches and cream that just seems to come off her skin. It's so intoxicating it makes my head spin.

"Why did it bite you?" She asks, leaning over to press the wad against my throat. It comes away red with blood.

"Someone hurt it," I grunt. "It thought I was going to hurt it, too."

Her eyebrows draw together. "What? Why would someone hurt a dog?"

"It was at a tourist attraction near the town. Dog-sledding. Some idiots were having a dog-sled race, and one of them decided to whip his dogs to make them go faster."

Her mouth falls open.

"The dog fell down and broke his leg," I continue grimly. "He ran off from the pack, and the injury made him aggressive." It took me hours to find him, and when I tried to get it into the kennel in the back of the truck, he full-on attacked me. Tackled me right to the ground.

"What happened?"

"I took him to the vet to get his leg fixed."

She looks upset. "They won't put him down, will they?"

"Put him down where?"

"Kill him," she rephrases.

I shake my head. "No. He'll just be retired. Will get to be a house-dog, instead of dragging around tourists for the rest of his life."

Her shoulders relax. "Thank God." She tears off a new piece of kitchen roll and dips it in the water, reaching for my cheek.

I flinch away. "What?"

"You've got blood on your face. How did you even manage that?" She strokes the paper towel under my jaw in slow, soothing strokes, wiping out the blood that probably got dried in my beard. Her tiny fingers brush my skin. Something tightens in my chest.

I can't handle this. I can't handle the way she's touching me. Even though her words are sharp, her fingers are ridiculously tender as she cleans my skin. I don't remember the last time someone touched me like this, and I don't want to. I'm not a porcelain doll. There's no need to *pet* me.

I jerk my head away from her. "Stop babying me."

She ignores me.

I grab her wrist. "Stop it."

She sighs, pulling back. "You'd rather sit around marinating in dried blood?"

"I can do it myself."

"I'm just trying to help."

"Well don't! I don't need your help!" I don't realise I'm shouting until she jumps. I take a deep breath through my nose, trying to calm down. "I don't need your help," I repeat. "Not now, and not an hour ago. I would've made it to the cabin fine. It was stupid for you to come after me."

I swear to God, when I saw her out there, my heart stopped. She was stumbling through the snow like bloody Bambi. She didn't have the right equipment on. She could've easily slipped, twisted her ankle, and froze to death before any of us knew about it. Hell, if it was ten minutes later, the visibility would've been so bad that she would've gotten lost and died.

She could've *died*.

She crosses her arms, standing her ground. "I'm trying to help."

"Well don't!" I snap. "You're not helping! You're a liability! We were fine before you appeared, and now everything's going to shit!"

Her eyes flash. "And how, exactly, is it my fault you got bitten by a dog? How did I cause the storm? It's not my fault you don't give a shit for your own personal safety. You spend all this time calling me stupid, and acting like I'm some dumb tourist, but you don't see me *walking around dripping blood*. I'm not going to apologise for not letting you kill yourself."

The firelight flickers over her face. She looks so small standing next to me. So *delicate*.

I don't see delicate shit. I'm used to everything around me being heavy and sturdy and strong. You have to be, to survive these conditions. And now Daisy's here, all five feet of her, soft and small and gentle. She's the worst possible combination: fragile, but too brave—or stupid—to care. She's half of my weight soaking wet, but she still assumes she can keep up with me and the others.

The realisation hits me hard. She can't stay here. If she won't look after her own safety, we have to get her out of the North. As soon as possible. Whatever she's running from back in England can't be as bad as her dying from her own stupidity.

"I've changed my mind," I announce. "We're not waiting for your car to get fixed. As soon as the snow clears tomorrow, you're leaving."

She sighs like I'm a difficult child. "Why?"

"Because we don't want you here," I emphasise.

"That's not true. *You* might hate me, but the others happen to like me."

I laugh. The sound is bitter. "Please. They're only letting you stay here because they want to sleep with you."

I know I've crossed a line as soon as the words leave my mouth. Silence falls between us. She blinks a couple of times. I watch throat contract painfully as she swallows.

She drops the napkins in the bin and leaves without a word.

"Wow," Eli says in the doorway. "I left you with her for ten minutes, man."

The door to the guest room slams shut. Even though the sound is muffled, we can both hear when she starts to cry.

CHAPTER 17
DAISY

I sleep with Riven and Eli that night, tucked between their bodies. Or rather, I share the bed with them. I don't sleep at all. Even after being shagged into oblivion and coming multiple times, my mind won't turn off. I lie between them in the dark as they breathe against me, staring at the ceiling, hearing Cole's words over and over again.

They're only letting you stay here because they want to sleep with you.

It's a long, long night.

I give up on sleep at about five in the morning, slipping out from under the boys' arms to pad to the kitchen. I make myself a cup of tea and sit by the window, looking out. The snow is still falling, but nothing like the blizzard yesterday afternoon. Now, the flakes look delicate and gentle as they flutter innocently to the ground. I sip my tea, remembering the awful, gut-wrenching feeling that hit me as soon as I recognised Cole struggling through the storm, barely a blur in the distance.

Cole said the problem was with visibility. Normally, he would drive the car straight into the barn, but he couldn't, because the snow was so thick he couldn't even see where he was driving. He'd had to abandon the car halfway down the drive.

It seems ridiculously dangerous to me. If the guys can't see where they're walking during a storm, they could die. But none of them has set up any kind of safety measure, in case that happens. It's dumb.

I come up with a plan. Grabbing a bit of paper from Riven's desk, I start drawing a map of the yard. Then I tiptoe back into the bedroom. The boys are still fast asleep.

I creep up and poke Eli lightly on the shoulder. "Eli," I hiss.

"Wha'?" He grumbles.

"Do you have any really long rope? And some metal hooks? And a hammer?"

"Tools are all in the porch," he mutters, reaching out blindly for me. "Come back to bed."

"Nope. I wanna make a safety line from the drive up to the house. Kind of like a handrail. Is that okay?"

"Go nuts," he mumbles, rolling over and shoving his face back in his pillow.

By the time I've found the rope and some tools, it's getting bright outside. I pull on my snow clothes and head out into the yard, trailing the rope behind me. I start off right outside the house. It takes me almost twenty minutes to hammer a hook into the doorframe and tie the rope to it. Hopefully the boys don't mind; the cabin is pretty weathered on the outside, so they don't seem too precious about it. When I've tightly secured the knot, I lift the rope and follow my map, making a trail down to the drive. Every so often, I'll wrap the rope around a tree, fastening it tightly.

It's not long until I come to the barn. I drop the rope and survey the doorframe, looking for a good spot to fasten the rope. Maybe it would be better on the inside? I step through the door and start scanning the walls.

"What are you doing?" A deep voice asks.

The hairs all over my body prickle and stand up. I set my jaw, turning to Cole. He's sitting crouched on the barn floor, surrounded by thin planks of wood. He's hammering them into a square. It looks like he's making some kind of picture frame.

They're only letting you stay here because they want to sleep with you.

Because that's all I'm good for, right? I don't have any other good, non-vaginal qualities. Why else would a man want me around?

I lift the rope. "Making a safety line. Got any idea where I can hammer in the hook?"

He straightens. "You shouldn't be out here."

"I know, right?" I sigh. "I should be sucking the other guys off. Luckily, they're both pretty tired out, so I've got a quick break from shagging their brains out. It's tough work, being a walking, talking fleshlight."

He sighs, rubbing a hand over his mouth. "I didn't mean it like that. What I said last night—wasn't true. They're not just keeping you around to sleep with them."

"Well, I figured. Unless Eli has some kind of UNO fetish he hasn't told me about." I study the heavy beams making up the barn's doorframe. There are already a few metal rings buried deep into the wood, I guess from where they used to hang equipment. I give the biggest one a tug. It's not going anywhere. "Can I use this one, do you think?"

He grunts.

"Very insightful. Thanks for your input." I put down the toolkit and tug the rope taut. He watches as I start to wrap it around the hook. I can feel his eyes on me, like laser-points on my skin. I sigh, turning to face him. "*What*?"

"Just…" He grimaces. "Don't do that again. Don't come after me. Don't put your life in danger, just to help me."

"I'll make the decisions about who I want to risk my life for, thank you."

His face darkens. "I wouldn't have died."

"Probably not," I agree. "But you definitely would've been more seriously injured. Riv says if you stayed out there much longer, you would've probably gotten hypothermia. You would've lost more blood. Lugging that pack around was tearing open the wound. If I hadn't gone to get you, you wouldn't be sitting in here, chopping logs right now. You'd be getting driven down to a hospital for a transfusion. I'm not expecting a *thank you*, but it would be nice if you stopped calling me an idiot for three seconds."

He doesn't respond to that. We're silent for a few minutes, as I twist the rope into a tight double constrictor knot, then step back, testing it out with a few tugs. The knot holds fast.

"I'm not… good with people." He starts.

I relent a bit. "Oh, I don't know. I think you're better than you give yourself credit for. You have your charming moments."

He raises an eyebrow. "Really?"

"No. They shouldn't let you out in public." His lip twists. I look around at the mess on the floor. "What are you making? Furniture?"

"See for yourself. There's a couple finished ones back there, under the tarp."

Intrigued, I go to lift up the blue plastic sheet. My eyes widen. "Oh my God." Underneath the tarp are three canvases arranged in a pile, from biggest to smallest. "Did you make these?" I lift one up to examine. It's perfect. The wood has been sanded down. The fabric is perfectly taut, stapled into the frame on the back. It looks even better than the canvases I would buy at the store—professional-grade, but just a little rugged. Perfect for mountain landscapes.

"Figured it would keep you quiet," he says gruffly. "You can't just wander around the place getting in everyone's way. They better be good enough, because I'm not doing them again."

"I thought you were throwing me out," I remind him, running my finger down the line of perfectly even staples.

"Doubt the others would let me."

I glance at him. "Is this your way of saying sorry?"

He turns his attention back to the nail he's hammering. "I've got nothing to apologise for."

I scoff. "Yeah. Sure."

I'm pretty sure it is an apology. Cole's not exactly the best at saying things out loud, but actions speak louder than words, right? He saw that I was upset about my broken canvases, and he decided to fix the problem. That's an apology.

"Thank you," I say quietly.

He nods, then jerks his head towards the knot I made. "Where'd you learn to do that?"

"Oh." I look back at it. "My dad was in the navy. When I was little, he used to practise his knots with me. I learned every one in the book."

"You're close?"

My throat tightens. "We were."

"He's dead?"

"No. Just… we're not close, anymore." I remember the last time I saw my parents. It was only about a week ago. The look of utter disgust on my dad's face when I turned up crying on their doorstep flashes in front of my eyes.

Neither of them have called. I don't think they've even noticed I've left the country.

I shake off the clawing sadness. "What about you? What's your family like?"

He shrugs. "Didn't have one."

"No one at all?"

"No siblings, and all my mum cared about was whatever boyfriend she was with at the time. I pretty much raised myself."

Explains a lot.

"Eli's mum took care of me, when I was in school," he continues. "I spent half my childhood at his or Riv's house."

"And you've been living together since?"

"On and off." I wait for him to elaborate, but he turns back to his work. This conversation is clearly over.

I look out of the doorway, back at the gently falling snow. "I was thinking of putting that shack thing on the safety line. Eli said you don't use it, but it would be a good shelter, if you can't drive the car up all the way to the house."

"No point. I'm the only one who ever goes that direction."

I narrow my eyes. "So? You might be a prat, but you don't deserve to die any more than the others."

"Waste of time," he repeats.

I sigh, picking up the rope. "Whatever. I'm doing it anyway. Thanks for the canvases."

He doesn't respond, and I head back into the yard, trailing rope behind me.

Eli comes out of the house, yawning, just as I'm finishing up. The rope line looks perfect; sitting at about waist-height, it runs taut around the edges of the yard, stretching all the way from the bottom of the drive to the house. It's discreet enough to blend into the trees unless you're actively looking for it.

Eli looks impressed. "Holy shit." He gives the rope a tug. "This is really smart."

"Yeah?" I dust snow off my gloves. "Think it'll help?"

"I don't see how it couldn't." He presses a kiss to my head. "Thanks, baby."

"You're welcome." I roll my shoulders. "I didn't sleep good. I think I'm gonna go take a nap."

He gives my bum a playful smack as I pass by him into the hall, shaking snow off my body. After all that work, I'm dead on my feet. I trail through the corridor to my guest room, ready to crash on the portable cot.

But when I open the door, the bed is gone. Instead, the room is set up like a little studio.

I look around with wide eyes. While I was in the yard, Cole must have brought all my paint in here. He's stacked the pots against the wall, next to the pile of canvases and my folded drop-cloths. My easel is standing proudly in the middle of the room, with a little stool set next to it. There's a battered-looking desk and chair pushed into the corner, and he's added a couple more lamps so I can adjust the lighting.

Suddenly, I don't feel tired at all. Excitement fires up in my stomach. I bend to pick up a canvas and put it on my easel, then start rooting through my paints.

CHAPTER 18
ELI

I am so Goddamn bored.

I wander through the cabin restlessly, picking things up and putting them back down again. There's nothing for me to do. It's been over a week since the last storm, so I've spent the last eight days at work, giving private ski lessons. Today is my day off, though, and everyone else is too busy to hang out. Riven's working. Cole is outside the barn, skinning some game a hunter brought him. Daisy's painting.

My feet take me through the corridor to her door. Daisy's left it open, so I lean in the doorframe and watch her. She's painting a woman sitting at a dresser, pinning up her hair. The reference photo her client sent in is clipped to the top of the canvas, and she checks it over and over as she works. The painting's obviously not done yet, but even half-finished, I can't help admiring how realistic it is. You can practically feel the soft texture of the woman's skin.

Daisy reaches for a clean brush, executing a little twirl. She's dancing around as she works, shaking her hips to some crappy pop song playing over the radio. Her hair is pulled back in a bandana, and she's got pink paint smeared on her cheek.

It's cute as Hell.

She's been with us almost two weeks, now, and it's been heaven. There's been a lot of sex. A lot. Morning sex, midnight sex, after-noon-quickies-before-work sex. It's more than that, though; I just like being around her. I like having someone to come home to. We hang out all the time, cooking, playing games, watching movies. Most nights, we spend hours talking, letting the hours go by. I'll say it now; I have a massive crush on the girl. I don't know what I'm going to do without her. I'm seriously consid-ering bribing the mechanic to break her car again.

As I watch, her phone bleeps. She puts down the brush and picks it up, checking the notification. Her shoulders droop as she reads.

Well, we can't have that.

"Everything okay?" I ask.

She jumps out of her skin. "Jesus, Eli! You scared the shit out of me!"

"Sorry, Tink. What's up?"

"Nothing. Just a text." She puts her phone in her pocket and smiles up at me. My heart patters in my chest. I can't handle the way she looks at me. There's so much softness and fondness in her eyes. "Did you need something?"

"Attention."

She laughs, crossing the room into my open arms. I kiss her, long and deep. She makes a soft sound, dragging her hands down from my shoulders to my biceps. I make sure to flex, so she gets the full experience of feeling me up, and she hums appreciatively. Her fingers trace over my tattoo.

"What was it like in prison?"

I feel like I shut down. I suddenly can't smile anymore. I can barely breathe.

I guess it must show on my face, because she looks stricken. "Sorry. Sorry, that was nosy. You don't have to tell me if it's hard."

"No." I frown. "No, it's fine. I can talk about it." I hate how I sound like I'm trying to convince myself.

She curls a hand around the back of my neck. "I don't want you to, if it'll hurt," she says quietly. My stomach bottoms out, looking into those melted brown eyes.

I remember what she said when I first told her about my prison time. *Whatever you did, it can't have been that bad, because you're not a bad person.* This girl, who had known me for literally three days at this point, believed me. I'd known Riven and Cole almost two decades, and they didn't believe me. My parents didn't believe me. Every person I met after I got out didn't believe me.

But she did. She saw right through me. If there's anybody I can talk about this with, it's her.

I clear my throat. "It was okay. Better than most other countries, I guess. Scandinavia is known for their prisons being humane."

"*Humane* is a pretty low bar," she points out drily.

"There was some violence, some drugs, but overall, it was a nice prison, I guess. But I was still… you know. Imprisoned." I rub my tightening chest. "I spent a lot of the time alone. I didn't have anyone who could come and see me. My parents cut me off. Riven and Cole were both mad at me. So I was just… alone." God. I hate thinking about this. My heart is battering out of my ribs. "It was hardest on, like, my birthday, and Christmas, and shit. The other guys would get visitors. These were guys who had drug empires and forty-year-long sentences. They blackmailed mules and sold drugs to minors. Their parents would still come. They had girlfriends, friends, siblings. No one ever came to see me. It—" I have to stop talking to swallow. My mouth is dry. "I don't know. Being locked up in a cell and then left by everyone who loved me, when I did nothing wrong —it hurt pretty bad. Took me a while to get over it."

I'm not sure I have, completely. How can you trust anyone to really love you, after that?

Daisy doesn't say anything. I turn to look at her. Her big brown eyes are shining.

"Oh, baby. Don't cry—"

"That must have killed you," she whispers. "It's the worst thing someone could possibly do to you."

I don't deny it. "It happened. I can't get that time back. All I can do is get over it and move forward."

She wraps her arms around my neck and tips her face up to kiss me. She's so short that even on tip-toe, she's practically strangling me. I wrap a forearm round her waist and pull her into me. As our chests crush together, my eyes widen. I pull back, suddenly feeling a lot brighter.

"You're not wearing a bra."

Her eyes twinkle. "And risk getting paint on it? They're expensive, you know."

I growl and spin her in my arms, so her arse is pressing up against my growing hard-on. She happily grinds back into me as I tug the neck of her shirt down, letting her full, heavy tits fall free. I cup one in each hand, squeezing softly. God, she's so, so *soft*. I run my thumbs lightly over her hardening nipples, keeping my touch feather-light and teasing. She moans, arching into me, trying to get some more pressure.

"I don't think I want to talk anymore." I mumble into her skin. "What do you want? My fingers?" Her hips buck against me, and my dick twitches at the friction.

"My mouth?" I continue, trailing my lips down the side of her throat. She tips her neck back, giving me better access, and I press a hot kiss right over her pulse point.

"Or my dick?" I grind into her again, rubbing up against her.

She lolls her head back on my shoulder, looking up at me with glassy eyes. "Why choose? You've got all three, haven't you?"

I smile, sliding one hand down her stomach and under the waistband of her little shorts. She sighs as I stroke her through her underwear, tension melting out of her muscles.

I unbutton her shorts, helping her step out of them, then hook a finger under her pants and tug them down her thighs. She goes to kick them away, but I grab them, scrunching them up in a little ball of wet lace. "I can keep these, yeah?" I stick them in my pocket before she can argue, then resume playing with her, parting her lower lips with my fingers. She's so wet that my fingers glide slickly across the hot, delicate skin.

"Oh!" She bucks in my arms. "Please!"

"Please what?"

"Touch me. Properly."

I lick the pad of my thumb, then start drawing it in slow circles across her sweet spot. She shivers all over, and I watch a pink flush climb over her soft, white tits. I reach up with my free hand to palm one, feeling her heart hammer away in her chest. "That feel good?" I murmur in her ear, increasing the pressure slightly. She squeezes her thighs together and just moans.

My thumb still working, I start dancing my fingertips around her entrance, swirling over the sensitive skin. When she bucks again, I slowly begin to tease my fingertips in and out of her, keeping my touch light and tickly, until she's squirming. I have to squeeze my eyes shut as her firm, tight ass rubs up against my crotch. I'm painfully hard, and hearing her moan and cry out is not helping.

"Oh *God*. Put them *in*," she orders. "Now!"

Outside in the hallway, I hear Riven start talking. He's using his doctor's voice, so he must be on the phone. I tut. "That sounds important. You should be quiet. I'm sure his patient doesn't want to hear you getting fingered."

She twists and gets my shirt between her teeth, biting down on it. Even with a mouth full of cotton, she still can't stop gasping as I slide my fingers into her. She's burning hot and sopping wet inside.

She cries out as I increase my thumb's pressure, squirming desperately. "I can't, I can't Eli—"

"No?"

"No," she practically sobs.

"If you can't come quietly," I offer, not slowing my pace, "maybe you should just hold it in."

"No, no, I can't—"

I put my mouth right by her ear. "If you hold it off," I promise, "I'll switch out my fingers for my dick."

"If you don't get me off, I'll punch you *in* the dick," she growls, but I can feel that she's trying to slow herself down. Her hands grasp weakly in my shirt. I press an open-mouthed kiss to her throat, smile, and curl my fingers, massaging her G-spot.

It's cruel, really. No matter how hard she tries, she can't stop the explosion. She falls apart against me, burying her face in my shoulder and shaking completely silently as I finger her through the release. It just keeps hitting her in waves. Every time I think she's done coming, her walls ripple around my fingers again, and she just keeps shuddering.

Eventually, the climax finally fades. We both stand in the middle of her paintings, panting. She flops back against me, shivering and shivering.

There's a creak in the doorway. We both look up to see Riv standing there, watching. He runs his eyes all over Daisy as she blinks back to reality.

Aching, I slowly pull my fingers out, trailing her wetness up between her folds until she shudders. She holds out a hand to Riven as I suck off my fingers. "Wanna join?"

He clears his throat, shifting his weight uncomfortably. "As much as I'd like to, I have an emergency appointment in Kiruna. Do either of you feel like coming to town for a few hours?"

We both hesitate. I'm so hard I'm throbbing. My balls are aching so bad I'm in actual, physical pain. Every cell in my body is begging me to just grab Daisy, flip her over, and plunge myself into her. But it's been ages since we went to town. I know Daisy wants to get out. I don't want her getting bored of us and leaving.

Anyway, I'm a big fan of delayed gratification.

I push her hair behind her ears. "Let's do it. Assuming my dick doesn't die and fall off while we're out there, we can get back to this later."

"Get your clothes back on, then," Riv says, his voice a little hoarse. "We're leaving in five." He heads down the hall. I catch him subtly adjusting his pants as he leaves.

Daisy sighs. I dip to press a quick kiss to her boob. "I'll miss you," I whisper, tucking it back into her shirt. "See you soon."

"You're so dumb," she mumbles, leaning against me.

"You noticed!"

Cole disappears as soon as we park up in Kiruna, to do whatever it is Cole does. I take Daisy's hand and lead her through the streets, showing her all the places Riven, Cole and I used to go when we were growing up. I point out the cafe we went to after school. The park we played football in. The library we spent endless hot, sleepy afternoons in, curled up under the radiators as we tried to do our homework. She listens to everything with stars in her eyes.

"It's so cute that you all knew each other back then. I wish I could've seen you all as kids."

I shrug. "We were pretty much the same. Riv was a bit less serious. Although he did used to yell at me for running with scissors or not tying my laces, shit like that. Cole was just as grumpy and quiet as he is today. He was the shyest kid I ever met."

She tilts her head to the side, her long braid swinging. "I never thought of him as shy," she says thoughtfully.

"That's because he's a big muscly man, now. But back then, he was just a skinny kid with dirty clothes and an attitude problem."

"Huh." *Interesting.*

We pass a lingerie shop I never noticed before. Normally I would walk right by, but today, something in the window catches my eye. In between all of the inhumanly skinny mannequins modelling bras and robes, there's one, right in the middle, dressed in a peach-coloured silk slip embroidered with tiny white daisies.

I can't help but imagine it on her. The pale fabric would just melt over her soft skin. It would cling to the curves of her tits and hips, and the hem would probably just graze the bottom of her perky little asscheeks.

I realise I've been staring at it too long when she nudges me in the ribs. "Do you wanna try it on?" She drawls.

"As pretty as I would look in it—" I glance back at the window. "Do you like it? The middle one?"

"It's gorgeous."

I grab her hand and tug her inside. The bell jingles as we step into the small shop. I lead her right to the rack. "Pick your size."

She laughs. "Eli, I'm trying to save to fix my car, I'm not spending money on lingerie."

"It's a gift, baby."

She frowns. "I don't want anything from you. You're already giving me a free place to live, for God's sake. I'll never be able to pay you back, as is."

"Trust me." I slide a hand up the back of her coat. Her skin is burning hot under all the insulating layers. "I will definitely be benefiting from this gift. If anything, it's a present to me."

"And Riven?"

"Maybe. If I feel like sharing you tonight."

She pops up and presses a kiss to my Adam's Apple. "Thank you, then. Let's do it."

I pay for the slip, insisting they put it in their fanciest gift wrap, then we step back outside into the snow. As the door swings shut, I spot Cole and Riven crunching towards us. Cole looks pointedly at the shopfront.

"Eli's experimenting with his look," Daisy explains. "I was just helping him find his bra size."

I kiss her ear. She's wearing tiny, sparkly little earrings shaped like stars. Maybe I should buy her some earrings, too. I wonder if I could get away without her noticing.

"Are you shopping?" Riven asks, eyeing the bag. "Do you need more clothes?"

"We're going to have some fun tonight," Daisy says sweetly. "Eli wants to finish what he started."

His eyes darken. He clears his throat. "Well, then. Ah. Are you hungry?"

"Starving."

"We can get some food before we head back home. What do you feel like?"

"I vote pizza," I chime in.

"You always vote pizza," Riv mumbles.

Daisy glances across at Cole. "What about you, Cole? What do you want?"

Cole doesn't say anything. Which isn't particularly unusual; he's not exactly the chattiest man. "Cole," I prompt. "Daisy asked where you wanna eat."

He still doesn't answer. I turn to look at him. He's staring grimly at something across the street. I follow his gaze, and my stomach bottoms out.

No. No way. It's not possible.

Our ex-girlfriend, Johanna, is standing just a few metres away, studying the window display of a sports shop. I guess I must have killed a bunch of kittens or something in a past life, because just as I'm staring at her, she glances up at me, her pale blue eyes meeting mine. Recognition sparks in her face. She starts making her way over. I have to fight the urge to just grab Daisy and run.

"Johanna," Riven says calmly, as she steps up to us. Her blonde hair is a bit longer, and there are few more lines on her face, but for the most part, she looks exactly the same as the last time I saw her, in the courtroom.

"Riven. Cole." She doesn't even bother acknowledging me.

I dated this woman for two years. I've been inside her hundreds of times. But she looks right through me as if I'm not even here.

Which is fine. I'm used to it.

My heart feels like it's bursting out of my chest.

Her eyes fall on Daisy, tucked between us. "Wow. You're still doing this, then?"

"We don't want to talk to you," Cole mutters.

"There's no need to be rude," she says coolly, turning to Daisy. "How's it working out? Have they moved you in, yet?"

Daisy just blinks back at her, not understanding. "Um. *Förlåt.* I don't speak Swedish."

Johanna's pink lips part in surprise. "A foreigner? You're shipping them in from overseas, now?"

Riven moves to step in front of Daisy. "Don't talk to her," he barks. "What are you even doing up here?"

Johanna blinks. "Oh. We're just on a little visit home."

"We?"

She nods, looking over her shoulder. "Rickard!" She calls. "Come over here and say hello!"

A little kid with white-blonde hair unsticks himself from a shop window and runs toward us, stumbling a bit in the snow.

"Hello," he says cheerfully, pulling up next to his mum. "Who are you?"

All of the colour drops out of Cole's face. He actually takes a step backwards, staggering back in the snow. My heart twists for him.

Johanna starts messing with the kid's hair. "These are some old friends. They knew you when you were a baby. This is Riven, and Cole, and—well, Elias, I guess you never met Rickard before, did you? You were still in jail."

I feel like I've been slapped. Riven sucks in a deep breath. Cole's hand clenches into a fist. Daisy looks between us all, clearly confused.

Johanna smiles blandly. "Good to see they let you out."

I swear to God, my vision goes dark at the edges. My ears fill with static. All of a sudden, I can't do this shit anymore. I *can't*. Dropping Daisy's hand, I turn on my heel and walk away, pulling out my phone to call a taxi.

I don't even register the drive. It's like I black out. My brain just switches off. The next thing I know, I'm at the rental desk at the slopes, bargaining with my coworker Carolina.

"I need to rent equipment," I tell her gruffly. I'm leaning on the counter, shaking and sweaty. It feels like my heart is whirring out of my chest. I knock my fist to my sternum, trying to get it to slow the Hell down.

She looks over me, concerned. "Eli, I don't think that's a good idea."

I push my hair back with a trembling hand. "I need equipment," I repeat.

"Honey, what you need is to sit down. You look like you're gonna pass out." She reaches for my shoulders to push me into a chair, but I just shake her hands away.

"Give. Me. The. Equipment," I bite out. "*Now*, for God's sake!"

Her eyes widen. I'm not surprised. I never talk to anyone like that. I'm gonna feel like such a prick tomorrow, but right now, I'm just not feeling very charming. I feel like my head is about to explode.

She checks out some equipment for me, and I head up on the gondola, navigating to our hardest double-black diamond. No one else is up here. I ski over to the start of the trail and look down. The slope is steep; almost a direct vertical drop right down the mountain. Trees line either side, narrowing the path, and a sharp cliff's edge drops off at the end.

I pull down my goggles. Time slows down. My chest tightens. I can hear my own shaky breaths in my ears. Carolina was probably right; I shouldn't be doing this right now. I'm not in the right headspace. My reaction time will be all screwed up. I should go do a few easier trails until I've calmed down.

But right now, I don't give a shit. I push myself off the edge, flying into the air, then feel myself start to fall.

CHAPTER 19
DAISY

I wander through the ski resort, winding my way through groups of people holding snowboards and ski poles. My head is spinning. I have no idea what just happened. Who was that blonde woman? Why did she have such a massive effect on all the boys? Cole and Riven headed back to the car as soon as she left, but I asked to get dropped off here, instead of going to the cabin. I figured if Eli was upset, this is where he would've come.

Crossing the road, I spot a couple of blonde girls wearing jackets emblazoned with the resort's logo, and stop one of them. "Excuse me. Do you know where Elias Sandahl is?"

She huffs. "God. If I had ten crowns for every time some girl asked me that."

"He's on the slopes," her friend says. "He's been up there a while." She turns and squints at the mountains looming over us. "Hm." She scans the view, then points. "There! That's him, there, in the green jacket."

I follow her finger, and my heart squeezes as I spot him. Holy shit.

Eli's barrelling down the mountain impossibly fast, tilted sideways so his body is almost brushing the ground. As I watch, he straightens out just in time to fly over a ramp. His skis slide out from under him, and my mouth drops open as he tumbles, flipping backwards lazily in midair. He lands effortlessly upright on his skis, zooming around a corner.

"Is that safe?" I squeak, as he shoots downhill.

She laughs. "I think he can manage himself fine."

I watch with bated breath for him to get to the bottom of the slope, then force myself to turn away. He obviously needs to let off some steam, so I text him that I'm here, and head into the nearest apres-ski bar to wait.

While I'm waiting, I pull out my phone to check my commissions email. I have to stifle a groan when I see three new messages from Sam. I don't know why the Hell he won't leave me alone. I obviously don't want to talk to him. Inwardly wincing, I slide to open the message.

Baby I know you're there. Please reply. We need to talk

What the Hell does that mean? My hands sweating, I type back a terse response.

We have nothing to talk about. Stop trying to contact me. This is my work email.

The reply comes back almost instantly.

> *Thank God you're okay! I was so worried. Where the Hell are you?*
>
> *I know you're mad baby, and I'm sorry. I was childish. But we can move past this. We work so well together*

Rage floods me. How can he talk like this, as if he didn't ruin my entire life? He got me fired, he turned all of my family and friends against me, and now he says that we should just 'move past' it?

> *I'm seeing someone else. Even if I weren't, you are the last person on the planet I would date. Leave me the Hell alone.*

I send the email, then power down my phone and put it back in my pocket. I'm so angry I can barely see straight. I can't believe him. He seriously wants to get back together, after humiliating me in front of everybody I know? I grip the counter, seething silently.

"Daisy?" A heavy hand lands on my shoulder.

I turn to see Eli, still in his skiing clothes. Without even thinking, I surge upwards and kiss him. His lips are freezing; there's still ice in his hair and snow melting in his clothes. He's still for a moment, like he doesn't know what to do; then he sighs and opens his mouth, letting me kiss him properly.

"Well," his green eyes shine when we finally pull apart. "That was the best welcome off the slopes I think I've ever had."

I lean into his side. "I was so worried about you. You looked so upset."

"Oh, Tink." He turns to the server, who's watching us both with an amused look on her face. "Maria, can you get us some *glögg*? I think my organs are frozen."

"Coming right up," she says brightly, and turns to ladle some steaming liquid out of a big silver pot on the stove. Eli shakes off his ski jacket, then grabs my stool and drags it closer, wrapping his arm around my shoulders. I snuggle into him, breathing in the warm scent of pine needles.

"What is glooog?"

"*Glögg*. Hot red wine, with… stuff in. Spices and shit."

"Like mulled wine?"

"Sure, I guess."

"Here you are." Maria puts two steaming cups on the bar in front of us.

I take a cautious sip, then smile. "It's delicious."

"Yeah," Eli says softly, staring at my face.

I take his hand and entwine my fingers through his. "Are you okay? Why did you come here? Who was that woman?"

He blinks, looking down. "That was our ex. Johanna."

"Oh." I mull that over in my head. "*Our ex? As in, all three of you?*"

"Yep."

I suddenly feel a stab of jealousy towards the woman. She got all three of them. Cole wanted her as well. "Did you love her?"

He nods, fiddling with the handle of his drink. "We all did. A lot."

"Sounds serious."

"It was pretty serious. Lasted two years. Well—" he pulls a face. "My relationship with her lasted two years. The other two were with her longer."

"Why's that?"

He shrugs tightly. "She got bored of me."

My mouth drops open. "How is that possible?"

He laughs. *"Du ser ut som en fågelholk."*

"What?"

"You look like a birdhouse." He nudges my mouth closed with his knuckle. "You're cute."

"How could anybody get bored of *you?*" I burst out. It seems impossible. He's one of the most energetic, fun, charismatic people I've ever met.

He sighs heavily, taking another deep sip of *glögg*. "I know it's hard to believe, but yes, even with this much charm, wit, and good looks, people do still get bored of me. It truly makes no sense."

He's deflecting. I touch his arm. "Well, I think she's mental to not want you."

He snorts. "Yeah?"

"Yeah. I saw you coming down the slopes earlier. You're crazy talented. And you're handsome and smart and sweet and charming—"

"I've got a big dick," he adds.

"—You've got *such a big dick, Eli*," I echo. "Really, you're the whole package. Any woman—anyone at all—would be mad not to want you in their life."

He ducks his head, but he can't hide the smile spreading over his face. "Thanks, Tink. You're sweet." He slaps a hand on the bar. "C'mon. Finish your drink, then let's head back. I think me and Riven should tell you the full story."

When we step back into the cabin, all of the lights are off. It looks cold and empty.

"Riv?" Eli calls.

"Hi," a voice comes from the kitchen table. I turn to see Riv, bent over a pile of paperwork in the dark. His voice is dejected.

"Where's Cole?" Eli asks.

He jerks his head at the window. I can hear a steady *thwack* sound coming rhythmically from outside. "Hacking an innocent tree to pieces."

"Is he okay?" I unwrap my scarf from around my throat.

Riv shrugs. "He will be. He just needs to axe something." He runs a hand through his hair. He looks so sad and worn out.

Stepping out of my boots, I cross the room and slide into his lap, winding my arms around his neck.

He stiffens in surprise, then relaxes. "Hello," he murmurs, pulling me into his chest.

"Are you okay?"

"Why wouldn't I be?"

"I told her we'd tell her about Johanna," Eli says, stepping into the kitchen and flipping the lights.

Riv frowns. "What? Why?"

"Don't you think she deserves an explanation, after today?"

"Is that a good idea, though?"

Eli snorts. "Do you think she's gonna get inspired to turn evil, or something? I don't see how there's any harm in telling her."

Riven pulls back slightly, reading my face. I stay quiet. I'm dying to know the story, but I'm not going to press them for it.

"I guess not," Riven says quietly. "I'm gonna need a drink for this conversation, though."

"On it." I turn and see Eli pulling a cocktail shaker out of a cupboard. "I'm making these *strong*."

CHAPTER 20
DAISY

T wenty minutes later, the fire is crackling in the grate, we're all on our second whiskey sour, and we've migrated to the couch. I'm sitting cuddled up against Eli, watching as Riven sits down stiffly. He looks like a man who's just been sentenced to death.

"Let's get on with it, then," he mutters.

I reach across and squeeze his hand.

"Right." Eli strokes my arm. "Well. We met Johanna down in Kiruna, seven or eight years ago. Cole and I were both working at a sports centre, and Riv was doing his *allmäntjänstgöring*." I nod sagely, and he tilts his head. "It's like… the internship you do after medical school, to get your license. Johanna moved into the flat next to ours. She was pretty, and sweet. We fell for her immediately, and it got serious pretty damn fast. We actually spent Christmas that year with Riv's family in America, all four of us."

"Oh." My eyes widen. "You guys are open about this?"

"It's not like we're doing anything to be ashamed of. The next two years went by. She eventually got bored of me and dumped me, but we were all living in the same flat at that point, so we were still roommates." He clears his throat. "One day, the police knocked on the door. I'd rented a car earlier that day, and the rental place found a massive baggie of coke stashed down the back of a seat. Johanna had also used the car, but it was rented in my name, so I ended up getting arrested. Nobody believed me when I said it wasn't mine, I got sent to jail—you know that bit of the story."

I nod, squeezing his thigh.

"Right after the trial, Johanna told Riv that she wanted to be exclusive with him. She wanted to dump Cole and get married. And Riv was head-over-heels for her, so he proposed, and they moved out and started planning the wedding. The only problem was that a few months in, she found out that she was pregnant. She did the calculations, and said that *Cole* was the father."

I take a sip of my drink. "This is like Eastenders, or something."

"Glad we're entertaining you," Riven says drily.

Eli elbows him. "Riv wasn't thrilled about it, but it's a risk of what we do. They only went exclusive after the engagement, so it wasn't like she cheated on him or anything." He downs the rest of his glass. "The baby was born. Rickard. Johanna and Cole worked out an arrangement where Cole looked after him on weekends. He was so excited; he renovated a room in his flat into a nursery, bought all this baby shit. And *then…*" he pauses dramatically. "One night when Cole was on baby duty, a man arrived on his doorstep and told Cole that *he* was really the father. Cole was furious. He loved this kid *so much*. He almost beat the guy down in the street. When Johanna came to pick Rickard up, he told her what happened, and she got all weird and defensive. So he demanded a DNA test, and lo and behold— Cole wasn't the father."

"She was cheating on you?" I ask Riven. "Um. Both of you?"

Riven nods.

"But I don't get it. Why would she say the baby is Cole's and not Riven's?"

Eli gives me a pointed look.

"What?"

"Riven's black," Eli says kindly. "Cole is white."

I flush. "Oh. Right." Duh.

"Didn't you notice?" Riven drawls, taking another deep swig of his drink.

"I try not to look at him."

Eli guffaws. "Anyway, it hit Cole hard. Like, *really* hard. He felt like he'd just lost his kid. He just disappeared. Up and left town. Meanwhile, Riven couldn't believe his fiancée was cheating on him, so he started searching through her stuff, looking for evidence. And guess what he found?"

"Do you have to make this so interactive?" Riv mutters. I peer up at his face. His eyes are pained. He really isn't enjoying this.

I push away from Eli and go to snuggle under his arm instead, putting my head on his chest. He presses a kiss to my hair, breathing me in.

"He found baggies of coke," Eli continues. "A lot of it. She was stashing it for a party she was going to."

My eyes are probably the size of plates. "She set you up."

"My dad knew that Eli was innocent," Riven forces out. "He defended Johanna in court for free, because my parents hated the fact that I had group relationships. They saw it as an opportunity to get me locked down with a smart, beautiful, educated woman." He flicks the rim of his glass. "Dad told her that he would do the case *pro bono* if she agreed to dump the other two and get married to me. And I fell for it." He swallows thickly. "As soon as I realised the mistake, I tried to visit Eli in jail, but he wouldn't see me. I found him months after he got out. He was unemployed, drinking himself to death in a motel room."

"It's pretty hard to get a job with a drug charge," Eli shrugs. "But it's okay, because after that, he fixed everything."

I heave a sigh of relief. "Yeah?"

Eli nods. "Anybody else would have just given up on us and moved on. But Riv tracked Cole down in Stockholm, and took us both up here, where we grew up. He got me a job as a ski instructor at the resort. Vouched for me to the owner. And he bought this place." He waves around the cabin. "It was falling apart, but we fixed it up together. And the rest is history."

"Wow." I slump back against the sofa cushions. "That's the most wack relationship story I've heard in my life." It makes my bad breakup look tame. "At least it has a happy ending." Riven scoffs. I look across at him. "Don't you think so?"

"No," he says shortly. "It's not a happy ending. Eli was wrongfully imprisoned. Cole lost a kid. None of that had to happen, but I let her manipulate me."

"It wasn't your fault, man," Eli protests. "That's why it's *manipulation.*"

"I get it," I chip in. "I've been manipulated by an ex, too. When you love someone that much, they have so much power over your thoughts. They don't even have to get inside your head; they're already there."

Riven frowns, his gaze focussing on me. "Who manipulated you?"

I look down, examining the slice of orange in the bottom of my glass. For a second, I think about actually telling them what happened with Sam. But the words die in my mouth.

I can't. It would ruin everything. I wouldn't be able to stay here with them anymore, if they knew.

"Just an ex who didn't want me to leave him. It was a while back." I clear my throat, looking for a quick way to change the subject. "Um. Well. Thank you guys for telling me." I set my glass down and slide out from under Riv's arm. "You know, Eli got me a present, today."

Eli grins, perking up. "I definitely did."

"Do you want to see it?"

"Okay." Riven looks bemused.

"One sec." I practically run to the bathroom to freshen up, then trip along to my bedroom to get changed. Riv's left the lingerie bag on my bed, and I quickly unfold the white, sparkly tissue paper, pulling out the slip. I run my hand over the fabric. It's unbelievably soft and silky, a delicate, ballet-slipper peach. I wriggle into it, not bothering with underwear, then brush on a touch of makeup, spritz some perfume into my hair, and run my fingers through my curls, loosening them. When I check myself out in the mirror, I'm impressed. I look hot.

Something pangs in my stomach as I study my reflection. I do. I look *hot*. I look hot and sexy and kind of... beautiful. I reach out, touching the glass with my fingernail.

I'd never admit it, but before I left for Sweden, I didn't think I'd ever find myself sexy again. I couldn't even look at my body in the shower. Everyone that I thought was my friend was suddenly talking behind my back, calling me a slut. Journalists on the news were talking like I was some kind of sexual deviant. Everywhere I went, I felt men looking at me, undressing me with their eyes. My body didn't feel sexy; it felt used, like a bit of trash at the bottom of a rubbish bin.

But now my body feels like it's mine again. I'm flushed and turned on and excited. And that feels incredible.

Fluffing up my hair, I pad back into the living room barefoot. The guys are chatting over their drinks. Riven spots me first, and he freezes, mid-word.

CHAPTER 21
DAISY

Eli looks over. "Oh, *baby*. It looks even better on you than I imagined." He reaches out for me, and I walk into his arms, letting him rub his fingers over the fabric on my hips. "God. You're so damn gorgeous."

I sway into him, then jump as I feel hands on my shoulders. Riven turns me gently to face him, spinning me in place like a ballerina. He runs his eyes over me slowly, drinking me in so thoroughly that heat rises to my cheeks. He notices, and lifts a hand to stroke a thumb over my cheekbone, his Adam's apple bobbing. "You have good taste," he tells Eli drily.

Eli doesn't respond, too busy smoothing his hands over the silk on my ass. He cups my cheeks, squeezing, then gives me a little stinging pinch, making me jolt. Riven slips a finger under one of the little lacy straps, tugging it off my shoulder. Then he pulls me closer and buries his face in my tits. I actually cry out, overwhelmed by the feeling of his hot lips trailing down the sensitive skin. His stubbled cheeks rough against me as he mouths at my cleavage, breathing hard.

Behind me, Eli slips a hand up the inside of my thigh, reaching between my legs. He slicks two fingers between my folds, sucking in a breath. "Baby. You're *soaked*."

I shiver and don't say anything as he trails his thumb around my entrance, teasing me until I buck my hips back into him. He lifts up the hem of the slip and nips at my buttcheek, making me yelp.

"What do you want," Riven says, kissing his way over my chest. My eyes flutter closed as he licks over the silky fabric of the slip, wetting my sensitive skin underneath.

"You. Both. Now."

"Why don't you take her first?" Eli says, slowly pulling away. I watch as he sprawls back on the couch, throwing an arm around the back of it, and licks his fingers off lazily. "I'm quite enjoying the view."

Riven looks at me, and I nod, running a hand through his curly hair. "Condoms?" He rasps.

I consider. We've already had The Bareback Talk; Riv produced bloodwork results for both of them, and I got tested right after breaking up with Sam. I've had the coil for the last couple of years, so we're in the clear to do whatever we want.

Whatever we want.

I want a lot of things.

"I want you to come in me," I decide.

Riv makes a noise at the back of his throat, then wraps his arms around my waist and picks me up, right off the ground. I yelp as he spins me around and slams me up against the wall, so his chest is pressed against my back, and his erection is rubbing between my asscheeks. Sliding a hand under the slip, he feathers his fingers between my lower lips. "You're so wet," he mutters. I push back into him, keening as he grinds up against me, lining his cock against my fluttering entrance. His hands rove all over me, cupping my ass, squeezing my hips, and I clamp my eyes shut, feeling waves of tingles rush over my skin. His hard tip presses between my legs, teasing me until I start bucking back onto it, trying to take it inside me. Riv swears in Swedish as he gives in and pushes into me slowly. I feel myself opening up for him, blooming like a flower. He slicks his thick shaft inside of me, inch by inch, and my mouth falls open at the intense feeling of fullness. My hands fly out. I grasp onto his taut, trembling bicep, and for a moment, we're still.

"Good?" He murmurs, and I nod.

"Please. Please, please."

He flattens a hand on the wall and presses a kiss to the nape of my neck. "Sweet girl," he whispers, then starts to fuck me with strong, heavy thrusts. I let my head fall back on his shoulder as he drives into me hard, melting in his embrace. I can't do much else; I can barely stand. His fingers clench on my hips, and I feel the muscles in his chest and arms flexing as he pounds into me, his hard rod sliding against my sensitive walls over and over and over again. My toes curl, and I choke for breath as I feel my release already shuddering up inside me, dangling over my head, just out of reach. I squirm, but I just can't get there. "More," I rough out.

He obeys, pressing me even harder into the wall. My breasts are crushed up against the wood panelling. His hot breath stutters against my neck as he picks up the pace, battering into me. I start to moan over and over as each thrust draws me a tiny bit closer to the edge. Riv licks his finger, then reaches down and drags it around my sweet spot.

It's too much. I jerk against him. "Oh, *God*, Riv—"

"Shh," he whispers, nipping at my earlobe. He starts lightly stroking between my legs in time with his thrusts. His touch is teasing and frustrating, too light to do anything but inflame me more. I wriggle against him, gasping and sighing. He just keeps thudding that perfect spot deep inside me, smacking the sensitive nerves, sending pleasure sparking through me. Right when I think I can't handle it anymore, I'm *actually about to murder this man*, he gives in and rolls his thumb over my clit. I half-scream when my climax hits me, bursting up in my stomach and shooting all through my body. I collapse against Riv's chest, and he holds me up as I tremble and writhe, grinding back on his dick, clawing at his forearm. His thrusts are getting shaky and uneven. He's close, but he's trying to hold back. I push my butt back into him, rubbing into him as my climax fades, and I think I hear Eli wolf-whistle in the background.

"You're sure?" Riven rasps against my ear.

"*Yes*. God, just *come*, Riv. Come in me."

I cry out as he digs his fingers into my hips and finally lets go. His release is a full-body shudder, and warmth spreads through my belly as he spills into me, filling me deep. I close my eyes. It feels incredible. He keeps pounding into me as he comes, grinding against my G-spot, panting into my hair. Eventually, though, his thrusts slow to a stop. We both stand, panting, our hips still making tiny little rocking motions against each other.

He rubs his lips down my neck, across my shoulders, his hot breaths fogging against my shivery skin.

"You're a dream," he rasps.

"Good show?" I call weakly to Eli over my shoulder.

"Critics give it ten out of ten." He stands, shaking his auburn curls out of his eyes. His bottom lip is red, like he's been biting it, and he's breathing too hard. He takes my hand. "My turn, I think."

Riv touches his lips to the back of my head, then pulls out slowly. I rub my thighs together, trying to fill the empty ache he's left behind. Warm, sticky wetness dribbles down my legs, and I smile. My whole body is humming. I feel hot as Hell.

Eli gently eases me out of Riv's arms, tugging me into a tight hug. I'd honestly expected him to just toss me onto the couch, so the gesture is kind of heart meltingly sweet. I snuggle into him, feeling my breathing settle.

"How d'you want it, sweetheart?" He whispers in my ear. "From behind?"

"On my back," I order. "Wanna see your face."

"Who wouldn't?" He grins, pushing me toward the sofa. I'm spread out on my back, my legs draped over the armrest. Riv, still sweating and breathing hard, slips a couple of pillows under my shoulders as Eli gets into position between my legs. I dig my heels into the muscled V of his back, trying to pull him into me, and he rubs his hard-on against my lower lips, making me moan and squirm.

"Eli… please…"

"Come on, honey. Get me all slick for you. Don't want you getting sore." He rolls his hips again, spreading my wetness down his length. I don't know how he's handling it. He's so hard it looks almost painful, his thick length flushed and weeping. As I watch, he reaches down and cups his balls, a look of discomfort flitting over his face. The poor man's probably been hard half of the day.

"Does it hurt?"

"Like shit. I'd rather be kicked in the nuts." He grins. "Not for much longer, though, right?" He reaches down between my legs. I tremble, moaning as he strokes through my slick folds, and his smile gets even wider. "These *noises* you make. Can I record you? Make you my morning alarm?"

"No you bloody cannot."

Riv slumps back into the armchair to watch. Out of the corner of my eye, I watch him stroking himself back to hardness. I choke as Eli gives me a little pinch. *"Elias Sandahl,"* I bite out. "Get inside me. Now."

He laughs, lining himself up. He doesn't need to ease himself in like Riv did; I'm already loose and aching for him. Instead, he grabs my knees, pushes them apart, and then spears into me in one solid thrust. I gasp, every nerve in my body electrifying as he starts up a punishing pace, slamming into me repeatedly, lighting my insides on fire.

"Higher," I moan. He lifts my hips a little, hitting a better angle, and I just about melt into the couch. "Oh… Please…. Please… Please…" is all I can say, as he drives himself into me. It feels incredible.

I'm so distracted, I barely even notice the creak of the kitchen door opening. It only registers when Eli freezes mid-thrust. My heart drops into my stomach. Slowly, I tip my head back to see Cole, standing in the kitchen doorway, holding a glass. He's shirtless, dressed only in a pair of jeans. His blonde hair is damp, and his bright blue eyes are wide as he looks me over. Holy shit, the guy is *jacked*. His abs are like a pile of bricks stacked on top of each other, and his arms are roped with muscle. I glance up to his shoulder, and see Riv's taken his stitches out; the bite is already fading to a reddish scar. It fits right in—he's got scars all over him, some new, some old. He looks like some kind of Viking warrior.

He doesn't say anything as my eyes finally climb back to his face. The others are still frozen around me, waiting for me to say something.

I hold my hand out to him. "Wanna join?"

CHAPTER 22
COLE

Every muscle in my body stills as I take in the scene in front of me. My grip tightens on my cup.

I'm tired. After seeing Johanna and the kid in town, I came back and chopped us a good month's worth of firewood. We don't even need it, but I had to do something physical.

Now I'm exhausted, more than ready to turn in. I just stepped out here to get a drink of water; but instead, I find my three housemates rutting frantically in the living room.

Suddenly, I don't feel so tired anymore.

Daisy licks her lips and extends a hand out to me. "Wanna join?" She asks, her voice deep and husky.

I run my eyes over her slowly. Riv and Eli have *ruined* her. Her skin is flushed and glistening with sweat, and her brown hair is falling in tangled curls around her face. She's wearing lingerie—something pale and silky. I watch her tits tremble against the lace on her cleavage as she pants for breath.

"You want that?" I ask, eventually. I've been so rude to this girl. There's no reason she should want anything to do with me.

But she bites her lip and nods, her eyes dropping to the growing bulge in my jeans. "A lot."

I consider for a few seconds, then nod, stepping forward. Eli graciously goes to stand, offering up his place between her legs, but I shake my head. "No." Daisy is stretched across the sofa, her head pillowed against the armrest. I come to stand by her face. "I want your mouth."

Her eyes darken. I reach down and touch my thumb to her bottom lip. "You want that?" I ask again.

She nods, slowly. I run my hand down her throat, down past her collarbone, in between her soft tits. She wriggles under me as my fingers slip over the slick fabric, looking up at me from under her lashes. I thumb at one of her nipples, making her gasp.

"Then take this off." I tug at the strap of her little nightdress. She sits up and slips out of it, and I settle back into position behind her head, unzipping my jeans. I'm already painfully hard.

"You, too," she says.

"What?"

She scowls. "What, you think you're just going to unzip your jeans and screw me with half your clothes on? If I'm naked, everyone is."

I stare at her. She stares right back, narrowing her eyes. Slowly, I push down the waistband of my jeans, letting them drop to the floor. Her eyes fall between my legs, and her lips part.

"Will your ego explode the cabin to bits if I comment on how big it is?"

I grunt. "You'll manage. Open up."

She tilts her head. "When was the last time you had sex?"

"A while ago."

"It shows, smooth talker. You sound like a goddamn dentis—" she suddenly yelps as Eli, who has been quietly dying, half-buried inside her, apparently decides he can't take it anymore. He grips her hips, thrusting into her.

"Can you two flirt *while* I fuck you?" He mutters through gritted teeth. "I'm losing the will to live." He rolls his hips, grinding up against her, and Daisy's head lolls back with a gasp. I keep stroking myself, just enjoying the view for a moment, before she reaches back for me. I help her guide the head of my cock to her lips. She plays with it for a few seconds, kissing the tip, running her tongue across my slit. I close my eyes as she licks me, all the way from my balls up to my shaft, then takes me into her mouth slowly, not breaking eye contact as she inches her lips down my shaft. I hiss. Her mouth feels incredible; scaldingly hot and unbelievably soft. I expect her to stop at the head, but she just keeps going, pulling almost all of me into her mouth. "Don't hurt yourself," I mutter. She rolls her eyes, going even deeper. I swear softly under my breath as I slide against the back of her throat. Jesus. Does the girl not have a gag reflex?

Slowly, she pulls out again, and pushes back in, her head bobbing. I swear stars burst behind my eyes.

Her eyes flutter shut, and she hums softly as Eli hitches one of her legs higher, pounding even further into her. Whatever he's doing, he's clearly doing well; every time he thrusts into her, her breath hitches, and her whole body jerks a little. God. I love this. Love feeling her reactions to him screwing her, through her mouth.

"You know," I curl my fingers under her jaw, "I think I like you better when you can't talk."

She pulls back and says something that sounds an awful lot like *do you want me to bite you?* But I can't really pay attention, because the vibrations running down my dick pretty much zap my brain dead. I grip her head, forcing my hips to stay still and not batter into her mouth. She probably wouldn't appreciate that.

Suddenly, she starts moaning loudly, gasping around me. I feel her body tightening, and look up to see Eli grinding his balls up against her. She flings out a hand, grasping at the air, and without thinking, I reach down and squeeze her fingers between mine. She clings to my hand, her moans getting louder and louder, and then her whole body arches and shudders as she comes, crying out.

Holy shit. I twist my spare hand in her hair and pull out a bit so she won't choke. Never, in all our time doing this, have I felt a girl come while I was in her mouth. It rocks over her in waves, leaving her shaking and flushed and hot, gasping around me. I squeeze her hand the whole time, drinking in the sight.

Eventually, she calms down, making tiny little whimpering sounds. I let her hand go, stroking through her long hair, and Riv steps forward, palming at himself. He's already gone, judging by the sticky come glistening between Daisy's thighs, but he's hard again. I can't blame him, after that show. Daisy reaches for him, waving him to the side of the sofa. When he gets close enough to touch, she wraps her hand around him and starts stroking him rough and fast. He chokes, running a hand over his mouth.

There's a few awkward seconds when she tries to keep up the rhythm of jerking him off while simultaneously sucking on me and getting pounded into by Eli. She quickly realises that she's not coordinated enough, and pulls her mouth back, kissing sloppily up to the tip of my dick, licking and sucking the head. "Fuck my mouth," she murmurs huskily.

I swallow. My dick twitches against her lips, and she smiles. "Don't wanna hurt you," I rough out.

"Do it," she orders. When I hesitate, she glares. "If I tell you I can handle it, I can handle it."

Groaning deeply, I grab her head, hold it steady, and thrust into the hot wetness of her mouth. Again. And again. I try not to go too deep, but she doesn't even flinch when I lose control and my hips smack forward. She feels incredible, shivering under me as Eli keeps jackhammering into her. And the whole time, she keeps rubbing Riven.

It's apparently more than he can take. He tips his head back, square jaw clenching. "Can I—"

"Come on my tits," she breathes, twisting her hand over him. He grips a hand onto the sofa arm, bracing himself. The thick muscles in his arms shake as he hisses through his teeth and spills over her chest. Daisy squirms and sighs under him, rubbing his come into her skin, and the visual is too much for me. I feel my balls tingle and tighten painfully.

I can't hold on much longer. I tug her head back to look at me. She's nodding before I even open my mouth. "Yes."

I nod, gritting my teeth as I thrust into her, once, twice, three more times—

I lose it.

I feel myself spill into her mouth, my hot come sliding down her throat. Her eyes flicker shut as she swallows, sucking at me, and the sight is so damn hot I can't help grinding up against her face. It feels like I come for goddamn *years*, all of the tension leaving my body as I drain myself into her, but she doesn't pull back as I spasm in her mouth. In fact, she seems to like it. She starts to moan around me again, staring up at me, squirming against the couch cushions she's laid on as her cheeks flush red. From her trembling thighs, I can see she's building up to another release. My brain still hazed up with endorphins, I bend and start groping her tits, tugging hard at one of her nipples. She cries out, arches, and comes again with a scream, her mouth falling open as she convulses. Opposite me, Eli shouts as he grips into her thighs and explodes into her, his whole body shaking. Daisy keeps on coming right through it, moaning and gasping underneath us both. I squeeze her breasts, feeling her heart hammer under my fingers, and she twists, grabbing for my hand again, clinging to it.

Eventually, she calms down. We're all silent for a few seconds, panting. I rub my eyes, carefully pulling out of her mouth. I feel lighter than I have in years. All the colours in the room seem too bright around me, as if I'm in a dream.

Daisy sighs under me, curling up on the sofa. "I dreamt of this," she says breathily, wiping her red lips with the back of her hand.

"All of you together like this. I dreamt of it." She tugs my hand down and traps it under her cheek like a pillow, then tilts her lips up for me. "Kiss me?"

I hesitate. God, I want to. She looks so sweet, spread below me like this. I don't even remember the last time I kissed someone, but my eyes are drawn to her soft mouth like magnets. I clear my throat. "I don't kiss the girls I sleep with."

"What, not ever?"

"No."

"You got really bad breath, or something?" I roll my eyes. She stretches. "Seriously, I just sucked you off, and you won't even give me a peck?"

"No."

She frowns slightly. "You're weird, Teddy," she whispers, snuggling her cheek into my hand.

"Don't call me Teddy."

She hums. Her eyes flutter closed.

I raise an eyebrow. "Tired?"

"She's worse than us," Eli puts in. "Always wants to fall asleep right after." He gives the arch of her foot a squeeze, and she shivers deliciously. "What do you want, Tink?"

"Cuddle me!" She orders, tossing her arms out dramatically. The other two both laugh.

I extricate my hand and stand back, hating the way I'm still trembling slightly. Riven and Eli curl around her as I pick up my pants from the floor. Riven dabs come off her skin, while Eli presses kisses into her hair, making soft, comforting sounds. She smiles under their hands, basking in the attention.

Shucking on my shirt, I turn, leaving them to it. I don't cuddle after sex. I don't *coddle.* If she wants kisses and caresses and comfort, Riven and Eli have her covered.

"Stay," she says quietly, as I head for the door.

I pause in the doorway, my heart pounding in my chest.

"Please?" She whispers. "You don't have to cuddle. Or kiss me. You can just stay."

I grit my teeth and leave.

CHAPTER 23
RIVEN

The next ten days pass in a blur. The sky stays clear of storms, and Cole, Eli and I go about our routines like normal. Eli drives down to the ski slopes to give his private lessons. I head into the nearby settlements to visit patients. Cole spends his days chopping wood and performing his duties as a ranger. Every night, we eat together, hang out for a few hours, then go to bed. It's a familiar routine.

But everything is different now, with her. All the boring shit I used to hate, like shovelling snow and doing the dishes, is suddenly exciting just because she's nearby. When I'm signing off prescriptions or doing paperwork, she's curled up at the end of the sofa, or humming to herself in the hallways. Every night, instead of lying in a cold bed alone, she sleeps between me and Eli, exhausted and glowing with a post-sex flush.

We've had her in every possible position, all over the house. She's screamed our names in every room of the cabin. We've touched every inch of her body. Sometimes Cole joins in, sometimes he doesn't. There's a sizzling tension between him and

Daisy that seems to get stronger every day. He's still refusing to kiss her, and only ever sleeps with her when Eli or I are also there. I was worried it would piss her off, but I think Daisy sees his aloofness as a challenge; she's been trying harder and harder to pin him down and get him alone. He's resisting, but it's only a matter of time before he breaks down. Any idiot can see he's dying to touch her.

It's not just sex, though. I've never seen the other two so happy. Eli especially. He's clearly falling for her. The first thing he does when he gets home from work is track her down and snuggle her. He's always bringing her things, little soaps and chocolates and gifts he's picked up from the resort shops. The two of them can spend hours together, laughing and joking and flirting.

Cole is harder to read, but he's more relaxed now than I've seen him in years. He's been spending a lot of time in the barn, building more canvases for her. He's currently working on a new set of drawers for her to store all of her paints. I'm not really sure why he's bothering. It's not like she'll stay long enough to use it. All of us are ignoring the fact that this is all temporary. She'll be gone soon, and we'll be alone again.

We finally end up discussing it on Thursday evening. After a couple of hours of getting bent over the bed by each of us in turn, Daisy falls asleep, exhausted. It's only eight PM, so we leave her cuddled up in Eli's room, and relocate to mine so we don't disturb her. Eli sprawls himself across my bed, bouncing a rubber ball against the wall. Cole's pacing up and down, wearing a hole in my rug. I'm trying to focus on my copy of *Treasure Island*.

It's a comfortable routine. I can't begin to guess how many times we've hung out in each other's rooms like this, ever since we were children. But today, the mood is tense. As we were all collapsed in Eli's bed, trying to catch our breath, Daisy sleepily announced that her commissions were finished and dry, ready to be shipped tomorrow. She's just waiting on the final payments.

We all know what that means. And none of us like it.

Cole stops pacing abruptly by the window, staring out at the snow, and growls something.

"Use human words, Nalle," Eli mumbles. "We've been over this. We don't speak bear."

He raises his voice. "She could stay."

I glance up from my book. "What?"

"She could stay here," Cole repeats.

"Like… officially?" Eli asks. "We ask her to move in and date us?"

Cole gives the tiniest of nods. They both look at me.

My gut twists. "I don't think that would be a good idea," I say slowly.

Eli snorts. "Of course, *you* don't. But I seriously doubt she's a Johanna 2.0. Unless we have literally the worst luck on the planet."

I pull off my glasses and rub my eyes. "It's not just that. Think about it. She's got a job. Students. She has a life she needs to go back to. We can't ask her to leave London and live in the *Arctic Circle*."

Eli sits up. He looks a mess. His t-shirt is crumpled, his hair is practically standing on end from when Daisy wrapped her fingers into it, and there's hickeys all over his neck. "Of course we can *ask*."

I shake my head, my temples aching. "Even if she said yes, she'd be miserable. She's enjoying herself now, because she's on holiday. But she doesn't know the language. She wouldn't be able to work. She'd have no friends. She'd be completely isolated from society. She'd just be stuck up here with us three, all day, every day. She'd feel trapped. And she'd start to hate us."

"But—"

"We knew from the beginning that this was only ever going to be temporary," I say as gently as I can. "You promised her that."

Eli looks down. A muscle tics in Cole's jaw. Once. Twice.

He turns on his heel and leaves, letting the door slam shut behind him.

The next day, the forecast says we're due another storm. I spend the day in town, shipping Daisy's parcels, checking in on people, and picking up some fresh food to tide us over. By the time I'm parked back at the cabin, the snow has started up again, and it's already getting worryingly thick. I heave the shopping out of the boot and head to the house, but I'm only halfway there when my phone buzzes in my pocket. The old stone shack is nearby, so I duck inside to take the call.

"Hello?"

"Hello," a man says in Swedish. *"This is Ulf."*

The mechanic. "Ulf," I greet. "Why are you calling me? You're not sick, are you?"

"No, no, I was calling about the girl's car. I know she is staying with you, and she has not been answering her phone the last few hours."

I've noticed that about Daisy. Even when we have signal, she's terrible at answering her phone. Most of the time, she just leaves it switched off, letting all her texts and emails build up. "I think she must be busy."

"Well, her car is ready to pick up. It will have to be after the next storm has cleared, though. Looks like it already started."

I look out at the white sky. "It's not so bad here."

"It will be," he warns. *"My mother lives further north, the storm's already hit her. She says it's the worst one we've had all winter. You guys should stay safe. Get all your supplies ready now."*

"I'll keep that in mind. Thanks. And thanks for the work on Daisy's car."

"No problem. Goodbye."

"Stay safe." I hang up, then shove the phone back in my pocket. My heart is thudding.

Her car is ready. She can go.

She's going to leave.

I traipse back inside. I need to find her and tell her. I'm not sure exactly where she is — Eli texted me a while back, saying he and Cole were going to the village to sell some skins, but I assume they didn't take Daisy in the truck. I doubt she would've enjoyed sharing the backseat with a bunch of animal hide.

The first room I check is her painting room, but she's not there. I take a quick look around the room, marvelling at the amount of work she's managed to do in just a few weeks. I don't know much about art, but her work still takes my breath away. The painting balanced on her easel shows the mountains at dawn; big swathes of stippled blue, silver and white, with gold sunlight trickling down over the crevices in the rock and snow.

I'm about to leave, when I notice the portrait balanced against the wall in the corner of the room. My heart stops.

It's of me.

Actually, it's of all of us. Me, Eli, and Cole, all sitting around the table in the living room, laughing over our *snaps* glasses. Our faces are lit up orange in the firelight, and the window behind our heads shows a white blizzard of snow. The detail is incredible. She's got the colour of Eli's eyes exactly right, and the sardonic twist of Cole's mouth. There's a little piece of paper pinned to the bottom of the canvas. I lean in for a closer look. In faint pencil, she's written the word *Home,* with today's date. My throat squeezes so hard I can barely swallow.

She thinks of this place as her home?

My lungs feel too small. I wipe a hand over my mouth. If that's true, then maybe Cole and Eli are right. Maybe she does want to stay here. Maybe, if I ask, she won't say no.

Giving the painting one last look, I head back into the hallway.

I finally find her in Eli's room. She's in his bed, curled up, scrolling through her tablet. She glances up at me. "Riv! How was work? You look frozen."

"Just got in. Work was fine." I run my eyes over her. "Why are you lying down? Do you feel okay?"

She groans. "Eli cooked so much food. I think I need to hibernate to digest it all."

My lips twitch. "He thinks that fattening you up will increase your chances of surviving up here."

"Will it?"

"Probably."

"I thought he just wanted me to have a bigger ass," she mumbles. "Whatever. I'm not complaining." She yawns, stretching delicately, then curls up in a tiny ball. Her hair is down, and it's spread over the pillows in loose, chocolate-coloured waves. I stand in the doorframe and just watch her. I can't move.

I really, really don't want to tell her about the car.

I don't want to lose her, I realise. I can't stand the thought of never seeing her again.

"It's kinda hard to sleep when you're being creepily watched," she mumbles into the pillow.

I clear my throat. "Sorry. Can I warm up with you?"

Her smile brightens her whole face. She holds out her arms. "Please."

I strip off my jumper and socks, sliding into the bed next to her. She cuddles up to my chest, and I wrap my arms around her, drawing her close.

"You're so cold," she whispers, tipping her face up to kiss my neck. She presses tiny, fluttery kisses up and down my throat, her lips barely brushing the skin. They feel good, but I don't reciprocate.

She frowns, pulling back. "Wait. Was that not a come on?"

"I'm just…" I close my eyes. "I just want to hold you."

"Oh," she whispers. "Okay, then." She tucks her face into my neck. "Hold away."

God, she's cute. "Baby."

"*Baby.*" She snugs closer. "I like that."

I steel myself. "I have something to tell you."

"Hm?"

"I got a call from the mechanic. Your car's ready." She tenses. I keep talking through the lump in my throat. "As soon as the snow clears, you'll be free to go. You got the money for your commissions, right?"

She nods slowly. "Came into my account this morning."

"Well, then. What are you going to do?" I stroke through her hair, pulling it away from her face.

She's quiet for a bit, thinking. "I don't know. I'm not ready to go home, yet. I guess I'll just book into the Airbnb down in Kiruna. Maybe I'll get lucky and finally get a glimpse of the lights."

"You could go to Eli's ski resort," I offer. "Have him give you some lessons. I know he's dying to get you on the slopes."

She shakes her head. "No. No. I... can't stay anywhere near here."

My heart contracts. "Why not?"

"I just can't."

I take a deep breath, cupping her cheeks to make her look at me. "I saw your painting of us all."

She groans. "Riv! It was meant to be a surprise!"

"Sorry." I'm not sorry. "It's beautiful. But... why did you paint it?"

"I thought it would be something to remember me by, when I'm gone. And a thank you for all of you, for helping me out for so long."

"You called it 'Home'."

She squirms a bit. "Mm. I thought about something a bit more descriptive. Like *Three Swedish Mountain Men,* or *Snowed In,* or something. But 'Home' felt better."

I lick my lips. "You could stay here. Right here."

She smiles sadly. "I can't," she whispers. "I'm sorry."

"Why not?" I'm getting kind of desperate. "Eli wants you to stay. Cole, too, even though he'd never tell you. You could stay here as long as you like."

"Riven—"

"Obviously, we won't charge you rent, but if it bothers you that much, you can pay it," I try. "After the Northern Lights end, there are other things you can paint. The midnight sun is pretty incredible, too." It's not, it's actually bloody annoying, but I'll say anything to make her stay right now.

She shakes her head, putting a hand over my mouth to stop me. "I can't, Riv. I'm sorry."

I nod, my stomach sinking. "Right. Of course." I was right, last night. She has a life she needs to go back to. This could never work.

"I can't just stay here," she continues. "Like I'm on some extended holiday, shagging you all until you get bored of me."

I frown. "Daisy—"

"This has been so fun for me," she pushes on. "Really. It's been an incredible experience. But… I don't know how much longer I can have sex with you all, and not develop feelings. It would kind of break my heart to stay here, having 'casual' sex, while I slowly fall for all of you."

"Daisy, you don't understand. I'm asking you to stay here for a relationship. As a romantic partner. As a girlfriend."

She sits up. Rumpled curls fall around her face. "*What?*"

I rewind what I just said in my head. "I… don't know how to say that any more clearly."

Her eyes are wide. "It's not clear *at all!* You want me to date you?"

"Not just me. All of us."

She just stares at me blankly.

"It's really not that hard to understand," I say gently.

She glares. "Okay, pro tip, maybe don't call a girl stupid when you're asking her out?"

"I'm not calling you stupid. I just mean—we'd be doing the exact same thing we've been doing these past few weeks."

"But instead of it being casual," she says slowly, "I'd be your girlfriend."

"Yes."

"We'd be exclusive."

"God, yes."

"I would have three boyfriends."

"*Yes,* baby." She presses her little pink lips together, her eyes roaming my face. I wish to Hell I could read her better. "It's unconventional, but we've done it before. It works for us. The question is just whether it works for you."

"What about the others?" She demands. "How do you know they *want* to date me?"

"We talked about it last night. They both agreed."

"Even Cole?"

"Cole was the one who brought it up." I rub my throat. "I'm not up to date on the law, but you're an EU citizen, so I think you can stay here for six months before finding a job, or starting studies. Depending on how much your paintings make, that could be enough for you to get residency. Or, we have *sambo* visas for couples in relationships, you don't need to get married to get a visa, here." She doesn't say anything, her brown eyes glistening. I swallow. "So, what do you think?"

She throws herself at me, and I choke as she pushes me flat on my back, knocking all the air out of my lungs. "Yes! Of course! I would love to!"

Relief floods me. I catch her hips and pull her more firmly into my body, moulding her against me. She cups my face and kisses me deeply.

"You're happy?" I check, after we gasp apart.

"So so so happy," she breathes.

Warmth spills through me, filling my veins. "That's all I ever want," I tell her quietly.

She grins and wriggles on top of me, rubbing against my crotch. "Really? But I have so much more to offer. And I want celebratory boyfriend sex."

I growl, pulling her closer.

We're just getting handsy when we're interrupted by loud fizzing static coming from the lounge. I pause, listening, but the sound melts away again. Shrugging, I turn my attention back to Daisy's neck. She sighs, shuddering against me, and I feel myself twitch in my pants. Shit. I have to have her. I slide my hands down the waistband of her sweatpants, grabbing her ass and kneading her soft cheeks.

Suddenly, the radio squawks again. This time, a voice makes it through.

Dr Nilsson. Can you hear me? Come in, Dr Nilsson.

I frown. The message is in English, which is odd. Daisy gives my cheek a quick kiss, then pushes me off the bed. "Go get it," she says. "Go save lives."

"I hope it's not as serious as all that," I mutter, grabbing my shirt and padding barefoot to the living room. Heading to the desk, I pick up the radio. "This is Dr Riven Nilsson. Over."

"Oh, thank God," the man's voice gushes. *"I've been trying to get through for hours. Do you have Jenny with you?"*

"Jenny? I'm sorry. I don't know anyone with that name. Over."

"Jenny Adams. I tracked her up here. I'm up in a settlement north of Kiruna. I showed her picture to some of the people in the village, and multiple people said that they saw her with you."

"I guess you must have gotten the wrong information. Sorry. Over."

"Please!" He half-shouts. *"The mechanic said he saw her. And a woman in a pub. Charlotte Lundquist?"*

I frown. Charlotte wouldn't get me mixed up with someone else. I've probably been in her restaurant a hundred times. "If you give me her description, and your phone number, I can keep an eye out for her. But I seriously doubt I will have seen her. We keep to ourselves up here."

"She's English. Very, very short, long brown hair, brown eyes. She drives a beat-up old orange car. She's got a little tattoo of a fairy behind her ear."

I'm silent for a moment. "I'm sorry, what did you call her?"

"Jenny Adams? Jennifer? Please, if you know where she is, tell me. She just disappeared a few weeks ago, I've been going mad, worrying about her."

"Who are you?" I demand.

"I'm her boyfriend."

I feel like I've been slammed into by a truck.

There's a footstep in the corridor outside. Daisy sticks her head in the doorway. "Sorry to interrupt," she whispers, her dark eyes shining. "Can I call the others and tell them?"

I turn to her slowly. She frowns. "Baby? Are you okay?" She steps into the room. "God, it's not bad news, is it?"

"Who's Jenny Adams?" I ask. All of the blood rushes out of her face.

CHAPTER 24
DAISY

"Wh-where did you hear that name?" My eyes flick to the radio in his hand. "Who are you talking to?"

The radio fizzes with static. *Is that her? Oh, thank God. Jenny, baby. Jenny, pick up the radio. Tell me you're okay.*

Sam. I take a step back. *No. No.* Riven holds the radio out to me, his face blank. "You should answer him."

No. No. I lick my lips. "No," I force out.

"Apparently he's your boyfriend," Riven clips out. His voice is utterly expressionless. "He sounds worried about you. You shouldn't let him worry."

"He's not my boyfriend."

The radio crackles. *Jenny, baby, it's so good to hear your voice. Are you okay? What the Hell are you doing?*

"Take it," Riven says, thrusting the radio at me. I pull away, letting it clatter to the floor. Sam's voice cuts off. "*No.* I'm not talking to him. And he's not my boyfriend, he's my ex."

"Really." Riven's voice is flat.

"Yes! Really! Why would you believe him over me, you don't even know him!"

"It sounds like I don't even know you." He shakes his head. "What's your name?"

"D-Daisy Whittaker."

His lips press together as he surveys me. I shiver as his cold eyes assess me. The man in front of me looks nothing like the man who was laughing into my neck just minutes ago. He looks furious. Like he hates me.

"Give me your wallet," he says suddenly.

"What?"

He looks around the room, spotting my handbag hung over a kitchen chair. He goes to pick it up, rooting through it until he finds my wallet.

I lunge for it. "What the Hell are you doing? Give that back!"

"Stop," he orders, opening it and shaking all of my cards onto the table. He looks through them slowly, examining my driver's licence, my library card, my debit card. Reading the name printed on all of them. *Jennifer Adams.*

Ice slides down my back. "I can explain," I whisper.

He ignores me, checking inside my purse again and finding my passport. He flips through the pages, checking my name and photo.

"Sure looks like you," he says flatly. "Well. I suppose everything makes a lot more sense, now." He tosses the passport onto the table.

"Riven, I swear, it's not what you think—"

"Is anything you told us true?" He demands. "Anything at all? Do you really live in London?"

"No," I whisper. "Brighton."

"What?"

"I don't live in the city. I live by the sea, in Brighton."

"I see," he says, his voice icy. "What about your job? You're an art teacher? Are you really here on holiday?"

I hesitate.

His eyes narrow. "Tell me the *truth*, Goddamnit."

"I am an art teacher. Or I was," I admit. "But I'm not on holiday. I was fired."

A muscle twitches in his jaw. He turns away, taking in a deep breath. "Jesus *Christ.*"

I close my eyes, tears streaming down over my cheeks. I don't know what to do. I don't know what to say. I can't explain what happened without telling him the whole story. And then he might see the video. I'd rather die than let him see the video.

"Stop crying," he barks, pulling himself upright. He towers over me. It feels like he's filling up the whole room with his cold fury. "Who *are* you? Why are you here? Why the Hell did you come here? Making us all care for you, when it was all just a lie?"

I reach for him. "Riven, I'm so sorry—please let me explain—"

"*No.*" He snatches his arm back. "I don't want you to explain. I don't want to hear your excuses."

"But…"

"*NO!*" He roars, and I flinch back, horrified, as his voice echoes around the lounge. "You've been lying to me this whole time! I don't want to listen to any more lies!"

I close my mouth. Riv's never shouted at me before. I didn't even think he could. But now the calm, gentle doctor has been stripped away, and I don't recognise him anymore.

He's silent for a moment, chest heaving. Then he turns and heads for the desk, opening up his laptop.

Fear gushes through me. "No. Please don't look me up."

He ignores me. I grab his arm, trying to pull him away from the laptop. "Riven, please, please, *please,* if you care about me at all, *do not look me up. PLEASE!*"

He shakes me off. "I need to know who the Hell I've been keeping in my house all this time. I want to know who I've been letting into my *bed every night.* What, are you some kind of criminal? Are you in trouble with the police?"

"No, I—"

"Then why do you care if I search your name?" He opens a web browser.

Fear bolts through me. I can't stop him. He's going to see the video.

He's going to see the video.

I have to get out of here. I can't be here while he watches it. I can't.

I barely even think as I run to my room. I ignore my suitcase. I don't care about it. I just have to get out of here. I can barely breathe. I pull on an extra sweater and a second pair of socks, then rip out a page from my sketchbook and scribble a quick note. In the hallway, Riven barks something I don't understand. I jump, heart thudding. *"Eli,"* he growls. There's a radio hiss.

Shit. He must be telling the others to come back. I skitter through the living room, grab my wallet, and pull on a pair of snow-shoes, bundling into my coat. When I push open the front door, I have to lean against the wall for a few seconds. I feel weak. My chest is burning. There are tears rolling down my face.

The snow is heavier than it was this morning, but it should be fine to walk in. Riven was out here an hour ago. All I need to do is get to the village; then I can find a place to stay until the weather clears up. I can get my car, and drive away to some new town, and forget any of this ever happened.

I push myself off the wall and start trekking through the snow. I can't be in that house with him anymore. I can't just sit there while he watches that video of me. Even thinking about it makes my lungs squeeze and my stomach flip.

My vision starts going dark at the edges. Fat frozen flakes sting my eyes and cheeks. I swallow down a sob as I plough forward.

Oh my God. I'm all alone again.

CHAPTER 25
ELI

Cole and I heave the moose hide out of the car, then I stand back as the man counts out some cash. He's one of our regulars; a craftsman who makes clothes out of the skin. Cole was called to clear up the roadkill a few days back, and now the hide is going to good use.

I cross my arms over my chest. I'm freezing. The snow is coming down much thicker now, and the wind is getting uncomfortable.

Cole finishes the transaction. The man thanks us, then looks at the sky. "You need to go home," he says grimly. "The roads won't be safe much longer."

We both nod. It's pretty clear that the storm that's about to hit will be a bad one.

"We'll have to finish off after the snow clears," Cole shouts over the wind as we head back to the car. I nod, too cold to talk, and slide inside, slamming the door shut. Immediately, I notice a frantic beeping. The radio we have in the dash is going haywire. I pick it up.

"Hey—"

Riven's voice barks down the line. *"Come home. Now."*

"I know, I know. We're not gonna get caught in the storm." Cole sparks the engine, and we reverse onto the road. "We're on our way back now."

"I don't care about the bloody storm," he spits out. I frown, sitting up straighter. It's been a long, long time since I've heard Riven sound this pissed. He always keeps it together in a crisis. Which means whatever's wrong must be very, very wrong.

"Wow, man," I say lightly. "Thanks for the concern over our safety. For a second there, I thought you cared."

He huffs a deep breath. "It's Daisy."

Cole looks over sharply. "What about Daisy?" He asks, raising his voice. "Is she okay? Did something happen?" He taps the gas a little, speeding up.

"She's been lying to us."

"About what?"

"About everything." We turn a bend in the road, hitting the forest, and the radio crackles in my hand as we lose connection. I look up at the sky. It's darkening worryingly fast.

"Are we gonna be alright?" I ask Cole. "I've never seen a storm come on this quick."

"We'll make it," he mutters.

We drive out of the copse of trees and Riven's voice starts back up.

"Everything he said about her was true. Everything. He—"

I cut him off. "Look, man, we didn't get any of that. Just hang on and wait until we get there. It can't be all that bad."

"No, I—"

"Cole is trying to drive through a blizzard. Shut up until we get there." I slam the radio back into its holster.

When we make it to the cabin, the snow is coming down really badly, and the wind is picking up. We don't have time to park the car in the barn; we have to abandon it in the driveway and stagger the few metres to the door. As soon as we step inside, I see Riv pacing up and down in front of the fire. He doesn't even wait for us to take off our shoes.

"She *lied* to us," he announces, spinning on his heel. "Her name is *Jenny Adams.*"

"What?" I unwind my scarf, then push past him to the fire. "Can you give me a second to warm up?"

"Daisy," he insists. "Her real name is Jenny Adams. She never lived in London. She didn't work at the school she told us. She isn't on break, she was *fired.*"

I frown. "Wait, what? How do you know all this?"

"I spent the last twenty minutes talking to her boyfriend on the radio. She suddenly disappeared, and he was worried sick, so he tracked her all the way up here."

I feel like I'm falling.

"Her *what?*" Cole growls.

"Her boyfriend," Riven snaps. "She has a boyfriend. Hell, the way he was talking about her, I think they're pretty damn close to getting engaged."

My heart thumps. Daisy doesn't have a boyfriend. There's no way.

"I checked her passport and driving license," he continues. "Everything he said was true."

"Why would she lie?" I ask. "She must have had some reason. She did mention having a manipulative ex; maybe that's him?"

His eyes are burning. "I don't care. As soon as the storm is over, you're driving her straight to the airport."

"We need to talk to her," Cole says. "She can explain herself."

I head for the corridor to find her, but Riv grabs my arm. "There's no point. She's already proven that we can't trust her. She'll just lie even more to get herself out of it."

"You don't know that—"

"*Yes*, I *do*," he growls. "It's happened before. Or have you forgotten?"

I frown. "Daisy's nothing like Johanna."

He shakes his head. "We're not talking to her. We need to find the truth ourselves." He holds out his hand. "Give me your phone."

"What?"

"Give me your phone. It's better at picking up signal than mine. I want to connect the laptop to the hotspot."

I check my screen. "I don't have any bars."

"I'll find somewhere in this Goddamn house which has signal. Give. Me. Your. Phone."

Sighing, I give it up. He sits at the dining room table and fiddles with it, connecting it to the laptop, then opens up his browser. When the page doesn't load, he slams his hand down on the table. "*Shit!*" He bellows.

I jump. "Jesus, man!"

I've never seen Riven this angry. Not even close. He looks like he's about to lose it. I put a hand on his shoulder. "Calm down. What the Hell is up with you?"

He runs a hand over his face. "I almost did it again."

"Almost did what again?"

"Almost screwed us all over. I just—" He takes a deep breath, trying to calm himself down. "I just asked her to stay with us."

"What?"

"To move in. To—date us. Officially. I asked her literally an hour ago."

My heart leaps. "What did she say?"

"Does it matter? It's obviously not going to happen now." He scrubs a hand through his hair. Underneath all the anger, he looks completely miserable.

"You love her," I realise. "Holy shit. You're completely in love with her."

He presses his lips tightly shut, not denying it. "I should've known," is all he says.

I frown. "We don't actually know *anything,* yet. This might all be some big misunderstanding."

He scowls up at me. "How? I saw her ID, she gave us a fake name! Why are you on her *side?*"

"She believed me when I told her about my jail time. I literally told this girl that she was trapped in the mountains with a *criminal,* and she didn't even flinch. I think she deserves the benefit of the doubt." He doesn't say anything. I sigh. "Look, Johanna lied to you for years. But I told you, man, that wasn't your fault."

He clicks to refresh the webpage over and over. "It was. *I* was the reason everything happened. I was the one who proposed to her. I was the one who testified against you in court. Everything was fine, until *I* fell for her."

I shake my head. "*She* was the reason everything happened. Not you. She was the evil bitch."

"I told myself I'd never let a woman trick me like that again. And *Jenny* did. She did it *so much worse* than Johanna. At least Johanna told us her real goddamn name!"

Suddenly, the laptop screen flickers white as Google finally loads up.

"*Finally.*" Riven leans forward and types *Jenny Adams* in the search bar.

I drop into a chair and watch, my heart racing. I have no idea what's going on, but the one thing I do know, is that I trust Daisy. I know whatever it is that she's done, she's a good person.

The name pulls back thousands of results. I squint at the first headline. It's a news article from The Express. *High School Teacher Fired After P*rn Star History is Revealed.* "Daisy does porn?"

"*Jenny*," Riv insists. "Her name is Jenny."

"She's Daisy to me." I reach over his shoulder and click on the article, skimming it.

> *In Brighton, a high school art teacher is currently under fire after adult videos of her were leaked to the faculty and the parents of several students. One mother, who received the inappropriate content in an email, expressed that she was 'horrified' that 'someone so depraved would be allowed to educate teenagers,' while another worried that the 'screening processes for teachers aren't severe enough.'*
>
> *After a thorough investigation, Alton Secondary School quickly dismissed Miss Adams, leaving a class of A-level students in the lurch, just months before their exams.*

I squint. It's hard to imagine Daisy as a porn star. I mean, she certainly has the body for it, she's sexy as Hell. But I remember how angry she got when Riv asked her to take off her shirt.

"I guess this is why she didn't want us knowing her real name," Riv mutters.

"But why? Why would we care about her doing porn? It's her business." Like, yeah, it's really awkward and shitty that the videos were sent round to the parents of her students; but the article said they got *leaked*. It's not like she was playing them in her homeroom.

Cole doesn't say anything.

Riv goes back to the search page and scrolls through the results. There's a *lot* of porn sites listed. He clicks on one at random.

I grimace. "Dude. Shouldn't we go get her for this? She's literally in the next room. It feels weird to watch a video of her having sex without her."

"I want to know the truth," he gets out. I sigh as Daisy pops up on the screen. Riv's always been like this. When he's faced with a problem, he has to solve it. He's going to Sherlock this mystery until he's worked out exactly what's happening.

I focus on the video. It's of Daisy sitting on a bed in a t-shirt and underwear, kissing a guy. I'm surprised by the jealousy that stabs through me when I see his hand on her thigh.

"Do we have to watch this," I moan. "I said I like to watch, but not just random guys—"

"Shut up."

"He's completely missing that spot on her neck she likes—"

"Eli. Shut. Up."

I sigh, slumping back in my chair, and let the tape roll. I've got a bad feeling about this. The further on we get into the video, the worse it gets.

Not to brag, but I'm pretty familiar with porn. I'm honestly somewhat of a connoisseur. I prefer to have an actual, real-life woman in my arms, but after five years of living in the wilderness, stuck inside during bad weather, I've become pretty familiar with sex tapes.

This isn't a sex tape.

This isn't sex tape sex. There's no dirty talk or strip teases. None of it seems performed. She's not trying to position herself so she looks good on the camera, arching her back or sucking in her stomach. She's wearing plain black underwear. Yeah, it obviously looks amazing on her; but if I were a woman filming herself having sex, I'd probably pick out something a bit nicer.

The two of them start messing around. As she rolls on top of the guy, I hear she's talking about her classes for the day. His face has been cropped out, but hers is perfectly clear.

This isn't porn, I realise. It's not performed at all. It's just domestic, comfortable, loving-partner sex. She doesn't look at the camera once as she reaches for the hem of her shirt. As she starts to lift it up, I slam my finger on the space button, pausing it. I feel sick. "Dude. I don't think she knew that was being filmed."

Cole stands up, scraping out his chair. "Screw this. I'm going to find her. Turn that shit off."

Riven frowns. "Wait—"

"No," Cole snaps, leaving the room. "*Off.*"

I x out of the clip, checking the rest of the page, and feel myself go cold as I see the number of views on the video. Oh my God.

Riv pulls off his glasses and rubs his eyes. "She said someone used her," he says quietly. "Remember? The first night we slept with her."

"Apparently, *someone* is the whole bloody internet," I get out through gritted teeth. "She's hit the trending page." I guess after she got into the news, the video must have blown up. I scroll down to the comments.

Heard u r a teacher. Ur next video should be u spanking urself with a ruler in a schoolgirl costume

Came here from the express article, holy shit didnt expect an arse like that.

I'd go to town on you, you dirty little slut

I have to look away as nausea rises in my throat. *God.* How long has she been putting up with this? I check the upload date. The video was only released about a week before we met her. Everything starts falling into place. Someone posted this video of her online and sent it to the faculty of her school. It went viral after a bunch of news sites reported on the story. She packed a bag and just left.

"She said she had an ex manipulate her to stay with him," I remember. "Do you think *he*—"

The colour drops out of Riven's face. He stands, but before he can go find her, Cole reappears in the doorway.

"You idiot," he snarls. "You. *Fucking. Idiot.*"

"Where is she?" Riven asks quietly.

Cole doesn't say anything. Just slaps a piece of paper onto the table and storms towards the front door. He starts rooting through the coats. Riven doesn't move, so I pick it up to read aloud.

"Cole, Eli, and Riven. I just wanted to say sorry. I'm sorry for lying to you. None of you deserved it. You've all been so kind, and I took advantage of that. You three saved my life, and the last few weeks have helped me more than you can understand.

Pretty much everything I told you about myself was a lie. Where I lived, where I worked, why I'm here. My name. I really never meant to hurt any of you. But I broke all of your trust, and that was an awful thing to do. I'm going to catch the next flight back home.

I'm so, so, so sorry,

Daisy."

I put the paper down. Silence fills the room.

"No," Riven says. His voice is low. "No."

I turn to look out of the window. The storm has hit us full force. The wind is screeching, and the snow is falling so thickly all I can make out is white.

I can't speak. My heart is thumping out of my chest.

"Her coat, wallet and shoes are gone," Cole says, stamping towards us. "How long ago did she leave?"

"I don't know. I—I didn't see her going."

"She obviously left in a hurry. She didn't take any of her things." Cole's blue eyes burn. "When did you fight with her?"

"I guess… thirty minutes ago?"

I close my eyes. She's dead. There's no way she'll have made it to the village in time. And there's no way she'll survive in the blizzard for that long. She would've gotten caught in the storm before she even got to the road.

She's dead.

Riven surges to his feet and heads to the front door. "I'm going to find her." He grabs his coat from the peg and shrugs it on, his hands fumbling with the buttons.

"No." Cole pushes him back. "You'd be useless. Stay here in case she comes back." He pulls on his own boots. "Eli, where are my survival packs?"

I don't say anything. I keep staring out of the window. I feel like my insides have been frozen.

She's *dead*.

She's dead, and I'm pretty sure I'm in love with her.

"Eli!" Cole barks. "Where are the survival packs?"

I force my mouth to work. "Top shelf."

He grunts and grabs one of the backpacks, slinging it over his shoulder.

Riven goes to take one, too. "Eli can stay here. I'll come too."

"No!" Cole turns on him. "*Listen to me.* This is my *job,* so let me do it!"

"But she could be dying!"

"You'll just slow me down. I'll have two people to keep alive."

"I can look after myself."

"It would be a suicide mission."

"I don't *care*."

Cole's nostrils flare. In one quick movement, he grabs Riv by the front of the shirt and slams him hard into the wall. "You're. Staying. Here."

"But—"

"I'M NOT LOSING BOTH OF YOU!" Cole roars, getting right in his face. "YOU'VE ALREADY TAKEN HER AWAY FROM ME, YOU'RE NOT FUCKING DYING AS WELL!"

Riven pales. Cole holds him in place for a few seconds, chest heaving. Finally, Riven gives him a small nod.

"Go," he says hoarsely.

Cole steps back, pulls on his goggles, and unlocks the front door. Instantly, the wind slams it open. The noise is deafening. Snow whirls into the corridor, flying over the two men, covering the floor.

I close my eyes. There's no way she made it. No way in Hell.

Cole tightens his hands on his pack and steps outside. Riven heaves the door shut after him. When the roar of the wind cuts out, the house is eerily silent.

"I shouted at her," he says, his voice empty.

I wet my lips. "I think I loved her."

He puts his face in his hands. "I'm so sorry," he rasps. "I thought—"

"You *thought*." I jump to my feet. Anger burns in my throat. "You *thought*. You didn't *know*. You didn't even *ask* her, for God's sake." I turn to go.

"Eli—"

"Don't fucking talk to me."

I head to my room, leaving him standing alone in the living room, with the laptop still open on the video of her.

CHAPTER 26
COLE

I'm lost.

I've been out here ten minutes, and I'm completely lost.

The most dangerous thing about a snowstorm isn't necessarily the cold, or the wind. Humans can survive that, as long as they get back inside fast enough. It's the disorientation. When everything around you is white and moving, you can barely tell up from down, or left from right. You could leave your house to put the bins out, then die ten feet from your door, because you can't remember which direction you came from.

When I first stepped outside, the visibility was near zero. I'd hoped that Daisy would have left some sort of trail; but of course, her footprints were long covered. All I could do was plough forward through the wind, trying to navigate from memory.

By my guess, she would have made it almost to the road before she realised that she wouldn't be able to get any further. I try to hold a map of the land in my head as I forge through the whirling snow, praying that I'm heading in the right direction. Strong wind buffets me back, and icy snowflakes sting the tiny amount of skin left uncovered by my goggles and scarf. I'm losing hope. For all I know, I could be going in circles. I could arrive right back at the front door at any second. I could—

I almost fall over as I slam right into some bushes. They're completely covered in white, and I'm so snow-blind I can barely see them, but I recognise them as the bushes lining the end of the road. I have been going in the right direction. A thought occurs to me. Daisy's smart. If she got this far, she would've hid under the bush for cover.

And if she hasn't made it to the bush, then she's dead. So I don't have a choice.

I start walking alongside the hedge, looking for lumps in the ground. I barely make it ten steps before I trip over something soft. I drop to my knees, scooping frantically at the snow. A smear of pink appears under my hands. Her coat. It's *her*. She's covered in snow, but the shelter from the bush has stopped her from becoming buried in it. I wipe her face clean. There's snow in her hair, falling down her coat, sticking to her eyelashes. Her eyes are closed. She's as still as a corpse in my lap.

"Daisy," I breathe, stroking her face. "Daisy. Daisy, please. Come on, baby. You're not dead."

After a few terrifying seconds, her eyes flicker open. She opens her mouth, but no sound comes out. I could cry with relief.

I look her over, cataloguing her blue lips and skin. She's not shivering, which is a very, very bad sign. She's hypothermic. I need to warm her up, now. The fastest way would be through my own body heat, but for that to work, we'd need to strip off, and we can't do that until we're somewhere dry.

I give her a little shake. She lolls in my arms, blinking sleepily. "Daisy. Can you stay awake? Can you talk to me?"

Her blue, chapped lips move. I bend, putting my ear right by her mouth.

"Teddy," she mumbles. My heart clenches.

"Yeah. I'm here. I'm here, you're going to be okay."

"Sorry." Her eyes flutter, but she doesn't say anything else. She's fading. Trying to balance my pack on my back, I wrap my hands under her armpits and pull her upright, swinging her into my arms. She barely weighs anything. My pack is heavier than her, for God's sake. As soon as I get her back to the cabin, I'm locking her inside and feeding her up. Maybe then she'll stop getting blown over by the wind.

"Hold on to my neck," I bellow. I feel her arms loop weakly around my neck, and turn, looking around. Everything is a white blur. Which way was the house? Hell, I can't remember. My tracks through the snow are already completely covered. I feel fear squeezing my throat shut. Forcing myself to stay calm, I take a second to reorient myself, then turn ninety degrees to the left. This should—*should*—be the way back to the house. I plough forward, stumbling through the snow. My shoulder burns as Daisy's weight tugs at my healing husky bite, but I ignore it. I have to get her back inside. I have to get her safe.

I grunt as something slaps into my hip. It's thin and taut, almost like a handrail or a clothesline. I frown, feeling along it, brushing off the snow. It's some kind of cord. The rope that Daisy set up to guide us towards the house when visibility is bad. My heart lurches.

I don't have a spare hand, so I lean on it with my hip, following it forward. I barely make it five steps before I fall, tripping over a rock covered by the snow.

It takes me almost thirty seconds to get back up. I pat down Daisy, checking that she's uninjured, then rearrange her in my arms and keep moving. The next time I fall, it takes a full minute to get my feet under me again. All the time, the snow is getting thicker and heavier. Every time we go down, it starts to cover us, threatening to bury us completely until I force myself back up again.

It happens again, and again, and again. We move at a snail's pace. It feels like with every step I take, I get weaker. My limbs are going numb. My body temp is dropping.

The next time I trip, I don't even fall over anything; I just trip over my own damn boot. I drop onto my knees again, doubling over. Daisy almost rolls out of my arms, but I grab at her, panting. My shoulder is burning like fire.

We're not going to make it. I know how far I walked from the house. It was this distance four or five times over. Even if I picked the right direction, we're not going to make it.

I've had a few near-death experiences before. I've been caught in storms, and beaten up in fighting rings, and attacked by wild animals. Each time, the second I realised I might actually die, a strange sense of calm came over me. I felt almost peaceful. When all choice has been taken away from you, there's nothing left to worry about.

But right now, I'm not peaceful. I don't give a shit if I die, but this isn't about me. It's about *her*.

There's no way I'm letting her die. Not while I have breath in my body. I'll fight to the very last second.

I roar into the wild wind as I force myself up again, heaving her into my arms. With first one step, and then another, I keep moving forward.

Slowly, through the snow, something grey looms in front of me. I squint, wiping my goggles clumsily on my shoulder. A few staggering steps closer, and it comes into focus.

It's the shack. The ramshackle, broken-down stone cave we abandoned when we first moved into the cabin. The stunning, kind, *genius* girl put the *shack* on the rescue route. Even though I told her not to bother.

Well, today, her own kindness is going to save her life. I stagger the last few steps through the snow, practically falling into the shelter. Instantly, the deafening noise of the wind outside gets muffled by the stone walls. It's still freezing in here, but at least we're protected from the wet and the wind.

I lay Daisy down on the floor. The ground has iced over, and I swear. I can't leave her on this.

"We need to get you off the ground," I tell her, stroking her cheek. Her eyes have closed again. I'm too scared to take her pulse. Of course she's alive. There's no alternative. "You're losing too much heat," I say. "Just hang on a second."

She doesn't respond.

I head back outside and hack some leaf-covered branches off a nearby bush. I can barely see what I'm doing, and I almost slice my damn thumb off, but eventually my arms are full of twigs. I carry them back inside. Daisy hasn't moved.

"I'm going to make you a bed," I tell her. "One minute."

I lay the switches down on the ground, covering the frozen stone floor, then lift her carefully onto them. Then I turn to my bag. I keep a hypothermia first aid kit in the bottom of all of my survival packs. I unpack a space blanket, a chemical heating blanket, and a blizzard sleeping bag, unfolding them all. Even though each one is big enough to completely cocoon her, they're all folded and packaged in tiny little packets the size of envelopes, which are hard as shit to open when you're shivering convulsively. I grit my teeth, swearing, as my hands slip on the plastic wrapping for the fifth time. Eventually, I get them all rolled out. I turn back to Daisy.

Her clothes are wet with snow, so they have to come off. I start peeling off her coat, then her trousers and sweater. Even her underwear is damp. She must have gotten snow down her clothes when she fell. I pull off her little pink bra and pants, setting them aside, then wrap her naked body up in the blankets. When she's tucked in tight, I bundle her up in the sleeping bag, taping it shut so none of the heat can escape. She looks like a little orange burrito in my lap, only her white face peeking out.

I sit back on my haunches, panting, and close my eyes. I'm exhausted. My energy was already rock bottom by the time I found her. Now I feel completely drained. I just want to hold her and go to sleep, but I know if I stop moving, I'll end up as bad as her. I can't stop moving. I can't stop moving until she's okay.

I force myself to turn back to my bag, and pull out the small, two-person nylon tent, shaking it open. I use a rock to drive the stakes into the frozen ground. I'm getting really weak; I need to lean against the walls of the shack a couple of times, but eventually, I have the tent up. I lift Daisy carefully, laying her inside, then pull out a can of chafing gel and light it with a waterproof match. It won't do much to heat the tent, but it's better than nothing. Wrangling a couple of metal cans out of the pack, I head to the doorway of the shack and scoop up some of the fluffy white snow that's blown inside. She needs water.

When I crawl back into the tent, her eyes are half-open. I could cry with relief. I zip up the tent, then stroke her forehead. "Daisy. Sit up. You need to stay awake." I peel off my gloves to touch her face. I think she's warming up. The heating blanket must be doing its job. Her eyes flutter.

"Say something," I order, setting the can of snow on the heater to melt.

She groans.

I pat her face again. "Daisy. Say something. Or I'll pour snow in your face."

"S-s-s-say what?"

"I don't care. Anything. Tell me how you feel. Sing me a song. Just keep talking."

She obediently starts mumbling under her breath. I don't understand, and I don't care. "Good girl." I leave the can of snow on the heater until it melts and warms, then pour in a sachet of dried hot chocolate, mixing it up for her. "Here. Sit up and drink."

She looks down at herself. "Got no hands," she mumbles.

I realise her hands are trapped in the sleeping bag. I pull her upright to lean on me, holding the can up to her lips for her. She drinks slowly, choking a bit on the warm liquid. I give it to her in sips until the can is empty. She relaxes against my chest.

"You feel better?"

She nods, tucking her face in my neck. "Tired. But. Okay."

"How's your heart?"

Her lips turn down. "Sore," she whispers.

Shit. I slip my hand down her sleeping bag, peeling back the layers of heated blanket, and press between her naked breasts, feeling her heartbeat. She sighs, rubbing into my hand. At any other time, the feeling of her soft, warm tits against my palm would have me rock hard in seconds; but right now, I think my balls are frozen. Anyway, I'm not exactly in the mood. Her heart feels strong and steady. "What do you mean?"

"'S a bit broken," she slurs.

"I meant physically. Is it—clapping?" Shit. *Hjärtklappning*. What the Hell is it English? "Is it going too fast? Or missing beats?" I try.

She yawns. "No." She wriggles against my hand, and I stroke her chest as comfortingly as I can.

"Do you know what you did?" I ask. "Riven and Eli are going crazy. They think you're dead."

"Sorry." Her face crumples. "Sorry. I wasn't thinking. I c-c-couldn't br-breathe in there. I just—"

"Ran." I can hardly judge her for that. Hell, when I got my heart broken, I left civilisation completely. "They think it was their fault."

Her eyes widen. "God. They're not out here l-looking for me, are they?"

I shake my head. "They're safe inside. Climbing the walls."

She frowns. "Why did you come get me? You could've died."

"Not all of us are one-hundred-and-fifty-centimetre weaklings who can't walk in snow."

She looks down, her eyes shaded. She looks unbelievably sad. "I f-feel like I missed you all my life," she whispers.

"We just met," I say stupidly.

She sighs. "I know. I mean, I feel like something inside me was missing, but I didn't know what. And it's you. It's a-all of you." Her mouth turns down. "And now I've ruined it all."

My chest is burning. I have to swallow thickly. "No. No. You've not ruined anything, sweetheart. You've not done anything wrong."

Her eyes shimmer. She's quiet for a long, long time. I can practically see the wheels in her brain spinning.

I give her a gentle shake. "Keep talking."

"Did you speak to Riven?"

"Yes."

"Oh." She presses her lips together. "Did—you see the video?"

"The first few seconds," I admit.

She squeezes her eyes shut. Tears roll down her cheeks. Her breath hitches as she starts to cry. "I d-didn't take it. I didn't know I was being filmed."

Shit. I rock her gently. "Shh. Shh. I know. I could tell." I don't know what to say. This isn't my job. Eli is the one who cuddles and coddles. Riven can calm people down when they're in pain. I'm usually the one who hurt them in the first place.

But I'm the only one here right now. So I have to do something. I pull her closer into me, and she snugs into my chest. "I f-f-feel disgusting," she sputters.

"You're not."

"I *know* I'm not. But I feel it. I feel... used. Like a used tissue. A bit of trash."

"I'm sorry."

She shakes her head, sniffling. "Thanks. For turning it off."

I frown. "Sweetheart. Of course." What kind of guy does she think I am?

She shivers delicately. "I love when you call me that." She yawns again. "I think I'm drunk. But I didn't drink anything."

"Stay awake. I'm going to make you some food." She's not sleeping until her skin turns a normal colour. I root back into my rucksack. Eli thinks that I'm paranoid about the survival packs. Thank God I am. We have enough food to last us a few days. A week, if we really stretch it out. I seriously doubt we'll be here that long, though. The storms in this area tend to be short and sudden. A couple days at most.

I spread out the foil packages of dehydrated food. "Minced beef chilli or minced beef stew?"

"What's the difference?"

"One has beans in."

That gets a tiny smile out of her. "Whatever."

I melt some more snow, then pour a pack of stew into the can. This shit is pretty disgusting, but as the salty, savoury scent fills the tent, my stomach rumbles. I suddenly realise how hungry I am.

"Talk," I order, as I mix the brown saucy mush around with a fork. "Tell me about the video."

"Really?"

I raise an eyebrow. "You have something better to do?"

She hesitates, thinking, then sighs. "It was my ex-boyfriend. Sam. He recorded it secretly, back when we were still together. Must have set his phone up on the bookshelf, or something."

Anger roars up in me. What is this guy's problem? The internet's full of porn, of women willingly taking their clothes off, and he had to trick Daisy into making him a sex tape against her will? It's disgusting.

"When I tried to break up with him," she continues. "He sent me the file. Said if I didn't stay with him, he'd put it online. I called his bluff. I didn't think he'd really do it. I didn't think someone I once loved could be that *evil*." She shivers. "He held it over my head for a few months, but when he realised that I wasn't going to come around, he did it. Put it on the internet, on a bunch of porn sites, and titled it with my real name." She looks up at me through her lashes. "It's Jennifer Adams."

"Riven told me," I say. Her shoulders slump. "Where did you get Daisy from?"

"It's my middle name. And Whittaker is my mum's maiden name." She coughs. "Sam said he'd only take the video down if I got back together with him. Obviously, I wouldn't, so... I guess I'd logged into my social media a few times on his computer. He had my passwords saved. He sent links to the video to everyone. All my Facebook friends. My family. Every single person in my work email list. All the parents of the kids that I taught. E-everyone." Her bottom lip trembles, and she looks down. "Sorry. I can't."

"Come here," I say roughly, pulling her into my chest. "You're okay. You're okay. It wasn't your fault."

As soon as I say those words, she just falls apart against me. She starts sobbing into my chest like somebody's died. I rub her back, feeling completely helpless.

"My mum and dad won't talk to me," she whispers. "They won't believe me, that I didn't film it on purpose. They think I did it for some easy money. M-most of my friends were other teachers at the school. They all blamed me. Said it was inappropriate for a teacher to be seen doing stuff like that. I had messages from pretty much every parent whose child I taught, calling me a slag, and a slut, and a 'danger to society'. I lost my job. My income. I was in the *news*, so many stations covered the story. *The Pornstar Teacher*, they called me. And every time someone looks up my name, they see a video of me getting b-banged from behind. I just—I don't know what to do."

I have nothing to say, so I don't say anything. I just hold her tighter, clenching my free fist so hard my fingernails bite into my palm.

When all of this is over, when Daisy's safe and warm and back in the cabin, I'm going to find her ex-boyfriend. I don't care where the Hell he is. If he's in Sweden, or England, or the bloody Amazon rainforest. I'm going to find him, and he's going to pay for hurting her this much.

Daisy makes a little noise against me, and I realise I'm squeezing her too hard. I force myself to relax my grip. The stew starts to bubble in the can, so I pick up the fork and feed it to her. She eats slowly, sniffling, then turns her face into my chest. "Can I please sleep now," she whispers.

I lay her down gently and wrap myself around her. With her all bundled up like this, it's like spooning a caterpillar. She falls asleep almost immediately, her breath still trembling with little sobs.

CHAPTER 27
DAISY

When I wake up again, Cole is huddled next to me, an arm slung protectively over my waist. Outside the tent, I can still hear the heavy fall of snow. I try to sit up, but I'm wrapped in about fifty layers of blanket. My arms are pinned to my sides by a bright orange sleeping bag. Frowning, I try to tug free.

"Don't," a low voice rumbles at my side. I look across at Cole. I thought he was sleeping, but his eyes are alert. "You need to stay warm," he mutters, reaching across to pull at the tapes tying the sleeping bag shut.

I feel plenty warm at the moment. If anything, I feel too warm; sweaty and gross and claustrophobic under all the insulating layers. "I'm fine."

"You're not fine."

"I can't breathe in here." I try to yank my hands free.

"You'd be dead without it."

"Please take it off? I'm really fine—"

"You're *not FINE!*" He roars suddenly, sitting up. My eyes widen. He looks furious. "You almost *died*, Daisy. If I found you any later, we would've spent tomorrow digging your dead body out of a snowdrift. So don't tell me that you're *fine!*"

The wind howls outside like a dying animal. The nylon walls of the tent flap violently.

"I'm sorry," I say quietly.

"*God.*" He shakes his head. "I'm not mad," he mutters. "Not at you."

"You should be. I was stupid."

"None of us saw the storm coming," he says gruffly. "Me and Eli almost got caught in it. Sometimes there's no warning."

I try to smile. "Sure you don't want to call me an idiot? That's your usual go-to. Don't go soft on me just because I almost died."

It's supposed to be a joke, but he wipes a hand over his mouth and swears again. "You really feel better?"

I nod. "Pretty much back to normal."

"Pretty much?"

"I feel kind of weak. But apart from that, I'm good."

He sighs. "Sit up, then."

I do, letting him unstrap me from my straitjacket. He leaves the blankets draped around me. I look down at myself. "You stripped me."

"Wet clothes will kill you." He fumbles around in his pack, pulling out a chocolate bar. He peels back the yellow wrapping and shoves it into my hand. "Eat."

"I'm not really hungry."

"You need energy to stay warm. *Eat.*"

So I do. I snap the chocolate bar into pieces and cram it into my mouth. "Can I have some water?" I mumble.

He hands me a can, and I thirstily suck it up, watching him narrowly. He's huddled in the corner of the tent, hunched over. Every so often, a flurry of shivers wracks his body, and he grits his teeth hard until they stop. I think he's trying to hide it, but he's freezing his balls off.

"Come share." I lift up the flap of my blanket. "There's enough room for two."

He shakes his head. "You should wrap back up. The temp might drop again."

For someone who spends so much time calling me dumb, he really is pretty thick. "You know it'll be good for me," I try. "Sharing body heat, and all that. I think this heated blanket is out of juice."

He sighs. "I'm going to have to take off my clothes," he warns. "Or it'll screw with the insulation."

"I hoped you would."

He glares at me, quickly pulling off his coat, then the layers of sweaters and thermals underneath. I rake my eyes over his naked torso, drinking in the sight of his solid abs and thick, muscled arms. "You could always take your pants off too," I encourage, my gaze drifting to his boxers. I thought penises were supposed to get smaller when it's cold. Trust Cole's to defy the laws of physics. "I really wouldn't mind."

He ignores my blatant come on, slipping under the blanket and opening his arms. "Here," he says gruffly. I obediently roll into him, and he pulls me closer, his chest against my back. I feel his sigh of relief brush through my hair as he relaxes slightly.

"I'm sorry," he says after a few heartbeats. "That I've been such a prick to you."

"What do you mean?"

"You think I'll call you an idiot for *this?* For being scared and hurt?" His voice is grim. "I must have been really shitty to you for you to think that."

"Just following the pattern," I mumble.

He shakes his head. "I've been too harsh on you, ever since we met you. I should have trusted you more. I'm sorry."

I take a breath. "Was it because of Johanna?"

He tenses. "What?"

"The other two told me about her," I pause. "And about Rickard."

"They're nothing," he spits out. "They don't matter."

I twist around so we're facing each other. Our chests press together. He closes his eyes as the bulge in his boxers rubs between my legs. "That's not true," I say quietly. "You can tell me."

"It seems like you already know the story."

"Not from you. I imagine you're the best person to tell it." He doesn't say anything, and I raise an eyebrow. "You have something better to do?"

He growls. I feel the sound rumbling through his chest, and press even closer. He hugs me tighter automatically, and sighs. "There's... not much to say. When we met Johanna—it was like she put a spell on us all. It was shitty when she got engaged to Riven, but I couldn't be mad at him for wanting to settle down with her. I would've, if she'd asked me instead." He swallows. "When she told me about the kid, though. That felt different."

"You loved him."

"I was a dad, for a bit. Or I thought I was." He squeezes my arm. "That was the hardest part. It wasn't losing a woman I loved. It wasn't even losing a baby. It was losing a—" he trails off.

"Family," I say softly. "For a while there, you had a family." A really weird one, where his baby-momma was getting married to his best friend; but a family all the same.

He doesn't say anything.

"It's okay to be upset," I tell him, tipping my face up to look at him. "It's cruel that it was taken away from you."

He shrugs a broad shoulder. "It is what it is."

"How philosophical." I poke him. "And, what? That's why you were so hostile towards me? You thought I was going to come between you all and destroy everything again?"

"Took me years to reach a point where I made a home. And I thought you were gonna screw with it. I thought you'd hurt

Riven and Eli." He cups my cheek, blue eyes meeting mine. "I'm sorry."

I consider, then sniff haughtily. "Well. I don't forgive you."

He looks down, dropping his hand. "That's fair."

"You're gonna have to make it up to me," I decide.

"How?"

"Kiss me."

His eyes darken. "What?"

"Kiss me."

"No." His gaze flicks to my mouth. "I told you. I don't kiss."

"Why not?"

"It's unnecessary. When I sleep with a girl, it's about release. Not playing-acting romance."

"I know you want to. Riven told me. He said that you'd talked about dating me. He said that you agreed."

Cole snorts. "That doesn't mean I want to kiss you."

"That's kind of exactly what it means."

He scowls. "You think because I saved you from freezing to death, I want to kiss you? It's my job to help weak creatures that can't handle the snow."

I refuse to be offended by his tone. "You're doing it again. Pushing me away, because you're scared. I'm not falling for it again. You can be as grumpy as you want." I slide closer to him, pressing my body against his, and put my head on his shoulder. "You know why I think you don't kiss?"

"I'm sure you're going to tell me."

"I think you're just scared of falling for someone. You're scared of romance, and love." I reach up and trace a fingertip down his cheekbone. "It's easier to just have sex, isn't it? That's just mind-less screwing. But when you look a woman in the face and kiss her, you're opening yourself up to her. You're treating her like you really care about her. And that means that she can hurt you."

"Very astute," he grinds out.

I press even closer. "But you don't need to be scared anymore. Johanna has moved on. It's time you did, too."

He bristles. "I don't want to talk about her."

"Too bad."

"*Excuse* me?"

I shrug. "I'm going to talk about her. And you're kind of stuck with me at the moment, aren't you? Unless you'd rather throw yourself into a snowdrift to avoid confronting your traumatic past."

"I should've let you die in that bush," he mutters.

"Hindsight is 20/20," I say sweetly.

"I can still throw you back out there."

"No. You can't." This man would hurt himself before he hurt anyone else, and we both know it.

I put my hands on his cheeks, forcing him to look at me. "I get it. She hurt you. You lost your family, and everyone you love. That doesn't mean you'll never love anyone again. The only person who's keeping you from having a family is *you*, now, Cole. You, pushing everyone away, trying to scare off people that care about you, isolating yourself in the damn *Arctic Circle* just so you never have to make eye contact with a woman again."

His eyes flash. He opens his mouth. I put my hand over it. "You can have a kid. You can have a wife, and a family. And yes, they might hurt you. We eventually lose everyone we love. That doesn't mean we should just stop *trying*."

He shakes his head slowly. "You don't know anything."

"I know *you*," I insist. "You don't hate people, not really. Deep down, you're kind, and gentle. So why not just give in to—"

"I can't do it again!" He snaps, cutting me off. "Did Riven tell you how he found me, after I realised the kid wasn't mine? I was living in a flat in Stockholm's red light district, getting the shit beat out of me every single night for fun."

I blink. "What?"

"I was in the underground fighting circuit. It was the only way I felt anything at all. If I'd kept at it, I would've died. I *wanted* to die."

Anger, twisted up with pain, rips through me. I drop my eyes to the scars stroking his chest. "These are from—"

"Yes." A muscle tics in his jaw. "I can't survive it again. I *can't*."

My nostrils flare. I get right in his face. "Yes. You. Can," I growl, practically baring my teeth. "For God's sake, you wrestle with moose and *wolves* and trek through storms for a living, and you think you're not strong enough to get your heart broken a few times? If the rest of the world can do it, you can. You're the strongest man I ever met." I'm so close to him, I can feel his heart battering in his chest. His icy eyes pierce mine as his hand slides down to my hip, squeezing. I push it away. "*No.* I'm not going to sleep with you. You think I want to sleep with a guy who's too much of a damn coward to kiss me on the mouth?"

His grip tightens on me. "I'm not a coward," he says, his voice dangerously low.

"So prove it! Pull yourself together and move on! Let yourself get out of this relationship with a ghost! There are people all over the planet who would want you in their family. Who would *love you*, Cole, if you just let them in—"

He cuts me off with his mouth.

CHAPTER 28
DAISY

It's crazy how three kisses can feel so different. Eli's kiss lit me up inside, filled me up with energy and happiness until I felt giddy and bubbly.

Riven's kiss had made the rest of the world go quiet, warming me up like a fire.

Cole's kiss makes me feel like a lightning rod in the middle of a thunderstorm. I moan into his mouth as our lips clash together. Every nerve in my body feels like it's on fire.

He forces my mouth open and pushes his tongue into me roughly. I shudder, melting as our tongues slide together. Cole kisses like he's fighting. Wrestling me, trying to get the upper hand. I love it. It makes me feel dangerous, feeding the wild streak in me, turning me into some kind of primal animal. He grasps my hair in his fist, holding it like a ponytail, and yanks my head back. I dig my nails into his neck, then rake them down his shoulders. He *shudders*, pressing in even closer. His kiss feels desperate, like he's been wanting it for a long, long time, and now he's finally doing it, he can't stop. We get closer and closer, kissing, nipping, sucking. I bite his lip, hard, and he makes a low noise deep in his chest, yanking me onto his lap.

Suddenly, his rock-hard erection is rubbing up against me. We both gasp, looking down. The only thing separating us right now is the fabric of his boxers. Slowly, Cole reaches out and touches my waist, cupping his big hands over my ribs. I close my eyes, feeling goosebumps prickle up all over my body. His rough, calloused fingertips swirl down to my hips, squeezing the soft skin, and I can't help myself from grinding down on him.

His hands pause. "What the Hell am I doing?" He mutters.

I peep open my eyes. "Feeling me up," I remind him. "Next, why don't you try touching my boobs? They've had great reviews."

He shakes his head, blinking hard, like he's dizzy. "You don't want to do this. You like the others."

"Is that so? What made you come to that conclusion?"

"You only fuck me when one of them is around," he says simply.

I stare at him. "Um. No. *You* only fuck me when one of them is around. I've been hoping for some one-on-one time with you for ages, but you disappear every time I try."

His jaw clenches. He grabs my face, forcing me to look at him. "Listen to me. Eli and Riven will be good for you. I won't."

"I'll decide what's good for me, thanks very much."

"Whatever you think it is you want from me—I can't give it to you. Hell, I only suggested 'dating' you because I knew it would make the others happy."

I'm offended. "Seriously? What was your plan? You'd let the others handle all the romance, and just use me as some kind of sex toy?" I rock my hips into him, and his mouth falls open. "You *asshole.*"

"It's not that I don't want—" he trails off, growling low in his throat. "I don't do *romance.* I don't do *soft.* I don't know *how.*"

"Evidently." I run my hand over his hard-on, feeling him twitch desperately under my palm. "Nothing soft here." My fingers trace up to the elastic waistband of his underwear. I snap it against his skin. "Take these off."

With a low groan, he does, sliding them down his muscular thighs. My mouth waters as he kicks away the fabric. He's so goddamn huge. I lean forward, reaching for him. "Can I?"

He grunts assent. I stroke his cock, gently at first, feeling the velvety texture of his skin, and he hisses, his whole body tightening. I dip my hand under to cup his heavy sac, feeling his shaft pulse. He shifts, teeth gritted.

"You want me?" I ask, giving him the tiniest squeeze.

His eyes don't leave mine, but a shudder runs through him. "Yes."

"Come take me, then."

When he doesn't move, I push his broad shoulders, shoving him down onto the floor of the tent and climbing on top of him. He growls as I grind over his crotch. My eyes flutter closed. God, I want him so bad. I can feel my core squeezing and aching and throbbing, deep inside. Drops of his precome mix with my wetness as I rub slickly up against him.

He grips my hips and tries to turn me over, but I don't let him. "Roll over," he orders.

"No," I snip back. "If you're screwing me, you're facing me."

He frowns. "I don't fuck like this."

I snort. "Yeah, I'm sure you don't. It's far too intimate, if you can actually look me in the face, right? Far too *romantic,* if we make eye contact, and you remember I'm a woman you actually care about, and not some hot wet hole for you to stick your knob into." I roll my hips, his tip sliding between my throbbing lips. "God forbid, you might even feel *emotions*." I drop my mouth to his neck and nip at his Adam's Apple, making him flinch. "And if I can make you feel something, I could *hurt* you, couldn't I?"

"Shut up." His fingers dig into my hips. His words have a warning edge. As if I should be *scared* of him. *Scared,* of this man who just risked his life to save me. I wouldn't be scared of Cole if he came into my bedroom with a chainsaw. He'd probably just be building me a bedside cabinet, or something. "I. Don't. Fuck. Like. This."

I sigh and pull away from him reluctantly. "Fine. I'll get myself off, then."

He frowns, swallowing convulsively. I can see his pulse beating in the hollow of his throat. "What?"

"I'm not going to make you do something you don't want to." I push my hair behind my ears and fan myself. "Jesus. This is an excellent hypothermia cure. You should write a research paper."

I sit back, spreading my thighs. His gaze focusses between my legs as I start to touch myself, slowly. I'm only half teasing him. After that kiss, I really, really need to come.

Cole's tongue flicks across his bottom lip. "You're seriously going to do this? I've seen Eli take you from behind. You like it."

"Yes, well, Eli shouts my name when he comes and kisses me whenever he sees me." I swirl my fingers in my building wetness, shifting slightly on the tent floor. "F-far too many men already see me as an anonymous shag. I'm not letting the men I actually sleep with do that to me, as well. I'm sure you can take care of yourself." I let my eyes fall closed and slip a finger inside myself. In my head, I'm not touching myself. Cole's big, strong, steady hands are doing the work for me. Several tense, heated seconds pass. I feel myself getting wetter as I fantasise. My breath hitches, my back arching slightly.

"Oh, for God's sake," he mutters, grabbing at me and pulling my body up against his. "You win," he growls. I growl right back, then climb on top of him, straddling him.

"Look at my *face*," I order, cupping his jaw and forcing him to meet my gaze. His icy blue eyes don't leave mine as I line myself up, then slowly lower myself onto his cock.

CHAPTER 29
COLE

Daisy feels blazing hot and soft as sin as she sinks down onto me. God, she's *tight*. I'm not even sure that she's going to be able to take me, but she just presses her lips together and keeps going, sliding down until she's completely full. Her lips open on a silent gasp. Her chocolate brown eyes melt into mine, full of softness and anger and passion that I sure as Hell don't deserve.

Why the Hell am I still looking at her eyes?

I grip her hips and thrust up into her, hard, pushing as deep as I can go. She keens, scrabbling at me. Together, we start up a fast rhythm that just gets more and more frantic. She rides me hard, rolling her hips. I grip my fingers in the soft flesh of her ass, then smack one of her cheeks, hard. She hisses in a breath through her teeth, and I smooth my palm over the skin, feeling it heat.

She looks absolutely unreal on top of me, her naked curves flushed and glowing with sweat, her long, dark curls tumbling loose around her shoulders. Her tits are in my face, trembling and bouncing with each thrust. I can see her pale pink nipples beading and scrunching right in front of my eyes. I lean forward and catch one in my mouth, nipping at it punishingly, and she moans, rubbing her tit into my mouth like she's desperate for more. "Cole," she gasps. "Cole. Jesus, I'm sorry, I can't... I can't..."

"Can't what," I force out, holding her tighter.

Her thrusts start getting jerky and weak, then she stops moving completely. She flops over me. "I can't—" she pants. "My legs—"

I'm so turned on, it takes a couple seconds for me to work out what the problem is. I grab her around the waist and roll us both over so I'm lying on top of her. The tent shudders as we slip around on the blankets. I plant my fist over her head and keep on pumping into her.

"You had hypothermia," I mutter between thrusts. "You think you have the energy to *ride me?* You can barely walk."

"Next time," she mutters, "I'm usually good at that."

"Oh, you're plenty *good* at it." She cries out when I lift her hips, changing the angle. The head of my dick finds the sensitive bundle of nerves inside her, and I hammer into it, over and over and over again. She shouts with every thrust, shivers running through her body. "Holy shit. Yes. *Yes.* Cole, God, you feel so *good—oh—*"

I love how loud she's being. With the wind howling outside, she may as well be. No one in the world can hear her but me.

I pull her closer, mouthing at her tit, tasting the soft warmth of her.

"Oh," Daisy gasps under me. "Oh, God. Cole." I can feel her weakening as the release builds. Her thighs start to tremble. Her hands slide off my back and cling desperately to my shoulders. "*Oh*. I'm gonna…"

"You're going to come," I rasp out, pounding into her even harder. My dick feels about ready to burst, like a champagne bottle that's been shaken up for half an hour. The pressure is damn near painful.

She squirms under me, hot and slick and desperate. "Please," she chokes out. "Please, Cole."

"Please what?"

She forces her eyes open and grabs at my face, dragging it to hers. I kiss her roughly on the mouth, and she just falls apart, convulsing in my arms. Her sex clenches, squeezing me in rhythmic waves. It's enough to send me over the edge. I tip my head back and shout as I explode inside her. She screams right alongside me, her fingernails scratching down my back.

For just a few seconds, my mind goes blank and white. I forget who I am. I forget my history. I forget that I absolutely should *not* be having sex with this sweet, kind, hurt girl in the middle of a snowstorm. For the first time in years, I have a woman I care about in my arms, and it feels like coming home.

And then the feeling fades, and I come back down to Earth. I look around the tent. Clothes and cans and other supplies are strewn everywhere. Daisy is lying underneath me, her chest heaving as she tries to catch her breath.

Shit.

I pull out gently, climbing off her. "We shouldn't have done that," I mutter.

She glares at me. "Fuck you," she spits.

Surprise jolts through me. "Excuse me?"

She pushes herself weakly up onto an elbow. Her eyes glitter. "I liked it. You liked it. So stop with the *that was a mistake* bullshit. I happened to enjoy myself."

"I *mean*," I grit out, "you're still weak. You just used a Hell of a lot of energy. You'll be lucky if you can walk tomorrow."

"At least I'm warm," she mumbles, rolling onto her side and closing her eyes.

I sigh and reach into my pack, fumbling with a packet of tissues. Pulling a couple out, I quickly dispose of the evidence, then swipe at some streaks of wetness on her thighs. She murmurs under the attention, curling up around my hand.

My heart stops. I have no idea what to do now. She clearly wants some comfort, and I'm not the person who can give it to her. "I don't hug after sex," I blurt out.

She looks up at me sleepily. "What do you do?"

"Leave."

"Alright, then." She waves at the tent entrance. "Off you go." I scowl at her. She scowls right back. "You've literally spent all night hugging me. But here is where you draw the line?" She rolls over, snuggling crossly into the blanket. "You may not have noticed this, but I didn't actually *ask* you for a hug. Prick."

"Good."

"Good."

We're silent for a few minutes. I tidy up the tent, then light up another cake of gel to keep us warm. Daisy stays still, breathing steadily, but I can tell she's awake. She's found her shirt, which has dried over the night, and is clutching it to her chest like she's covering herself. As I watch, she balls up even tighter, shivering.

My heart cracks.

She's right. I am a prick. She's cold and naked and scared. We're in the middle of a blizzard. She's probably worried about *dying*, and I won't even hold her after I fuck her. I close my eyes.

"Daisy."

She ignores me. A new thought occurs to me. Shit. Maybe I'm making her feel *used*. That's the last thing I want, after every-thing else she's been through. Setting my jaw, I lie down next to her. "Come here," I say quietly.

She doesn't move.

"I'll hug you."

She sniffs. "No need to force yourself."

Christ. "Come here, sweetheart," I try, keeping my voice soft.

She hesitates, then rolls into me, burying her face in my chest. She's asleep in seconds, her little breaths fluttering against my skin. I watch over her, my heart beating in my throat.

Sleeping with her was stupid. But if I'm honest, my biggest mistake was kissing her.

One kiss. That's all it took for her to unravel me completely.

CHAPTER 30
DAISY

The next time I wake up, Cole is sound asleep, his arms wrapped around me. For a man who apparently hates hugs, he's certainly a very enthusiastic spooner; he's clutching onto me like I'm a teddy bear, his face buried in the curve of my neck. He grumbles against my skin as I carefully extricate myself from his grip. Sitting up, I look at him, drinking him in. He's always so dark and tense-looking; I've never seen him so peaceful before. His face is easy, his full lips slightly parted. All of his muscles are loose and soft. His chest rises and falls slowly under my hand.

He's beautiful like this.

I'm thirsty. I look around the tent for one of the cans we drank from last night. I spot one and pick it up, but it's empty. We need more snow. I carefully stand up, wincing at the soreness between my legs. It's not a *bad* soreness, not really. In fact, I like the pinch. Even though Cole's fast asleep, it's like I can still feel him in me.

My mind flashes back to last night. I remember the way his hot hands cupped my breasts and shudder. *God*. I can practically still feel him on my skin. Heat flares through my belly, and I feel a little wetness touch between my thighs.

Jesus.

I don't have time for this. We need water. And food. And I should probably light another one of those little heater things. I spot Cole's thermal undershirt crumpled in the corner, and slip it on, along with my underwear and boots. Then I quietly zip myself out of the tent. The sudden rush of cold that rolls over my skin feels surprisingly good after being trapped in a tent for so many hours.

I cross to the mouth of the shack, already starting to shiver, and bend to scoop up some of the snow that has drifted in over the floor. I'm so occupied in the task, it takes me a second to realise that something has changed. I step out of the shack, wide-eyed.

It's stopped snowing. Everything is still. The sky is a very pale, clear blue, and the landscape in front of me is completely blanketed in white, several feet thick. All of the hedges and bushes have been covered. It's like someone's taken an eraser and scrubbed away half the mountain. The whole scene twinkles gently in the sunlight.

It's beautiful.

"Daisy!"

I turn just in time to get barrelled into by a giant, naked mountain man. Cole grabs my waist. "Are you okay?" He asks, frantic.

"Look! It stopped snowing!"

His eyes don't leave my face. "Are you okay?" He repeats, his voice rasping with panic. His hands smooth up and down my body, like he's looking for injury. "I woke up, and you were just gone. I thought you'd *left* again."

"I'm sorry, I was just—"

"For God's *sake*," he growls, pulling me into a bear hug that lifts me right off my feet. "The last time you disappeared, you almost died. Would it kill you to stay in my line of vision?"

"Sorry," I say, chastised. "I was just getting water. But look! Does this mean we can go back to the house?"

He puts me back down and surveys the landscape, his expression calculating. "Yes. I'll go back first, and then the others will come help you. Drag you over the snow on a sled."

I scowl. "Oh, Hell, no. I can walk just fine."

He sighs, shoulders slumping. "Fine. Get your clothes on."

I blink. "That's it? You're not even gonna growl at me?"

"There's no point. You'd just follow me, anyway."

I pat his cheek. "Aw. Teddy. You're really getting to know me."

I'm dying to get back to the cabin—some part of me is terrified that the snow will start again, and we'll be trapped even longer —but Cole insists that we eat something hot before we leave. After wolfing down a can of chilli and some freeze-dried coffee, we pack up the tent and all the equipment, preparing for the trek back to the house. Cole fusses over me like a mother hen, making sure I have enough layers, that my coat is zipped properly, that my scarf is tucked tightly around my neck. Eventually, I stop protesting and just let him have at it. I scared him. If this is what he needs to feel calm, I should let him.

It's almost forty minutes until we step out of the shack. The sun is fully risen, now, and I have to squint over the glare that shines off the snow. We're not too far from the house; only a hundred metres or so.

"Stay close to me," Cole orders, gripping the strap of his pack.

I nod. He gives me one last check-over, then we plunge into the snow. It feels almost like swimming; so much has fallen over the night that it's piled up to our waists.

Well. My waist. It's only up to Cole's thighs. He sees me struggling, and his mouth quirks.

"Why are you so small?"

"I shrank in the wash."

"Come on." He makes to pick me up, and I stumble back.

"No! Your shoulder!"

"It's fine. I don't want you getting too cold."

"I can make it," I insist. He reaches for me again, and I glare at him. "Pick me up, and I'll kick you in the dick so hard your balls fall out of your mouth."

Sighing, he turns around and keeps ploughing on ahead. I follow him determinedly, sticking to the path that his big body clears through the thick snow. I can feel the energy leaching out of me with every step. The cabin gets closer and closer, and nerves start to twist in my stomach. I remember Riv's face as he shouted at me. I shouldn't let myself get excited. I'm not expecting a warm welcome.

Still, I can't help the wave of relief that washes over me as I stumble the last few steps to the front door, leaning heavily on the wall. I'm shaking all over, sweating under my coats. I guess Cole was right about me still being weak.

"Do you have a key?" I gasp as he pulls up next to me.

"They will have left it unlocked for you." He hikes his pack higher onto his shoulder, but doesn't reach for the handle. I look up at him. "Open it," he orders.

My heart beating in my mouth, I close my fingers around the door handle and push inside the cabin.

The two men are in the lounge, sitting silently at the dining table with mugs of something in front of them. They both look up as we step inside. Eli's mouth falls open. Riven flinches like he's been hit.

For a second, we're all silent.

"I found her," Cole says gruffly.

I give them a weak smile. I'm not sure what to say. *Surprise? Sorry I almost died? My dramatic exit got interrupted, can I stay here a couple of days until I can try again?*

"You look like a birdhouse," I tell Eli. He shuts his mouth, standing suddenly, and crosses the room in a couple of long strides. I yelp as he grabs me around the waist, pulling me off the ground and into his arms.

"Don't *do that*," he orders, burrowing his face into my hair. "Don't *ever* do that again." He presses his lips to my forehead. He's breathing fast and jerkily, like he can't get the air in. His eyes are red. He's been crying.

I close my eyes, breathing in the soft pine scent of him. "Did you see the video?" I whisper.

He doesn't answer, pressing me close. "What the Hell happened?" He rasps. "Are you okay? How are you here? I don't understand."

"I'm fine," I say gently. "Eli. The video."

He pulls back so he can look at my face, pushing my hair behind my ears. His cheeks are wet. "I… yeah." He manages. "We saw the first few seconds. We stopped it as soon as we realised what it was. Sorry, baby. God. I can't believe you're okay."

I feel sick. "I didn't know he was recording—I… I..." I take a deep breath, the words drying up in my mouth.

"Her ex took the video, and put it online as blackmail to get her back," Cole says flatly. "She goes by her middle name to stop people from seeing it."

Trust him to be able to summarise the worst event of my life in two sentences.

"Oh, baby." Eli starts kissing frantically down the side of my face. "For God's sake, I don't give a shit about your name, or the video, or anything else."

A chair scrapes across the floor. I pull away to see Riven heading out of the room.

"Riv," I start, reaching for him, but he just shakes his head, leaving. I watch him go, my heart sinking. Cole mutters something in Swedish, kisses me hard on the cheek, and disappears too. It's just me and Eli, holding each other in the middle of the lounge.

Without a word, Eli pulls me against his chest and squeezes me. I press closer, breathing in his warm scent. Tears fill my eyes. I'm okay. I'm okay, and he's here, and he still cares about me.

I don't know how long passes as we cling to each other. Slowly, Eli's ragged breathing starts to even out. Eventually, he pulls back with a gasping breath, cupping my face between his hands. His green eyes burn into mine.

"You're okay?" He asks, his voice husky.

I nod. "I'm okay."

I gasp as he kisses me, hungry and desperate and strong. His hands rove all over my body, like he can't believe he still gets to touch me. "Baby," he mumbles against my lips. "Don't *do* that again. I can't lose you. I swear, my heart stopped." He grabs my hand and presses it to his chest. I can feel his heart battering away in his ribcage. "God, I love you."

"I love you, too," I say. I don't even have to think about it. I know it's true.

He winces, pulling back slightly. "Don't—you don't have to say that, Tink."

I narrow my eyes. "You think I'm lying?"

"Nooo," he says, drawing the word out. "But. *Me?*"

"Is it so hard to believe?"

He runs a hand through his hair, ruffling his curls. "Usually, girls prefer the others. I'm more of a... good time, than a serious commitment."

I reach up and cup his unshaven cheek. He turns into my touch, rubbing his lips against my fingers. "I think I love all of you," I say quietly.

There's no *I think* about it. I know I do. I just don't know what the Hell to do about it.

He makes a soft noise in the back of his throat and pulls me in for another kiss. This time it's gentle and lingering, almost unbearably tender. As our lips press together, a warm glow starts in my belly, heating me like a shot of cognac. I whine when he pulls away, stroking a hand down my arm. "I know, baby," he murmurs, "But you're frozen. Let's get a shower."

Before I can protest, he wraps his arms around my waist and lifts me up off the ground, carrying me bridal-style to the bathroom.

I shove his chest. "I can walk."

"Well done."

"Put me down."

He gives me a little shake. "I thought you were *dead*, woman. I need to fuckin' hold you."

I shut my mouth. He carries me into the shower, then strips us both off and comes in with me. I'm expecting some wandering hands, but he doesn't try to grope me at all; just lathers up soap in his palms and helps to wash me down. I think he just wants to keep touching me. The water streams down my back, hot and steaming, and I shiver as he gently massages shampoo into my scalp.

After I'm clean and dry, snuggled up in his hoodie, he heats us both up some leftover stew and pulls me into his lap on the lounge sofa. He sets up a movie on his laptop, but neither of us really watches it. We're just pressing ourselves into each other, breathing each other in. The crackling fire slowly warms my skin as his hands draw slow circles across my thighs and back.

I push back his auburn curls. "I love you," I tell him again. His eyes close. His arms tighten around me.

"You're so fuckin' special," he grates out, rubbing his rough cheek against mine.

"You, too."

He takes a deep breath, like I've knocked the air out of his chest. I know how he feels. I don't feel like I have enough breath in me, either. The fire spits in the grate, and I curl up in his arms like a cat, bathing in all of the love he's wrapping me up in.

I don't know if I'm going to be allowed to stay here. I don't know if Riven will come back in and kick me out any minute. But right now, I'm happy. And that will have to be enough.

CHAPTER 31
RIVEN

I squint at the patient log in front of me, but all of the letters blur together. This is the fifth time I've read through it, and I still have no idea what it actually says. I can't concentrate. My mind is somewhere else.

I keep imagining Daisy, hunched up in the snow, terrified as she feels her body starting to shut down. Resigning herself to dying out there, completely alone, frozen in the cold.

My bedroom door opens, and Cole strides right in, not bothering to knock. He raises an eyebrow at me, sitting at my desk in the dark. "Hiding?"

"Giving them some alone time," I say, keeping my eyes on the page. "I don't think Eli feels like sharing right now."

Cole snorts. "Liar."

I don't say anything. He comes to stand behind me. "What?" He asks brusquely. "She's alive. What do you have to be upset about?"

I lick my lips. "How did you find her?"

"I would've given her ten more minutes."

I close my eyes. "I almost killed her."

He doesn't deny it. Instead, he draws himself up. "She needs you."

I look up at him. His jaw is clenched. "What?"

"She needs you," he repeats firmly. "She needs you to hold her and tell her you still care about her."

I shake my head. "She doesn't want me—"

His eyes are serious. "Yes, she does. And you'd know that, if you weren't hiding in here like a scared rabbit."

"I—"

"Pull yourself together. You're better than this. You made a mistake. Apologise. It's that simple."

Before I can respond, he turns on his heel and leaves again, his heavy footsteps disappearing down the corridor.

I look down at my hands. They're trembling. I ball them into fists.

I've done a lot of hard things in my life. I've held patients' hands as they passed away. I've told people their loved ones have died. I once performed an emergency tracheotomy on the floor of a restaurant, cutting a hole in the throat of a woman who was choking to death.

I've never been more scared than I am right now.

· · ·

When I step into the lounge, Daisy is sitting squashed between Cole and Eli, cuddled up between them. Eli is playing with the ends of her hair, and Cole—

Cole has their clasped hands laying on his knee. I don't remember the last time I saw him hold hands with a woman. This might literally be the first time.

I stay back for a few seconds, just watching her. She looks so peaceful between my friends. The firelight flickers over her skin, licking her with a soft gold glow. She's the most beautiful woman I've ever seen.

And I almost killed her.

The thought makes me flinch, and she looks up. Her eyes widen. She slips off the sofa. "Riven," she starts. "I am so sorr—"

"Stop." I cross the room and pull her into my arms. She burrows into my chest, shaking slightly. I run a hand through her long hair, *hating* myself. "*I'm* sorry," I tell her, closing my eyes and breathing in her sweet peaches-and-cream scent. "I should've just asked you what was happening, instead of blowing up like that. It wasn't fair on you. I should have let you defend yourself."

She shakes her head. "It was a normal reaction," she mumbles into my sweater. "I'd be pissed if I found out a guy I'd been sleeping with lied to me about who he was. I'd feel mad. And scared. And violated. It was a shitty thing to do." She pulls back. There are big tears shining in her eyes. "I wouldn't have done it if I thought I had a choice. But if I'd told you my real name, you would've looked me up. To check out my Facebook, or look at my paintings online, or check I wasn't a murderer, or whatever. And I was trending in the local news, so I couldn't tell you where I lived, or the name of my school, either. If you'd done an internet search, you'd've found the video."

"I wouldn't have thought of you any differently," I say gently.

She frowns. "It's not just about *you.* It's about *me.* Don't you get it? So many men I've never met have seen me naked. They've jerked off to me. They've left comments, calling me a *dirty slut* and a *little whore.*" She shudders. "Every time someone watches that video, I feel completely violated. You think I'd feel safe staying in a house with three giant, strange men, knowing that sooner or later, they'll probably see me getting fucked from behind?"

"You could've told us not to watch the video," Eli says quietly. "We wouldn't."

"I didn't know you! How was I supposed to believe anything you said?" She crosses her arms. "I don't trust anyone who says they won't watch it. How do I know they won't just get curious? I would do *anything* to stop people seeing me like that. Anything. I feel dirty every time I think about it."

My chest aches. She wipes her cheeks off with the sides of her hands. "I meant what I said in the letter, though. I need to thank you guys. You didn't just save my life, you gave it back to me. These last few months, ever since Sam first threatened me, I've been so sad, and anxious, and scared all the time. I avoided people in the street. I was terrified of men recognising me. I felt so guilty. I was turning into a completely different person, and I didn't even realise it. I'm not a shy, scared person. I love sex. I love my body. I love being adventurous. Being up here, in a place where no one knew me… I got to be myself again. Thank you for that. Thank you. Even if you want to get rid of me, you've helped me a lot."

Eli chokes. Cole straightens, his gaze sharpening. All three of them turn to look at me.

Christ.

I cup her cheek. "Baby. We don't want to get rid of you."

Her lips part. "You don't? But—I lied to you all."

"Not to manipulate us, or trick us. You were just trying to keep yourself safe," Cole says, standing up. He puts his hands on Daisy's shoulders. "Look at me," he demands, and she tilts her head back, meeting his gaze. "You *always* do the thing that keeps you safe," he says gruffly. "Always. No exceptions. We will deal with the consequences after. You *never* jeopardise your safety just to make someone else happy."

She just looks up at him.

"You were right to lie to us," he continues. "We were strangers, and you were trapped here with us. You're right; as long as that video is up, you are more at risk to violence."

I remember the man yelling at her in the street, and my fists tighten.

"I would much rather find out that you lied to me, than find out you put yourself in danger. You did the *right thing*," Cole emphasises. "So stop apologising."

"Thank you," she whispers. He squeezes her shoulders and steps back again. Her lips press together. She looks down at her hands. "I don't want to live the rest of my life like this, though.

Hiding my identity to stay safe. Giving a fake name. None of this is my fault; it's not fair I have to do all this."

"You won't have to," I say. "Sharing intimate pictures of someone without their consent is illegal. If you took it to court, you could get the video removed, and probably hit your ex with some jail time." I try not to sound too excited about that.

She shakes her head. "He's got money. I'd never be able to afford a good enough lawyer to go up against him. All he has to do is say that I put the video up myself. I don't have any proof that's not true."

"My parents have been trying to bribe me to visit them over summer. They'll do this for me. They know some of the best lawyers in England. They will find you a lawyer, and they *will* sponsor your case." God knows they deserve to, after what they did to Eli.

I expect her to look relieved, but she wilts. "I don't know if I can," she says quietly.

I blink. "You don't want to?"

"Oh, I *want to*. But—I don't know if you understand what I'll have to do. I'll need to go through the video with the police. And then I'll have to stand in a courtroom, with Sam, while grown men argue over my head about whether or not I'm a liar. It's… how can you *do* that?"

Eli pulls her into him, pressing his lips to her temple. "It's the worst feeling in the world," he tells me.

I swear. Why the Hell does this have to be so bloody humiliating for her? She's done absolutely nothing wrong, and she'll have to go through so much pain, just to get justice.

"Well," I say after a moment. "Of course, we won't make you do anything. But it's probably the only way to get the video taken down."

She sniffles, wiping her face. "No. No. You're right. I have to do it. I won't be happy until I do." She somehow manages to look fierce, even with wet eyes and a pink nose. "I can do it. I'll probably need a lot of hugs. But I can do it."

"We'll be with you every step of the way," Eli promises. "Providing hugs." Cole nods. I reach across and squeeze her thigh. She smiles weakly.

"Thanks," she whispers. "Thank you."

The rest of the day passes lazily. We all huddle together in the lounge, only getting up occasionally to get food. After such an awful day, we all want to be together. Eli, Cole, and I sprawl on the sofa, and Daisy's bundled up in blankets and passed around between us. There's never a point where someone isn't holding her or touching her. She seems to enjoy it, nestling into all our arms. She obviously wants the comfort, and God knows the rest of us need it.

As the clock ticks into evening, we're all drinking mugs of hot chocolate, curled up together. Eli is telling some dumb story about one of his skiing students. I'm half-listening, watching Cole with Daisy.

He has her settled in his lap. Every minute or so, he presses a little kiss to her temple or cheek.

I haven't seen him be this tender with somebody since Rickard was born. It's so strange to see this side to him again, after all these years. Like meeting an old friend.

As I watch, his phone buzzes. He pulls it out, checks the screen, then stands. "I need to do something," he mutters. I open my arms, and Daisy climbs into them, snuggling into my neck. Cole gets dressed up in his winter clothes, grabs a shovel, and heads outside. This is pretty normal behaviour for Cole, so no one really questions it.

A few minutes pass, and then our conversation is interrupted by a scraping sound over our heads.

Daisy frowns at the ceiling. "Is he clearing snow off the roof? Right now?"

Eli and I both shrug. "He has odd priorities," Eli explains. "Hey, I have a question."

She settles closer in the curve of my arm. "Shoot."

"Do you want us to start calling you Jenny?"

She shudders delicately. "God. I don't even like hearing you say it. No. I think I like being Daisy better. It's still technically my name, and since I've been using it…" she shrugs. "I don't know. My life has been a lot better. I've stopped teaching and started painting. I finally drove up here to Sweden. I've started a new relationship. It feels like a fresh start. I look back at who I was before, and I barely even recognise her."

"Daisy it is," I promise, kissing the tip of her ear. She smiles, catching my hand and entwining our fingers.

The clanging stops, and Cole comes back inside, shaking snow off his boots.

"The storm has cleared," he tells Daisy.

She blinks. "Um. Yeah. I know. It was kind of an important part of my day."

"The skies are clear," he emphasises.

She nods slowly. "Good?"

He holds out his hand to her. "Come see."

Reluctantly, I let her slide off me and follow him outside.

Eli stretches next to me, letting his head loll onto my shoulder. "I can't believe how cute he is with her. I never thought…"

"I know." After losing Rickard, I thought he'd locked that soft side of him away. But maybe all he needed was her. Our missing puzzle piece.

My thoughts are interrupted by a gasp from outside. "Riven! Eli! Come look!"

Bemused, we both grab our coats and go to join them. As soon as we step outside, it's clear what has her so excited. The Northern Lights are out.

Even after living up here most of my life, they still take my breath away. They hang right over our heads, a glowing green curtain of light, like a rippling piece of silk. As we watch, the cold biting at our faces, they twist and shift, spreading over the dark sky.

Daisy makes a little noise, and I turn to look at her. She's crying, tears rolling down her cheeks. Her face is shimmering green and blue under the wash of coloured light. I put my hand on her back, rubbing circles through her coat, and she lays her head on my chest. "It's so beautiful," she whispers.

We stand there for five, ten minutes, as the lights burst and flame over us. She cries quietly the whole time, and we huddle around her to keep her warm. Eventually, though, she starts shivering too hard for us to ignore. I check her face. Her lips are turning blue.

"You need to get back inside."

"But—"

Cole puts a hand on her shoulder, turning her back towards the house. "I cleared the snow off the skylight in Riven's bedroom. You can see them there."

"Oh!" Wiping off her face, she practically runs back inside the house.

We all glance at each other, and none of us can hold back our smiles.

CHAPTER 32
DAISY

I curl up in the middle of Riven's bed, stretching my neck to watch the lights shifting through the thermal glass skylight. The boys traipse through the doorway, and I hold out my arms. "Come here." They all fall into the bed around me, huddling close enough that I can touch all of them at once.

"How long will they last?" I whisper.

"Hard to say." Riven shrugs. "Sometimes fifteen minutes. Sometimes all night. They're going strong, though."

"And now that storm season is finishing, you'll be able to see them pretty often up here," Eli adds. "Probably at least until April." He pauses meaningfully. "You know. If you stayed here."

"Because I *can* stay here," I say slowly.

"I might actually cry if you didn't," Eli says.

"And you all really forgive me?" I check. "All of you?" I don't want to beat a dead horse, but I can hardly believe it.

"Don't ask anymore," Cole orders, pulling me into his lap. "There's nothing to forgive."

I nod, looking down.

"How do you feel?" Riven asks. "Now that you've told us?"

I think, shifting a bit in Cole's lap. He grunts as I rub up against him, and I toss him a smile over my shoulder. "Great. Lighter. Like I don't have anything to hide from you guys anymore. Like I can do anything I want." I swallow, taking one of Cole's big hands and twisting my fingers with his. "I mean, deep inside me, obviously I knew I wasn't easy, or dirty, or what any of those people were saying about me."

"No," Riven says firmly. Eli starts stroking my ankle. Cole slips his spare hand down the back of my jeans, squeezing my buttcheek. I wriggle against him, feeling him harden under my ass. "But— everybody around me was saying it. Everybody that I cared about. It sort of felt like, it didn't matter what I believed. If the whole world believes something, the truth doesn't actually matter, does it?"

Eli frowns. "That's not how it works."

"No. It's not." I take a deep breath, looking between them. "Um. I think I want to try something, actually. If… you want to."

As if he knows what I'm about to say, Cole slides his hand between my asscheeks. I yelp as he kisses the shell of my ear, rubbing his thumb against my hole. I feel all the muscles in my behind clench.

"You like it?" He rumbles in my ear.

"Yes," I breathe. "I love it. But—"

"The video," he surmises. I look up at him with big eyes, and he scowls. "I didn't *watch* it. Riven told me what the guy in the square shouted at you, when we went to get your car fixed."

Riven winces. "That you liked—ah…"

"Getting fucked in the ass?" Eli offers.

Riven nods.

I sigh. "Yeah. I was having anal sex in the video. Honestly, I think that's kind of why no-one believed me when I said I didn't know it was being filmed. People thought, because I was having sex in an 'unconventional way', I *must* be some kind of depraved porn star." Cole pushes his thumb hard against my asshole, and I jump.

"You are quite depraved," he says in my ear. My eyelashes flutter. Honestly, right now, I'd have to agree. I push back into his hand and hear him hiss in a breath through his teeth.

"These poor people," Eli sighs mournfully. "I bet they all have unsatisfying missionary sex once a year, then lie awake at night dreaming of getting fucked in the ass. I bet—"

"Lube," Cole interrupts.

There's a few beats of silence.

"I know you're a bit of a caveman, Nalle," Eli says, "but that has to be the weirdest one-word sentence you've ever come out with."

Cole growls in my ear. "Does anybody have any."

Eli scoffs. "If you think that I'm sharing my extra-tingly, heating, cherry-flavoured super-glide female-stimulating lubricant, you have another think coming."

"You're willing to share a woman, but not your lube?" Riven says drily.

Eli just shrugs. "I own the lube. I don't own the woman."

Riven stands. "I have plenty of medical-grade lubricant in my kits."

"As *unbelievably* hot as that sounds," I interrupt, pulling off Eli's hoodie, "I have some. Can you get it? It's in my washbag."

All three men turn and stare at me.

I flush. "What?"

"That's hot," Riven says, leaving.

"Is it cherry-flavoured?" Eli asks.

"Nope."

He flops back in relief, eyeing me as I peel off my t-shirt. "Thank God. I still have something to offer in this relationship."

"Can we *get on with it*," Cole growls. I shake off my joggers and cup his square jaw, kissing him hard. He grips me tighter to him, thrusting his tongue into my mouth and twisting a rough hand into my hair. I keen as his big fingers tug at the roots, sending little sparkles of pain through my scalp.

By the time we break apart, gasping, Riven's back, dropping my little travel-sized lube onto the quilt. I rub my mouth, feeling my lips tingle.

"If you ever want *me* to shut up," Eli offers, shucking off his shirt, "that would probably work on me as well. I don't know. Maybe. I guess there's only one way to find out."

Laughing, I crawl forward to kiss him, keeping my butt in Cole's lap. I hear the cap of the bottle being popped open, and tense in Eli's arms, suddenly nervous. My mouth goes dry.

"I-it's been a while since I've done this."

"We'll go slow," Riven promises, unlooping his belt. He pauses. "Well. At least at the beginning."

"Then we'll go hard," Eli finishes with a grin, lapping at my bottom lip. I jump a little as Cole tugs down my underwear and gently parts my cheeks. Coldness touches my sensitive skin. He runs a slick finger around the ring of muscle, swirling my hole with slippery lube. With every circle he draws, he adds more pressure, until I can't help but whimper, twisting away.

"Relax," he mutters behind me. "You're too tight."

"I—I'm sorry. I just…" I'm surprised by how nervous I am. My heart pounds even faster in my chest. "I can't."

I *can't*. Holy shit. What's wrong with me? Even in a completely safe, supportive environment, it's like I can't shake off the last scraps of old embarrassment. I don't want to be ashamed to have sex. I don't want this to be a part of my life.

"Hey." Cole grips my hips. "You never apologise. You're not a sex toy. You don't do anything you don't want to do."

"But I *do* want to," I practically wail, bucking back into him. "I just… I guess I haven't done anything like this since Sam told me about the video."

"Move up," Riven orders, and Eli shifts, so they're both kneeling in front of me, just in their boxers. He cups my cheek, his thumb stroking my cheekbone. "It's okay," he says quietly. "Like I said. We'll start off slow." He glances at Eli. "Why don't you loosen her up a little?"

Eli grins, reaching out to touch my lips. I open my mouth automatically, sucking his fingers in, and watch his green eyes darken as I swirl my tongue over him. Slowly, he draws them back out again, and trails them down my body; between my breasts, over the curve of my stomach, then between my legs. I close my eyes as he starts playing with me, gently at first. His fingertips stroke up and down my sex, parting the soft lips, tracing over my hood. I watch his face, dark and intent, a hint of flush over his cheekbones, and feel myself getting hot all over. Behind me, Cole keeps rubbing around my asshole with thick fingers, making me tremble. Riv leans in and starts kissing my neck in slow, delicious suckles. Next to him, Eli draws circles around my entrance, teasing in and out, until I feel myself flutter and clench. Wetness is pooling between my legs.

"Just do it," I get out through gritted teeth. He grins, obediently pushing both fingers inside. I start to sigh, relieved, when suddenly, Cole adds more pressure. I jump, squirming, as the pad of his finger pushes inside of me.

Oh my God.

Eli has two fingers in my sex; Cole has one in my behind. I feel like every inch of my insides is getting slicky-wet and caressed. I'm suddenly so hot I don't know what to do. It's insane. I'm completely desperate for relief. I feel both of their fingers moving inside of me, sending ripples right through me. I try to grind down on Eli's hand and back into Cole's, rubbing desperately between them.

"Easy," Riven orders quietly, taking my face in his hands. "Kiss me."

I do. I kiss him hard, desperate, but it's just making it worse. I'm getting hotter and hotter as Riv's tongue slides over mine, and Eli curls his fingers inside me, massaging my G-spot.

Cole slides another finger into me, stretching me, and electricity sparks through my veins. Riv pulls me closer, sucking my bottom lip into my mouth, and the ache in me gets ten times worse, clutching at my belly. I have to pull back to moan. My head is spinning. I can't catch my breath. I shift my weight over and over, but I can't ease the pressure building inside of me. My pussy feels puffy and slick and angry, sopping wet. I can feel the tender skin twitching and aching. I can't do this anymore. The tickle of arousal in my belly gets worse and worse, flaring and burning, raging in me. I've never been teased so badly in my life.

Behind me, Cole adds a third finger. I tremble at the stretching feeling, then choke as Riv starts playing gently with my breasts. Heat wires right down between my legs. I can feel my climax starting, building up inside me, and I close my eyes, twisting my hands in the sheets, preparing for the wave to hit me—

And then it fades away again, as Cole and Eli simultaneously pull their fingers out. I whine, clenching automatically, trying to keep them inside of me.

Eli laughs. "Don't worry, Tink. There's more where that came from."

I *know* that, but it doesn't change the fact that I'm now gaping and aching and empty on two sides. I squirm, panting. I feel inflamed and trembly. I shove back into Cole. "Please," I gasp.

"You're ready?" He sounds skeptical.

"I don't know," Eli says slowly. "I think we could play with her a little more."

"It's better safe than sorry," Riv agrees.

"If no one puts a knob in me in the next five seconds I swear to god, I'll just snap them all off."

Three deep laughs rumble around me.

"I'm not joking," I hiss. "Please, just, *please*—"

"Shh," Cole murmurs in my ear. His big hands massage my cheeks. He gives one a sudden, stinging slap that has me gasping. "You want me in your ass?"

"Y-y-yes," I breathe. I hear the lube cap snap again, and then gasp as I feel his thick, slick head press against my back entrance. "*God.*"

I vaguely register Riv and Eli mumbling in Swedish. Pushing Eli off the mattress, Riv stretches out on his back down the middle of the bed, reaching for me. Pulling away from Cole, I obediently climb on top of him, straddling his hips. His strong, brown arms wrap around my waist as I carefully lower myself onto his dick, sighing when I feel how deeply he fills me. I swear, he's touching parts of me that have never been touched before. He apparently enjoys the feeling as well, clenching his jaw. Rolling my hips, I slowly start to ride him, letting my eyes fall shut. I've just hit a steady rhythm when Cole's rough hands touch my shoulders, bending me forward. Riv cups my cheek as I fold over him, baring my arse to Cole. I feel Cole's thick head press against my back entrance again — and then he pushes into me slowly. My mouth falls open, but no sound comes out as I feel him breach the tight ring of muscle. The stretching sensation is unreal— almost painful, but painful in a way that sends fire running through my veins. Cole is still for a moment, and I hear his low groan in my ear as he wedges himself into my tightness. Below me, Riv gets one of my tits in his mouth, nipping suddenly. I jerk, crying out, and Cole uses the distraction to push the rest of the way into my ass.

My eyes widen. I try to speak, but I can't make any words. I just stay there on all fours, filled from underneath and behind, frozen and gasping.

Full. I feel so full. I didn't realise my body *could* feel like this; stretched and jam-packed. Even my lungs feel full to bursting. The ache that the boys have spent the last half an hour teasing up in me dulls to a steady throb as I clench down. I hear a groan, feel Cole's hips jerk a bit as he tries to keep still.

God, I've *missed* this.

Someone strokes my face. "Is it too much?"

"More," I say hoarsely. "More, I need, I—fucking, *move—*"

Cole pulls out, then thrusts back in, and my eyes roll back. There's a deep, pounding throb in my belly as he thuds up inside me. Riven's face is sharp and strained underneath me as I slowly start to rock forward, gradually picking up the pace. I'm too overwhelmed to ride him properly, but he takes control, sliding his hands under my hips and thrusting up into me. The two men organise a steady tempo, Riv sliding out while Cole pushes in. I let my eyes fall shut, gasping and twisting as my body tries to understand so many sensations inside me, all at once. My heart is fluttering in my chest like a frightened bird. I grip onto Riven's shoulders so tightly my knuckles turn white.

"Breathe, Daisy," he orders, and I do, forcing myself to take a few deep breaths. It's hard not to get overwhelmed with all of the sensation rushing through me.

Suddenly, I feel something smooth and soft touching my lips, and look up. Eli is standing by the bed, his hand wrapped around his dick. Without waiting for him to speak, I open my mouth, swallowing him down. He's thick and throbbing against my tongue as I lick at him sloppily. I seriously doubt it's the best blowjob of my life, but he still shivers, his eyes falling shut. I twist my hand at the base of his shaft, pushing backwards as Cole and Riven both move in and out of me, one from below, one from behind. They're speeding up, getting faster and faster as they pound into me. I keep on rocking and riding, letting Eli thrust in and out of my mouth. It feels like every part of my body is being stimulated. Soon, I'm shuddering and twitching and gasping. I feel like I'm about to split out of my skin. I need release. As he rolls up into me, Riv reaches down and trails two fingers between my folds. I grind into his hand, helpless, and he groans.

"She's fucking dripping on me," he rasps.

Eli lets out a pained noise, and I slide my head up to suck on his tip. "Jesus. Baby."

I whimper. It's too much. Too much. I'm trembling all over. I can't *breathe*, my body is on fire. I need to come.

"Open your eyes," Cole orders, and I do, looking up at the skylight over my head. The lights are still going. They've changed colours slightly, from green to blue, with a pinkish aura down one side. I can see the stars through them. They're so beautiful I could cry. My breath hitches.

Tears fill my eyes. My whole body is screaming. I swirl my tongue frantically over Eli, lifting a hand to squeeze his shaft, cupping his balls.

"*Fuck*." Eli pulls out of my mouth, scrubbing a hand through his hair. "Kiss me, babe." He kneels down next to the mattress and brings my mouth to his. I try to kiss him back, but I can't focus on it. Riv is nuzzling over my cleavage, and Cole is massaging my asscheeks as they both batter into me. Pleasure is rippling and building up in my body. I can't make my lips work right. I tip my head back as every muscle in my body strains, desperate for release.

And then, beneath me, Riv lifts his hips, grinding against me. I snap forward violently, screaming as I come. Hands touch me all over me, stroking me, petting me as I gasp and writhe. It just doesn't stop. I clench and clench and clench, waves of pleasure hitting me, knocking the air out of my lungs.

Finally, the waves recede, and I flop, lifeless, on top of Riv. I try to heave in a shaky breath, sucking up the comforting, woody scent of his cologne, but I can't get a full breath in. It takes me a few mind-blistering seconds to realise neither Riven or Cole has stopped. Riv is still rubbing his balls up against me; Cole is still slamming into my ass. I shudder from the overstimulation, but I can't pull away from them. They just keep thrusting in and out of me. A tingle spirals through me, and I feel another climax start to simmer.

Eli stands and strokes my cheek. "Ready for me again, baby?"

I realise he's still stroking himself, and lunge forward, catching his dick in my mouth. He laughs and gasps in the same breath, grasping my head in both hands as I swallow him down. Behind me, Cole pinches my ass, pounding into me steadily. Riv starts stroking me with one gentle finger as he thrusts up, slapping repeatedly into my G-spot. I moan around Eli. It feels like every millimetre inside of me is pricking and tingling and aching, begging for more. I squirm, trying to rub up against all of them, to get the pressure I need, but I can barely move, locked in on all sides. It's torture. I can't handle it. I feel heat boiling inside of me again, bubbling to the surface.

I try to warn them. "I—I'm—oh, oh, *f-fuck*, ah…" I can't get the words out between my wildly hitching breaths and moans.

Eli pulls back a few centimetres to let me speak. "Baby?"

"I'm going to—I-I'm—"

Under me, Riv suddenly tugs on one of my nipples, hard. I shout, my hips jerking over his, pushing him even deeper into me—and that's enough to send him over the edge. His grip on my waist suddenly tightens, short fingernails digging hard into my skin as his whole body shudders underneath me. I feel him spasm as his hot come strokes into me, filling me deep. I sigh, loving the feeling. As if he set off a chain reaction, Eli groans, spilling into my mouth. I gasp, gulping down the salty hot come filling my throat. Every muscle in my body tenses as I get closer and closer to another climax. Cole chokes behind me as I clench down on him, groaning deeply as his hips stutter. I feel him harden, somehow filling me up even more; then he grips the ends of my hair and lets go. Silky warmth shoots deep into my ass, filling me up with wetness.

And then it's my turn. I'm still sputtering around Eli as I feel a wave of heat rising up through my body. It starts off in my toes and climbs higher and higher, tingling and burning over my thighs, my belly, my chest, until it finally hits me. I swear to God, I almost black out. I've never felt an orgasm like it in my entire life. It feels like it lasts forever, and I shiver and gasp through it, almost alarmed at how strong the feeling is. Hands stroke over my body, twitching my nipples, rubbing my clit, circling my asshole, as I convulse, and tremble, and shake, and finally, *finally* collapse, completely exhausted. I lie between them, sweat running down through my hair and over my skin. As I roll slowly over, I feel so full of liquid that I practically squelch. Someone makes a soft noise, stroking my wet face, and I realise I'm crying. But I'm not sad. I open my eyes and look up through the skylight. Lying there, as my boys huddle around me and the Northern Lights shimmer over my head—I feel happier than I can ever remember.

More than that. I never thought I'd have sex this good again. I didn't think I'd ever find people I trusted enough. I didn't think I'd trust *myself* enough. But I did, and I feel like my body is mine again. It's mine, and I can do whatever I want with it.

Blinking back tears, I grab the face closest to mine and pull it into a kiss.

DAISY

THREE MONTHS LATER

I'm shaking hard as we step out of the courtroom. Cole keeps a steady arm around my waist as he leads me back into the atrium. My head is spinning. I feel like I'm in a dream.

We barely make it three steps out of the door before Eli strides up next to me, tugs me right out of Cole's arms, and pulls me into a kiss. I squeak with surprise, then melt into him. Footsteps click on the marble floor around us as official-looking people in suits pass through the hall, but I don't care about all the disapproving stares we're probably getting. I'm too happy for that.

Eventually, we have to pull up for air. He touches his forehead to mine. "I'm so proud of you, Tink," he murmurs, pushing back a strand of hair that's fallen out of my bun. "You did so fucking good."

I burrow into his chest, breathing in his shirt. "I was so scared."

So scared. I haven't slept at all in two days, worrying about the trial against Sam. I spent most of last night hyperventilating on the floor of our Brighton hotel room. The guys took shifts, passing me between them, trying to soothe and comfort me—but I could tell they were almost as anxious as I was.

Eli kisses my hair. "I know," he rasps. "I know, baby. You were incredible."

Eli was the most stressed of all of them. I thought he was going to throw up when we stepped into the courtroom this morning. Which is understandable. The last time he was in one, a year of his life was sentenced away. The judge chose somebody else's story over the truth.

But not today.

Today, after a tense, heated, *long* debate, Samuel Warner was finally judged guilty of disclosing private sexual images, and sentenced with the full two years in prison. He's also being made to register as a sex offender, so even when he does get out of jail, his life is ruined. I was given the right to demand the videos be removed from websites and search engine results. Riven organised to have a man on standby, waiting for the all-clear to send the cease and desists, so it should be happening right this second. Even as we talk, all those images of me are getting wiped away.

I can practically feel it happening. It's like an iron band is unwinding from around my ribcage. I can finally breathe again.

I give Eli another peck, but pull away as I see my parents coming out of the courtroom, talking to Riven. I take a moment to appreciate how good Riv looks in his sharp navy suit. All of the boys are suited up: Eli looks like a model in his silvery-grey three piece, and Cole has somehow stuffed his broad shoulders and thick thighs into a stylish black ensemble. He'd flat-out refused to wear a tie, and with his shirt collar open at his throat, he looks incredibly sexy, and incredibly uncomfortable.

I force myself to stop checking out my boyfriends, and tune into my parents' conversation. "Thank you so much for supporting my daughter," my dad is saying. "She's so lucky to have you as a friend."

"Trust me," Riv says, "I'm the lucky one. There's nothing I wouldn't do for Daisy." He looks at me in Eli's arms, longing all over his face, and my mum gives him a sympathetic look. She clearly thinks he's pining away in unrequited love.

Little she knows. It's very, *very* requited. She steps forward, taking my hands. "Baby—" she starts. "We are so, *so* sorry for not listening to you."

I have to force a smile onto my face. If I'm honest, I don't forgive my parents. I know I will someday, but right now, the wound is still too raw. It's kind of heartbreaking that it took a judge and jury to convince them to believe me, when I've been telling the truth this whole time.

"You should've," Cole grumbles from behind me.

Mum looks up. "Excuse me?"

"You should've believed her," he repeats. "It's fucking ridiculous that you didn't."

My dad frowns, annoyed. "I'm sorry, who are you? And why are you even here?"

The boys all hesitate, looking at me. I haven't told my parents about our relationship yet. As far as my mum and dad know, they're just friends I made on my trip.

I think it's time I set the record straight.

"He's here because he's my boyfriend," I say, my voice very clear. Cole's face turns bright red under his beard. It's adorable.

My mum looks between me and Cole. "He's your boyfriend? *Him*?"

"Yep," I say simply. "We've been together for months, now."

"But…" Dad points at Eli. "Didn't you two just…"

"Kiss? Yes." I straighten my back. "I'm dating Eli, too."

Eli gives them both a shit-eating grin. "Surprise."

My dad's eyes widen. "You're *what?*"

"And—" I hold my hand out to Riven. He steps forwards and threads our fingers together. "Riv, too. I'm dating them all."

My parents look absolutely horrified.

In their defence, I guess it's a lot to spring on them at once. I actually wanted to tell them earlier, but the lawyer Riven's dad found me advised that we keep the relationship under wraps until after the hearing. Some bullshit about how the jurors might think I'm a sexual deviant, if it got leaked that I'm dating three men.

I think it's dumb. Let people love who they want, it shouldn't be this hard.

"All three of them?" Mum asks hoarsely, looking between us. "H-how is that possible?"

I shrug. "They each get two days a week with me, and they all share me on a Sunday."

Her mouth drops open. Eli snorts softly behind me. I sigh, feeling my shoulders slump. "I don't know what to say, Mum. I love all three of them. They all love me. That's all there is to it. I'm not going to apologise for who I love."

Dad's face is turning dangerously purple. "So, what? You're just going to live with these men up in the mountains? Alone? They could do anything to you!" He spins on Cole. "Look, I don't know what the Hell kind of crap you're pulling on my daughter, but—"

Cole's eyes blaze. "Crap *we're* pulling on your daughter?" He steps forward, looming over my dad. "*We* are not the ones who hurt her."

My dad bristles. "Don't use that tone with me. Neither am I. *I* didn't take the video."

"You hurt her." Cole insists. "You hurt her when you didn't believe her. The way you treated your own child is disgusting. She was a victim of a *sex crime*, and when she told you, you blamed her." He shakes his head. "And now, you think you can judge her for the relationships that she actually chooses? You think your opinion matters to her? To any of us? You don't deserve to be a member of her family. You don't deserve to be related to her. She's a better person than you'll ever be."

He steps back, his chest heaving. There's a very long, very awkward pause.

My dad licks his lips, slowly turning to me. "Sweetheart—"

"It's okay," I say. "Really. And I do care about your opinion. Not enough to change my mind about the guys, but I'd like for you to be happy for me."

"So… what? You're going to move to Sweden?" Mum asks, worry creasing her forehead.

I nod. "Yep. I'm already in SFI classes to learn Swedish—"

"She's terrible," Eli cuts in. "I've literally never met anyone with a worse accent."

"Sounds like she's gargling with rocks," Riven adds under his breath.

"I'll get it," I wave them off. "I'm moving into their cabin."

Her eyes widen. "But what will you *do* there, up in the mountains? How will you find a teaching position?"

"I never really wanted to teach, Mum," I say gently. "I always wanted to paint. And now, my oil paintings are giving me a pretty steady income." It's actually a funny story. When we were talking to his parents about finding me a lawyer, I told Riven's mum that I did oil paintings. She was so excited that she commissioned a portrait of him for his dad's birthday, and now all the rich hotshot lawyers that visit their house want their own pieces from the *hot upcoming artist.* "I'm thinking of doing a whole collection based on Kiruna," I continue. "There's so many beautiful things to paint. The Northern Lights. The midnight sun. The villages. Reindeers and huskies and mountains and…" I trail off, excitement flowing through me. "I'm *so* inspired up there."

"Plus me," Eli chips in. "I'm a great model."

My cheeks flush. The last time Eli modelled for me, I didn't get a whole lot of work done. He insisted on me painting him nude. It was pretty distracting.

My parents still look worried. I give them my most convincing smile. "I'm okay, Mum, Dad. Really. I'm happier now than I've been in years. I think—maybe ever."

Dad shakes his head. "We can discuss this back at home," he says flatly. "Come on. If we hurry, we can catch the fast train."

I take a step back. "I'm not going home with you, Dad."

His frown deepens. "Don't be silly. You flew all this way; the least you can do is stay with us. Maybe then we can talk some sense into you."

I shake my head. "I'm sorry. I can't. I promised I'd show the boys around Brighton before we fly back. We've already booked a hotel room."

"Of course," he mutters, wiping his forehead. "Just one room for the four of you."

"We had to get the honeymoon suite," Eli informs him. "It's the only one with a big enough bed."

I kick him in the ankle. "I'll come back sometime soon," I promise. "Just to visit, though. I've found my own home, now."

My mum blinks back tears. "We're not going to change your mind, are we, sweetheart?"

I shake my head. "If we could move past the arguing and straight to the accepting, that would save us a lot of time," I say hopefully.

She laughs tearfully. "You always were so stubborn." She looks over my shoulder, giving all three men a stern look. "You take care of her up there, okay?"

"Yes, ma'am," Riven says. Cole and Eli both nod.

"Alright, then." She wipes off her cheeks. "We ought to get going if we're going to catch the train, Harry."

"But—"

"Leave her. She's an adult. She gets to make her own decisions. I think after the last few months, we owe her some trust." She steps forward and squeezes me in a big hug. "He'll come around," she whispers. "He's just shocked. He never liked when you brought a boy home. I think three is a bit much for him to handle."

I nod. I know my dad just needs time. She steps aside, and he takes her place. We watch each other for a moment. I set my jaw, preparing for him to start arguing again.

Instead, he bends and tugs me into a rough hug. "You sure you can't come home with us?" He mutters in my ear.

"Nope. Sorry. We've got plans."

He sighs. "Okay." He pushes back, holding me at arm's length. "Call us tonight, okay? When you get back in."

I nod, and he presses a kiss to my forehead. "I'm very proud of you, Jennifer. You've been very strong."

My mum tugs as his sleeve, and he turns to go. I watch them push out of the big glass doors of the courthouse, feeling my heart swell in my chest. They made a mistake—a bad one—but they do still love me. I believe that. And that's enough for me. The doors swing shut behind them, leaving me with my three mountain men in the middle of the atrium.

"Great." Eli claps his hands together. "Can we please get out of here? All these lawyers are making me antsy. And Tink looks *really* hot in her court clothes."

We spend the rest of the day in Brighton, wandering around my hometown. I show them all the spots I went to when I was a kid. My old school, the arcade, the quaint little shops by the sea. When dinner rolls around, I introduce them to fish and chips. I have never seen Cole eat so much, so fast. After food, we head down the pier and onto the beach, stopping to get ninety-nines from an ice cream van. The sun is setting over the sea, reflecting off the gentle waves in gold and orange flashes. The air is warm and breezy. The guys all lose their suit jackets and roll up their shirt sleeves, and I kick off my heels, squidging my toes in the sand. Riven and Cole take my hands as we meander through the small clusters of people laying out on towels.

"I haven't had ice cream in *ages*," Eli practically moans. "It's too fucking cold back home." I pop up on my tiptoes to lick the sauce dribbling down the side of the cone. Then I lick a smudge off his bottom lip. He smiles, nuzzling into me. "Do legal matters make you horny, babe? You can barely keep your hands off us. Understandable, in my case, but I don't know about those two."

I run my palm up Riven's chest, feeling the muscle under the well-tailored shirt. "You all look so hot in your suits. I can't handle it." I tweak Riv's collar, and he catches my hand, brushing his lips over my knuckles.

"Those people are staring," Cole warns, and Riven freezes.

I look up and follow his gaze to see a couple staring at us, whispering to each other. As I watch, the girl points at me, giving her boyfriend a nudge.

All three men automatically move to stand in front of me. This still happens pretty often when I'm out in public. People will recognise me from the video. I hate it. I hate having people looking at me, judging me, mentally undressing me.

I'm pretty sure that's not why this couple is staring, though. It probably has more to do with me snuggling up against three different men. I wait for the pang of nerves and embarrassment to hit me, but instead, there's nothing. Just the warm glow of happiness in my chest, and the sweetness of vanilla ice cream in my mouth.

"I'll have a word with them," Riven mutters, dropping my hand.

"Wait." I grab his arm. "It's okay. I don't mind."

Cole frowns. "You hate when people stare at you in public. It scares you." His scowl deepens. "You don't need to be scared."

"Well, I guess I don't mind it anymore. I actually feel kind of… proud." Three sets of eyebrows rise. I shrug. "I didn't choose to put out the video. But I choose you. It's different." I glance back at the couple, who are still gaping like fish, and grin as an idea blooms. "Why don't we give them something to stare at?"

Before any of them can react, I go up on my tiptoes, wrap my hands around the back of Cole's neck, and kiss him as deeply as

I can. He yanks me in at the waist, and heat wires through me as his tongue roughly plunders my mouth. By the time we gasp apart, I feel hot and shivery all over. Next, I reach for Riv, twisting my hands in his collar and tugging him down to my level. He winds his fingers in my hair and slips his tongue between my lips, curling it against mine. His strong arms around me make me feel so safe and cherished, I can barely catch my breath.

Finally, I turn to Eli, breathing hard. He's watching with pink cheeks, his curls blowing over his forehead in the sea breeze.

"Saving the best 'til last?" He teases, as I stroke my hands down his chest.

"I told you. I'm not ranking your kissing techniques."

"Sure, sure. But that's just to protect their fragile egos, right?" He lowers his voice. "*We* know the truth."

"Oh, just fucking kiss me."

So he does. Passing the rest of his ice cream to Cole, he tugs me close and presses his mouth over mine. I lick into him, tasting vanilla and sugar—and then the world suddenly spins as he dips me right off my feet. My stomach flips as the sky tilts over my head. It's a proper romance-movie kiss, right in the middle of the pier. I'm laughing against his lips when he finally sets me upright.

"Wow. Holy shit, guys." I press a hand over my hot cheek, then straighten out my skirt. "Are they still staring?"

"Uh. Yes." Riv looks around. "Quite a lot of people are."

"Probably wow-ed by my kissing skills," Eli muses.

I shrug. We're standing on a beach, watching the sun set over the sea. Couples around us are snogging everywhere. Why shouldn't *I* kiss the men I love? "Good. Now everybody knows. Everybody knows how much I love all *three* of you."

They share a soft look over my head.

"What?"

"Nothing," Riven says. "You just seem so much more relaxed, already."

I look out at the sea churning over the sand. The wind picks up a bit, whipping my hair around my face. "I was so ashamed, for so long. But I'm not anymore. I just feel…" I trail off, trying to find the right word.

"Safe?" Cole guesses.

"Happy?" Riven offers.

"Horny?" Eli wonders.

"Free," I decide. "I've never felt so free. Like I could do anything I wanted. Anything at all."

Eli throws an arm over my shoulders. "Great. What shall we start with?"

I consider for a few seconds, then smile.

"Bet I can beat you all to the water." I take off, flying across the beach towards the sea. The boys may be better at walking in snow than me, but sand is *my* home turf. Eli catches up with me just as I'm reaching the surf. Swinging me up into his arms, he carries me into the waves, kissing me hard. Cole and Riv follow us in, rolling up the legs of their dress pants as we wade in deeper. They crowd around me, and I'm lowered into the freezing cold water. A wave sweeps me off my feet, and I fall back into somebody's arms. Someone kisses my neck, and someone else trails hot lips over my cheeks. Hands slide over my hips, my arms, my waist, keeping me upright. The sea burns orange around us, reflecting the setting sun. I let my eyes fall closed, just feeling.

"Us too," Riven says by my ear, his voice low and grating.

"Hm?" I loll lazily against a muscled chest, blissed out.

"We all feel free again, too."

I smile, and tip my face up for a kiss or three.

EPILOGUE

TWO YEARS LATER

"Excuse me, sir? Would you like a hot towel?"

Cole looks up at the flight attendant, irritated. "What would I do with a hot towel?"

The woman gives him a lipsticky smile. "Refresh yourself, sir."

"*What?*"

I lean over him. "We're fine, thanks," I say politely. She smiles back absently, not even bothering to look at me. Her blue eyes stay fixed to Cole's face.

This is the sixth time she's floated over to our seats to offer us something. Blankets, pillows, champagne, tissues, magazines. Every time, she takes the chance to touch Cole's shoulder, or lean over him to shove her boobs in his face. She's clearly shooting for a quickie in the aeroplane bathroom.

I'm not jealous; I honestly think it's pretty funny. Hell, if I were her, I'd be hitting on him, too.

But it's clearly annoying him, and this situation is stressful enough for him as is, so I step in.

"Would you mind leaving us be?" I ask, as kindly as possible. "My husband's a bit of a nervous flier, he's trying to get some sleep."

Cole grumbles when I say the word *husband.* I can tell he's pleased. He loves when I call him that.

"H-husband?" The woman stutters.

"Yep!" I show her my hand. She takes in the three gold wedding bands stacked on my ring finger.

The boys gave them to me just a couple of months ago. They did it one at a time; Eli, on top of a ski slope with the mountains all around us; Cole, on a walk in the woods; and then Riven, kneeling at the side of the bed before I went to sleep that night. Each ring has the man's name engraved on the inside.

Obviously, we don't have a piece of paper saying that we're married. But we have the love, and the commitment, and all the promises. Which seems like the most important part.

The flight attendant pulls herself up, suddenly professional. "Of course, ma'am," she says smoothly. "We'll be landing in Arlanda in forty-five minutes. Enjoy the rest of your flight."

"Great. Thank you!"

She sashays back down the aisle, and I turn to Cole. He looks kind of cute, with his massive body scrunched up into a plane seat. But I know he's uncomfortable. I tip my head onto his shoulder. "You okay?"

"I hate this." He looks out of the window at the fluffy white clouds and scowls. "Why the Hell would anybody do this?"

"We're almost done," I promise him. "You'll be hacking down trees and saving moose in no time."

He snorts. "I'm sure the moose are fine. You've been off the roads."

We've spent the last week in London. I had a showing for my paintings at one of the galleries in the city centre. It was incredible; tons of art enthusiasts and critics showed up to see my latest collection. A lot of the paintings got bought, and I had an awesome time meeting so many other artists. I can hardly believe that this is my life, now. Over the last year, I've also had shows in Dublin, Edinburgh, Gothenburg and Stockholm. Usually, Eli and Riven take turns accompanying me on the trips, but this time Cole offered to come with. I'm pretty sure he hated almost every single thing about London, but he stood by me the whole time, supporting me.

His eyes flick back out of the window. He scowls at the clouds like they've personally offended him.

"Until then," I put a hand on his thigh, "I can think of a way to pass the time."

He slides a hand round the back of my neck and tugs me into a rough, deep kiss. It's been two years, and his lips still make me feel like I've been set on fire. If anything, the feeling's just got stronger.

This time, when the flight attendant passes by, she moves right along.

From Stockholm, we have another two-hour flight up to Kiruna. The flight is delayed, and while I sit in the terminal waiting area, Cole spends the connection time grumbling and pacing up and down between the brightly lit shops and cafes. Every so often, he goes into a shop, buys something, then brings it back and dumps it onto the little plastic table next to me. So far, I've gotten two romance paperbacks, a cup of coffee, a salad, a cinnamon bun, and a pack of sweets. Apparently, trying to keep me happy is the only thing that's keeping him sane right now.

I sit back in my plastic chair and sip my coffee, watching him.

When he came to me and told me that he wanted to come with me on this trip, I was taken aback. I'd never invited him before— I honestly assumed he wouldn't want to go. Eli's right at home in the city, although he misses the slopes. Riven deals with it fine. But Cole just wasn't made for bustling crowds and queues and chain restaurants.

I watch as he steps out of a shop and comes back to join me.

"Here." He puts a plastic bottle of water down by my hand. "You should drink water."

"Thanks." He nods and turns to go again, but I catch his hand, pulling him down into the chair next to me. "It means a lot," I tell him sincerely, "that you came here with me."

"I wanted to see your work," he mutters. "You're incredible."

"Well, thank you for coming. You've been amazing."

He stares at me for a few seconds, ice-blue eyes piercing into me. Then he wraps an arm around my waist and picks me up. I squeak as I'm lifted onto his lap, right in the middle of the airport. Some people turn and stare, but I don't care. I don't care about other people judging me, anymore. It doesn't matter what other people think of me.

Cole visibly relaxes when we land in Kiruna. The drive back home is pretty much silent. I look out of the window, watching the snow get thicker and the trees get sparser as we climb up into the mountains. My throat tightens every time we pass a little village, or I spot one of the reindeer herders leading their animals home for the night.

I'm home.

It's dark outside by the time we finally pull up outside our mountain cabin. Cole goes to park the car in the garage, while I trudge through the snow to the front door. My stomach is twisting with excitement. I don't even have my key in the lock before the door flies open. Eli practically attacks me, throwing his arms around me and pulling me inside, right into his chest. I smile, breathing in the warm smell of pine.

"I missed you, Tink," he mumbles into my neck, squeezing me tightly. "God. Next time I'm coming with you, okay? I don't care whose turn it is. Me. My turn. I'm coming."

"Well, I don't know. Cole's such a seasoned flier, now. You might have to fight it out with him." I hug him tightly back. "I missed you, too. *So much.*"

He sighs happily, cupping my cheeks and tugging me into a deep kiss. I soften against him as he curls his tongue possessively between my lips.

"Eli," a cool voice says. "Share."

Eli grumbles and steps back so Riven can welcome me home. The man holds me at arm's length for a moment, running his eyes over me. His eyes catch on my slightly swollen breasts, and I wonder if the doctor will work out the secret I've been keeping over the trip. Judging by the tiny smile on his lips, he just might have. He pulls me into a warm hug, pressing a firm kiss to my lips. "We're not whole without you," he mumbles against my cheek.

Eli takes my hand, tangling our fingers together. I feel Cole come up behind me, his chest up against my back. Any tension left in my body fades away as I'm circled by my mountain men. My husbands.

Sometimes, I can't believe this is my life. I can't believe I got this lucky. I'm surrounded by love all the time. It cocoons me. It wraps me up and keeps me safe and warm. Our relationship is unconventional, but it's the best relationship I can imagine.

And I've never been happier.

AFTERWORD

Thank you so much for reading, and I hope you enjoyed! *Three Swedish Mountain Men* was my first reverse harem romance (and the second book I ever wrote), so I'm really grateful people are willing to take a chance on it!

Want to know what happens next for Daisy and her men? Sign up to my newsletter at lilygoldauthor.com to receive a FREE flash-forward short story!

Want to connect? Join my reader group at:

https://www.facebook.com/groups/lilygoldreaders

for cover reveals, updates, and behind-the-scenes content!

ABOUT THE AUTHOR

Lily Gold is an Amazon-bestselling contemporary romance author living in London, England. She has a soft spot for strong guys with big hearts, and thinks the only thing better than one book boyfriend is TWO book boyfriends... or maybe three.

When she's not writing, she's usually reading, accidentally killing her potted plants, or finding a pet to cuddle. You can connect with her at https://www.lilygoldauthor.com/

instagram.com/authorlilygold

Made in the USA
Las Vegas, NV
21 March 2023

69425597R00192